"ARE YOU FLIRTING WITH ME?"

"Yes," Jaspar murmured.

"It is most improper," Marianne said, still failing to command him to release her.

"I would apprehend you are not yet betrothed," he whispered.

"I am not yet betrothed."

And then he kissed her fiercely. She could feel all his love for her in every subtle movement of his body against hers. Of all the men she had kissed over the years, Jaspar outkissed them all, yet she could not say exactly why.

The mystery of her desire for him, of her delight in his kisses, swept her up in a whirlwind of passion. She could no longer think, only feel. He would love her so well and so completely—she would be happy with him. Yet Jaspar Vernham had been her father's stable boy!

Marianne drew back. "You should not be kissing me, Jaspar. Nothing will come of this."

He took hold of her arms. "How can you be so blind?" he cried. "Do you truly believe these kisses we share have no meaning for you?"

BOOK YOUR PLACE ON OUR WEBSITE AND MAKE THE READING CONNECTION!

We've created a customized website just for our very special readers, where you can get the inside scoop on everything that's going on with Zebra, Pinnacle and Kensington books.

When you come online, you'll have the exciting opportunity to:

- View covers of upcoming books
- Read sample chapters
- Learn about our future publishing schedule (listed by publication month *and author*)
- Find out when your favorite authors will be visiting a city near you
- Search for and order backlist books from our online catalog
- Check out author bios and background information
- Send e-mail to your favorite authors
- Meet the Kensington staff online
- Join us in weekly chats with authors, readers and other guests
- Get writing guidelines
- AND MUCH MORE!

Visit our website at
http://www.zebrabooks.com

A LONDON FLIRTATION

Valerie King

Zebra Books
Kensington Publishing Corp.

http://www.zebrabooks.com

ZEBRA BOOKS are published by

Kensington Publishing Corp.
850 Third Avenue
New York, NY 10022

First Printing: March, 2000
10 9 8 7 6 5 4 3 2 1

Printed in the United States of America

One

Marianne Pamberley stood with her hands squared on her hips and cast a defiant gaze upon her elder sister, Lady Ramsdell.

"Constance," she began heatedly, "I will say it again, only this time a bit more plainly, since you do not seem to comprehend me in the least. I refuse to descend the stairs and speak with that—that cretin!"

"Cretin?" Constance lifted her brow. "Are we speaking of the same man?"

Marianne felt her temper flare from the soles of her pretty, peach-colored slippers all the way to the tips of her elegant blond tresses. "Must you stand there in that wretched manner of yours, as though you are the keeper of all knowledge? You know very well we are speaking of the same man. Sir Jaspar Vernham may have humbugged the rest of you, but I know what he is—a dreadful creature, as arrogant as he is proud, who always knows what I am thinking and to what I purpose at any given moment of the day. He is a boor, an adventurer, and an impostor. You may think him a gentleman, but what I am about to tell you will utterly alter your opinion of him. Yes, well you may stare!"

"What did he do, Marianne?" Constance inquired calmly.

She tossed her head. "He kissed me!" she exclaimed. "Not once, but thrice—each assault as unwel-

come as the former. What have you to say to that?"
She snapped her fingers and, believing the subject
would now draw to its own natural close, resumed
packing one of several portmanteaus scattered about
her bedchamber.

Constance stepped toward her. "It is very true he
should not have kissed you," she said soothingly. "That
was very wrong of him, but did he not apologize each
time? I believe I know him well enough to presume
he did so."

Marianne sniffed, for it was true. He had apologized.
She did not say as much to Constance. "Rather like
telling me it had begun to rain once my clothes were
completely soaked through."

"Then you did not enjoy Sir Jaspar's kisses, even a
trifle?"

At that, Marianne paused in her careful rolling up
of yet another pair of fine silk stockings. She slid a
finger over the delicate weave, her mind suddenly
given to pondering her sister's question.

She had all the silk stockings she could wish for now,
as well as linen shifts, gowns in every imaginable color
and fabric, several extravagant muffs, and more bon-
nets than she had ever hoped to possess in her entire
life. Constance's marriage had changed everything—in
particular, Marianne's prospects. She had no intention
of letting any man's kisses deter her course. She would
be a fool to do so.

She cast a sidelong glance at her sister, wishing Constance were not quite so perceptive and intelligent.
Katherine, the middle sister of the five Pamberley siblings, would not have questioned her enjoyment of a
kiss, nor would her next youngest, Celeste. Her youngest sister, Augusta, might have done so, for she was
much given to the reading of books and study of every
sort.

Constance, as the oldest of the five beautiful Pamberley sisters, had always interfered in Marianne's life, in her comings and goings, and in the visits of her numerous beaux. She wished Constance was not to be her chaperone in London, for she was certain many of her flirtations—which she planned to conduct with the utmost discretion—would come to naught under Constance's careful eye.

However, her sister's presence in London could not be helped. As Lady Ramsdell, a married woman, Constance would have *entrée* into the highest of tonnish circles, and that was, after all, Marianne's primary objective.

Only why must Constance inquire now as to whether or not Marianne liked being kissed by Sir Jaspar Vernham? What did it matter whether she liked being kissed by him or by any man? By her estimation, given her ambitions concerning her forthcoming Season, kissing had nothing whatsoever to do with making a brilliant match.

She answered her sister's provocative question by saying, "I was far too angry with Sir Jaspar to know whether his kisses were tolerable, let alone enjoyable. On each occasion, he took sore advantage of me. I shall not easily forgive him for it."

"I see," Constance murmured. "Then there is nothing I can say to persuade you to speak with Sir Jaspar before we depart on the morrow?"

"Absolutely nothing. I spoke with him yesterday, bidding him a proper *adieu,* and what must he do but come the crab with me as he always does? No, I tell you. He can have nothing to say to me now of even the remotest interest."

"Very well, Marianne. I shall send him away, if this is what you truly wish."

Marianne whirled on her sister and sent a rolled-up

stocking flying through the air. "You sound as though I ought to care for him," she cried, "but I promise you, I do not give a fig for him or how he kisses or whether my knees tremble for days afterward—never mind that. Tend to your own concerns, Constance, and leave me to manage my life and my heart as I see fit. I am going to London. Do you not understand what that means to me? I have forever dreamed of sailing about the *beau monde* on gossamer wings, of forming my own court, of being petted and sought after by a number of eligible *partis*, of receiving and rejecting a dozen suits—" She broke off, swiping at sudden tears on her cheeks.

"I know you have, dearest," Constance replied, "which is why I have said nothing until now, but I feel I must speak. When I see you and Jaspar together, I am struck hard with the sensation you belong to one another, as I belong to Ramsdell and he to me."

Marianne felt as though her sister had struck her across the cheek with hard, deliberate blows. She fell into a chair in the corner, her chest leaden with an emotion she did not comprehend. "I know you mean well." She hiccupped. "But I believe with all my heart you are mistaken. Never will I condescend to marry our father's stable hand. I would not so dishonor Papa's memory."

She lowered her gaze from Constance's concerned face and watched tears splash onto the beautiful peach silk of her gown. "Now look what you have made me do. I have no intention of ruining my skirts because of *him*. And . . . and, Constance, I do not think that is what I meant to say—I mean about Jaspar and Papa." She looked up, but her sister was gone.

Marianne propped her elbow on the arm of the chair and rubbed her forehead with the tips of her fingers. She had told Jaspar not to call on her today, had begged him to stay away from Lady Brook Cottage. She wanted to leave the newly built home in peace, to forget the numerous quarrels she had sustained with him since his return to their small community last summer.

Her sole desire was to embrace a most beautiful future without encumbrance or even the smallest regret. She was going to London at last, and that was all that mattered.

Still, Jaspar had fairly insisted on a word with her before she departed. Oh, why couldn't he leave her in peace? She had begun to believe he had returned to Berkshire for the purpose of plaguing her to death.

Well, now Constance would know she was serious about not wishing to speak with Sir Jaspar and she could be assured he would quit Lady Brook. At least now . . .

She rose abruptly to her feet at the swift pounding of heavy boots on the stairs. She was vexed nearly beyond bearing. Sir Jaspar was taking the stairs two at a time. Now he was stomping down the hall.

"Marianne Pamberley!" he shouted. "Which door belongs to your bedchamber? Tell me at once or I shall . . . ah, Miss Katherine. Do forgive me. I must speak with your sister."

"Two doors down on the left," Katherine traitorously responded.

"Thank you. You are very kind."

Marianne was sorry she was past the age of being able to pull Katherine's braids when she was angry with her. It was the only punishment which could possibly atone for her sister's actually directing Sir Jaspar to her bedchamber. Her bedchamber!

She compressed her lips together, clasped her hands firmly in front of her, and waited for the most abominable man on earth to appear in the doorway.

* * *

Sir Jaspar Vernham, recently created a knight, knew he was behaving with little more decorum than the stable boy he had been so many years ago. Nearly two decades had passed. During that time, he had lived in India, made his fortune, taken hours of instruction for the purpose of losing a farmhand's accent, and returned to England to purchase a property as near to the Pamberley ladies as possible.

When he had finally come home to Berkshire with Constance's correspondence of many years packed away in his trunk, he thought he had returned for her. However, the moment he laid eyes on Marianne, he knew he would make her his wife if he could. But she had made it quite plain she felt herself and her prospects far above anything he might have to offer her.

Yet he had kissed her—not once, but three times— and holding her in his arms, feeling her respond so wildly—indeed, so wickedly!—to his embraces was all the assurance he needed to be convinced she was destined for him as he was destined for her. He had never been more certain of anything in his life. Yet why the devil could he not convince her of it?

And this—refusing to see him before she left! How he desired to wring her neck. She had blinded herself to the truth of their relationship. Her ambitions were founded on the worst of motives and purposes, yet she refused to listen to reason. Why could she not understand she would never know happiness by the mere getting of a handle to her name?

He strongly suspected her primary interest in doing so was to best her elder sister. If Constance was a viscountess, then Marianne would not be content until she was at the very least a countess. She had not confessed this to him, but he knew her. It rankled sorely with her that her elder spinster sister, who was not half as pretty as Marianne Pamberley, had actually become a viscountess.

Yesterday, he had tried to tell her the truth, to open her eyes to the serious flaw in her plans to take London by storm—that she would never be happy shaping her life around anything so trivial—but she had merely laughed at him. Well, she would not laugh today.

He paused, collecting his thoughts and his wits, both of which tended to scatter at but a glimpse of her beautiful face. After taking a deep breath, he gave her door a shove.

She stood beside her bed, the grayish glow of daylight from the window illuminating her peach gown. Her golden hair was caught up atop her head, and she was more beautiful to his eyes than even yesterday, if that were possible.

His breath seemed trapped in his chest, even if her expression was mulish. Memories sprang forth. She had worn that very gown last summer while walking with him beside the trout stream. The day, so full of bees, leaping fish, and birds on the wing, had mellowed both of them. They had not even brangled. Well, only a very little. He had told her anecdotes of his life in India. She had posed many intelligent questions and drawn him into talking of the adventures he had enjoyed during his long absence from England. He had made her laugh and he vowed her sweet laughter, like delicate bells caught by a gentle breeze, would make the angels weep.

He had stolen a kiss from her at that moment, the only one she had relinquished, without the smallest struggle. He had been consumed by the fire of it, by how nestling her in his arms had moved him beyond words and imaginings. Her lips, so pliant beneath his, had spoken the same language as his. She had slid her arms about him and returned his embraces without restraint.

In the end, however, she had run away, just as he believed she was doing now.

"I told you I did not want to see you again, Sir Jaspar," she began, perfectly composed. "There is no lecture you can pour over my head which will persuade me I ought to remain in Berkshire instead of journeying to London for the Season."

He was not daunted by her cool demeanor. "There is something I must say to you," he stated firmly. "Something I did not say yesterday, and which I believe must be said."

She rolled her eyes. "What? That I am being an insufferably spoilt child by hoping to marry well once I am in London? Or do you mean to tell me I have not dressed my hair properly? Perhaps you intend to recommend yet another book which might penetrate the dullness of my mind."

He snapped his brows together. "You speak as though I criticize you at every turn, and I do not. I swear I do not!"

"Then you do not listen to yourself when you speak," she returned heatedly.

"Marianne, if this is true, I do beg your pardon. It was never my intention to—to *scold* you."

"Yet you do."

"If I seem impatient, it is because I do not believe you are honest with your own sentiments. Can you deny that last summer, when I kissed you—"

She lifted an imperious hand and cut him off. "I have told you repeatedly that I cannot account for why I behaved so improperly. But I assure you, again, that my conduct did not reflect my heart as you insist it must have. The beauty of the day, the honey we stole from Mrs. Pritchard's hives, the poetry you read to me, all served to bewitch me. Yet I have considered, and considered again, my heart and my conduct. I promise you I was not in love with you then—as I am not now. Why will you not believe me? Why will no one believe me?"

Tears trembled on her lashes and her fingers had grown white because she had been clasping her hands together so tightly. He would never cease to believe the emotions evoked by his presence and a mere discussion of one of their shared kisses meant nothing to her.

"Marianne," he said hoarsely, "I love you. I am in love with you. I have been ever since Lady Bramshill's ball last summer, when I saw you for the first time since you were a child."

"Please," she begged him, "don't say such things to me. You don't know what you are saying. How can you love me when you despise me?"

"I don't despise you. I don't know why you would say that."

"Because you are always telling me such wretched things about my conduct and—and ringing a peal over my head for keeping so many gentlemen pinned to my side, and—and for the way I walk."

"I do no such thing!" He was shocked. "Whatever do you mean, the way you walk?"

Marianne opened her eyes very wide. "That is precisely what I wish to know, Sir Jaspar. The last time we were in Tunbridge Wells, you told me I had far too much bounce in my step to be ladylike."

"I did not," he countered carefully.

"Oh, but you did. I remember it very distinctly. We were walking along the promenade—"

"And I said, 'Marianne, if you walk with a brighter step you shall touch the clouds.' "

Marianne stared at him. "Is that what you said, indeed? Well, that does not sound at all aggravating, though it hardly matters—so you may remove that smile from your lips and do not, *do not,* come near me. I will not have a stable boy touching me as you have!"

She was scowling, her forehead all crinkled and pressing down on the bridge of her nose, yet she appeared more adorable than ever.

Jaspar narrowed his eyes, thinking she often reproached him with his former employ in her father's stables when she was afraid. Still, he felt he should address the subject. "So now we are at the truth, eh, m'dear?"

"And do not call me *m'dear,* as you are wont to do. It is most improper."

"Yet it is proper for a young lady to inform a gentleman he is unworthy of her because of his previous station in life?"

Marianne lifted her chin slightly, but said nothing in response. He could read the answer in her eyes. She felt he was beneath her.

He narrowed his eyes further. "You would do well to learn your manners a little better, for it is exceedingly unkind in you to remind me of my beginnings. However, I will tell you again. I love you more than life itself."

"Is that supposed to flatter me, sir knight, now I must learn my manners better?"

"Putting on airs does not become you, Marianne. You only look ridiculous." He advanced on her in two quick strides and grasped both her arms.

"Let go of me, you brute!"

"Not until I have had my say. You are willful and proud and beautiful. Perhaps you deserve all you aspire to, but I will tell you this, *m'dear:* With two hundred servants, a castle in the air, and a duke for a spouse, you will not be happy unless you love your husband with all your heart. Yet that will be utterly impossible for you, for you are already in love with me."

"Hah," she whispered, staring boldly into his eyes. "You are speaking complete nonsense, and well you know it!"

"Then why are you trembling? Why do you tremble every time I touch you or hold you? Have you never considered these things?"

"I am merely afraid you mean to hurt me."

"You know better!" he replied harshly.

"You are hurting me even now." She glanced down at his hands, which had imprisoned her arms.

He relaxed his hold on her a trifle. "Marianne, will you do me the honor of becoming my wife?"

Marianne blinked several times as she stared at Sir Jaspar. Had she heard correctly? Had the man now fairly holding her suspended above the floor offered for her? She had never believed in a thousand years he would do so. She had never believed she would hear such words pour from his mouth. "Marry you?" she asked, her voice hushed.

He nodded in response, very slowly. A faint, almost crooked smile appeared upon his lips. "I love you to the point of madness, and I am willing to overlook your dislike of my origins and make you my wife."

She compressed her lips again. "You are such a beast," she whispered. "For a moment, I almost believed you were serious in your proposal."

He shook her slightly. "I *am* serious, more than I have ever been in my life. We belong together, you and I. With a little attention to your tongue and your manners, I believe you will become the lady you hope a handle to your name will make of you." He was almost laughing.

"Stubble it!" she cried, jerking each arm out of his hold on her. "I would not marry you if you were a duke and had a fortune as large as—well, as large as Golden Ball Hughes. You think so poorly of me, Sir Jaspar, that I cannot begin to imagine why you would wish me to become your wife."

"Because I love you."

"Your love is mere foolishness. I will never be your wife. Never. I shall go to London and I shall find a man who . . . appreciates me for the woman I am."

He had the exceeding discourtesy to laugh outright. "A vain, conceited, looking-glass-hugging miss with no more sense than a gosling? I should like to meet such a man, for I tell you now he won't be worth a farthing."

Marianne hiccuped and compressed her lips tighter still. "Well. You have seen me, spoken to me, and insulted me. I trust you are finished and will now quit my bedchamber forever."

"Not before this." He dragged her suddenly into his arms.

Marianne fought him for what seemed like an eternity. She beat at his arms with her fists, tried to push him away, and kicked at his shins, but he merely struggled with her and laughed and told her he would have his kiss or he would never leave.

Shaking with rage from head to foot, she asked, "If I permit you to kiss me, will you then leave me in peace?"

He inclined his head.

She tilted her head, closed her eyes, and waited.

"What a ridiculous peacock you are!" he cried. "I shan't kiss you when you stand before me in that absurd manner."

"Oh, you are the most provoking man that ever lived!"

"Perhaps," he murmured. He slid his arms about her waist and drew her to him as he had done last summer.

Her shaking subsided. For some unaccountable reason, her anger fled as well. She found herself looking deeply into his eyes, which were amber brown and so extraordinary that she suddenly felt transported to another place and time, one in which she and Jaspar never quarreled.

He settled his lips upon hers. They were warm and moist and inexpressibly tender, so odd for a man who insisted on coming the crab with her and holding her captive with hurtful fingers. For a complete brute of a man, Jaspar Vernham could be inordinately gentle.

For the barest moment as he kissed her, Marianne felt an impulse to accept his offer of marriage. Perhaps he was right. Perhaps Constance was right. Perhaps being kissed in such a fashion was proof of love.

Yet she did not wish to be married to the man who had once mucked her father's stables and tugged on her braids and pinched her nose and kissed Constance in the trout stream. Constance should have married him.

She could recall that day so vividly, seeing Constance wading in the stream barefoot, her gown caught up to her knees. How scandalous—yet the day had been very hot. The sun had shone upon Jaspar's shoulders and he had been telling Constance how he meant to leave Lady Brook Cottage and travel to India, that he had booked passage a month past. Constance had been very sad and had said, "May I kiss you good-bye?"

How quickly Jaspar had gathered her up in his arms. She had always thought of Jaspar as belonging to her elder sister, but now Constance was married to Lord

Ramsdell and Jaspar was drifting his lips over hers in the nicest way.

She melted against him and slid one arm about his neck and the other about his waist. He held her tightly, and the sensation was nothing short of comforting, at least at first. To be held in the arms of a strong man with definite ideas about his future was a wonderful thing. She could feel his confidence, all the reasons he had been successful in making his fortune in a hot, tropical land. She wished he would hold her in this manner the rest of her life.

"Marianne," he murmured against her lips. His tongue touched hers as it had last summer, and for no reason she could explain, she parted her lips and permitted him to take possession of her mouth in the most intimate manner possible.

All the gentleness and comfort of the kiss ended, replaced with a fire that began in her stomach and raged upward to consume her heart and her mind. An intense passion took hold of her, dictating that she clutch at his hair and make odd warbling sounds in her throat and strain desperately against him. Some recess of her mind was shocked, but every other sensation swirled so swiftly about her that she was dizzy with exhilaration.

If only he might come to London with her!

The thought was almost as unfortunate as a tankard of cold water thrown over her head. She gasped and drew back to stare at Jaspar in absolute horror. "You did it again! You—you have tricked me in some stable boy's manner like you tricked Constance into kissing you."

"Constance?" He appeared befuddled and ran a hand through his hair. "What the devil are you at now? Your sister is married. I never kissed her."

"Oh, but you did!" she cried. "Before you left for India."

He laughed and shook his head. "Oh, that. But, Marianne, we were little more than children."

"I do not give a fig for it. You kissed her and you kissed me in the same manner and you tricked me. Now, please, take your leave."

"How can I take my leave? How can you be so obtuse? What we just shared—do you think that will happen with any gentleman who takes you in his arms?"

"I—I don't know. I have been kissed before, very nicely, too, but I confess you are the only man who has kissed me in this fashion."

"Oh, Marianne, you are such a child in so many ways."

"There you are out, for I am fully five and twenty."

"You are little more than a schoolgirl, but it is not your fault. You should have had your first Season seven years ago. You carry myths in your head about the way your future should be, fantasies you created when you were not yet a woman. At eighteen, after a few weeks in London, you would have thrust such air dreams aside and embraced what was true and real. At your present age, I greatly fear you will be doomed to considerable disappointment, particularly if you press on and marry for the reasons you carry in your heart. They are false and will serve you ill."

Marianne had lain awake for hours last night pondering the future, the forthcoming Season in London, and her desire to make a brilliant match. She had wondered just how realistic such hopes were. She hiccupped.

Jaspar approached her and possessed himself of her hands. "Marry me, my darling Marianne. Do not go to London. Stay here with me. Be my wife, fill my home with children—our children. Please."

She looked into his eyes. His pleading expression tugged strangely at her heartstrings. He had come home from India quite sun bronzed. While some of that golden color had faded, much remained. She saw in the feathery lines at the sides of his eyes that he'd had many adventures, had fulfilled his destiny.

What had her life been while he was making his fortune? She had cared for the poor in the many villages near Lady Brook, had mended her gowns until they simply fell apart, had watched all her friends marry respectably, had watched handsome beaux, upon discovering her circumstances, appear saddened as they bid her good-bye forever.

And she *was* beautiful. Everyone told her she was. Everyone had told her for years that were she to go to London, she would cut a dash as no other young lady before.

Now, with a proper dowry because of Ramsdell's exceeding generosity, she would be considered an excellent match. Now, with the beginnings of a fine wardrobe, to be augmented by a Parisian dressmaker on New Bond Street once she was settled in Grosvenor Square, she would be able to attract the most eligible gentlemen of the *haut ton*.

Jaspar had had his adventures, and now he wanted a wife to bear his children.

Well, she would not be his wife. She was not ready to set up her nursery. She wanted her own adventures, wanted a chance to make her own dreams come true.

So she lifted her chin and said, "I wish you every happiness, Sir Jaspar, but I cannot marry you. I do not believe I love you, and in station we are too far removed—as you well know—for me to consent to your proposals."

"You are set on going?"

"I am."

"Then I wish you every happiness, but I will tell you this: I am in need of a wife, and I will take one soon."

"I will wish you joy when you do."

He held her gaze for a long moment. The intensity of his expression caused her heart to quiver and a pulse to beat at her temple like a dull warning. He released her hands and was gone.

For no reason she could explain, she slumped into the chair by her bed and gave in to a hearty bout of tears.

Two

An hour later, Marianne descended the stairs slowly, pulling on her gloves of lavender kid. She wore a warm pelisse of soft gray merino wool and a straw bonnet decorated with purple and white artificial flowers.

Constance entered the expansive entrance hall just as Marianne reached the foot of the stairs. "Are you feeling better?" she asked gently.

"Very much so. I only wish Sir Jaspar had not insisted upon speaking with me."

"I tried to stop him," Constance said earnestly.

"I am certain you did. However, when I heard his boots fairly rattling the entire staircase, I knew nothing short of a cannon brigade could have halted his progress to my bedchamber. I . . . I would have called for your assistance, except that once he was before me I thought it best to deal with him myself." She could never tell her the truth—that not only had Jaspar kissed her again, but she had *enjoyed* his embraces and the warm strength of his arms.

Constance nodded. "I believe you were right to hear him out. He told me he offered for you and you rejected his suit."

Marianne withheld a very deep sigh. "Yes, he was so kind as to confess his love for me, as well as his dislike of my character generally, and to ask for my hand in marriage—I suppose with the firm belief that once we were wed I should become a woman he might one day admire."

"He did not." Constance clicked her tongue.

"Oh, indeed he did—perhaps not as meanly as I have expressed. However, I cannot be left in doubt of his true opinion of me. He believes me to be quite spoilt, besides harboring ambitions not in the least based upon what is real and proper."

Constance shook her head. "A most unpromising proposal. It is no wonder you refused him. Can there be a woman alive who wishes to have her lover inform her of her every deficiency *before* he begs for her hand in marriage?"

Marianne could not help but smile a little. She sighed and shrugged as she worked each finger into her gloves. "I expect he was right, for the most part. I do have any number of flaws. However, I simply do not love him, and he cannot comprehend that in the least."

"Where are you going now?"

"To the village. I promised Mrs. Applegate and her children I would pay a final call before leaving for London. Mrs. Applegate is fully convinced I shall be engaged before the end of May, and that by July I shall be whisked away to some county or other far from Berkshire and never see her or the children again."

For some reason, Marianne felt utterly disheartened by the notion. She should not have, for she always enjoyed having other people remark on her beauty and predict her success in society. Still, when she thought of moving very far from Lady Brook, she felt rather low spirited.

It was all Jaspar's fault. He had given her a fit of the dismals, and she was having a difficult time recovering her usual buoyancy. Ah, well. "Do you have any message for her which I might deliver?"

"No, but I thank you for asking. I paid my own visits this morning. She is increasing again."

Marianne smiled. "I know. This will be her four-teenth—no, her fifteenth child. Do you think you and Ramsdell shall have as many?"

She watched her sister blush and was surprised. Constance was rarely ruffled by anything. "I should like to have children, but not, I daresay, fifteen. I do not believe I am capable of such heroism."

Marianne's gaze drifted away slightly. "I should like to have that many," she murmured. "I have always loved children—being with them, holding them, playing with them." When she glanced at Constance, her sister's rather surprised expression made Marianne add hastily, "Do not pay the least heed to anything I might say this morning. Jaspar has overset my nerves abominably. Ah, I hear the carriage in the drive."

She tied the ribbons of her bonnet, and as she did so she twirled about in a circle, taking in the lovely balustrade of the staircase, the fine plasterwork on the walls and ceilings, even the elegant wood floor. "Oh, Constance, I am so grateful Lady Brook is restored to all her former beauty. When the fire erupted last summer, I thought I should perish watching our beloved home disappear into a jumble of scorched brick."

"As am I—and the work was done so quickly. We have Ramsdell to thank for that. He is so well-connected in London that we never wanted for laborers and we had the best architect imaginable. Really, the entire house is a miracle."

"You are happy with Ramsdell, are you not?" Marianne inquired, glancing at her sister curiously.

Constance smiled so sweetly that words were entirely unnecessary. She spoke anyway. "More than I could ever express to you or anyone. When we awoke that awful morning with every chamber full of smoke, my only thought was for Ramsdell. Believing he had perished in the blaze helped me see how much I loved him more than anything else in the world."

"I was never more frightened," Marianne said, "nor happier when he appeared, especially since he was carrying Mama. I admire him greatly."

"As do I."

With Constance accompanying her outside, Marianne addressed another matter entirely. "You received a letter from Mama recently, did you not? I have been so much engaged in preparing for London that I forgot to ask you. Is she well? Does she mean to come to London?"

Constance smiled and shook her head. "She will not leave Bath for some time, especially since Augusta is approaching her confinement. Mother is under the supervision of a fine physician and is taking the waters thrice daily. She even wrote part of her letter, so it would seem her every skill is improving steadily. She says she is recovering her speech and mobility more each day and has promised Augusta she will remain with her until her child is born. According to the doctor, that will be near the end of June."

Marianne considered Augusta and her happy marriage. Her thoughts turned quite naturally to Celeste. "Do you suppose we shall be hearing any day of Celeste's being in the family way?"

"I am in hourly expectation of an announcement, especially since there is an unusual bloom on her cheeks these days. Sir Henry seems rather content, as well."

"How I envy both Augusta and Celeste, to be so happily married and to be setting up their nurseries. How much our lives have changed," she mused. "I am going to London, Celeste and Augusta are beginning their families, and even Katherine is able to live as she has always wished—though how she could refuse an invitation to London I shall never comprehend."

"She loves her horses more than anything else in the world. She would not have been happy in London. She will be much more content visiting her friend, Miss Alistair, in Brighton and seeing if she can enter her gelding in the races."

"If that is what she truly wishes, then I am happy for her. Will your field be drained soon?"

"Yes, indeed. And with the increase in revenue, Lady Brook shall make a profit, besides being entirely self-supporting."

Marianne chuckled suddenly. "Do you recall how it all began? How Charles crashed his curricle through the fence, and later Ramsdell?"

"Pray do not remind me," Constance responded, slipping her arm about Marianne. "I still shudder when I consider how many young men nearly broke their necks because of Lady Brook Bend—"

"Which is no more."

"That it is not," Constance stated.

"The new lane is lovely, and with all of Finch's plantings, the old road has entirely disappeared."

"He has become a tyrant with three gardeners on his staff. He works them fiercely and is as happy as a lark, but I truly could not be more pleased with the results."

"Was Ramsdell disappointed that you insisted upon sojourning here for a few weeks before going to London?"

"Not at all. He is most generous and comprehends extremely well my love for this land. Besides, it afforded him the opportunity to fetch his cousin from Hertfordshire, which he had to do anyway in order to bring her to London. The timing was propitious."

"I shall be happy to have a friend in London," Marianne said. "Miss Theale seems to be a shy sort of person, not one to put herself at all forward."

Constance chuckled.

"Why do you laugh?"

"Only that I believe I understand the turn of your mind. You see her as a happy adjunct to your court—a lady-in-waiting of sorts."

"Now who is being fanciful? Of all the absurdities." Still, Marianne could not help but smile. Though the notion had not occurred to her before, she knew the value of having a rather retiring friend accompany her about London. Whenever she put Miss Theale forward, she would appear magnanimous, which could not help but enhance her own stature.

When the coach drew next to the steps, Marianne turned to her sister. "I am happy for you, Constance," she said, "and your most extraordinary turn of fortune. Have I thanked you yet for making it possible for me to go to London?"

"Only a score of times."

"I cannot believe I am truly going!" she cried. "After all this time!"

"And I have little doubt you will be the reigning beauty before the first fortnight is out."

Marianne smiled hugely. "Indeed, I hope you may be right!" She then turned toward the fine black barouche emblazoned with Ramsdell's crest and climbed within. The squabs were soft and oh, so comfortable. She leaned against them, hoping one day she would be sitting in her own coach and pair with an even more luxurious interior.

The coachman cracked his whip and called to his horses and the carriage moved into the drive.

* * *

Constance waved farewell, but remained on the brick steps to watch the coach pass into the lane and turn in the direction of Wraythorne. Once the barouche was out of sight, her thoughts turned almost immediately to Jaspar.

When he had returned from placing his proposals before Marianne, he had informed Constance of her sister's refusal. She had not been surprised, but she was frustrated that she could do little more than sympathize with his disappointment and hope that in time Marianne would come about.

"I do not believe she ever will," he had stated. "She has taken a notion into her head about what her future ought to be, and I do not figure into her schemes in the least. Besides"—here he picked up his hat from the table by the door and slapped it against his buckskins—"I am not certain we should suit. Marianne sees me as little more than her father's former stable boy. She is also rather vain. I am not certain she could make any man happy, for she thinks only of herself."

He had sighed heavily. "No, I do not mean that. I am excessively disappointed and wish I could fault her so I might be at ease. The difficulty is my own. But enough of that. I hope you enjoy your Season, Constance, for I recall distinctly from your letters that you enjoyed yourself immensely the one year you were able to attend all the delights of a London spring."

"I did, very much so," she had responded. "I might even more were Marianne just a trifle less enthusiastic about the experience." She had smiled, hoping to get over rough ground lightly, but a cloud quickly gathered over Sir Jaspar's brow.

"I have little doubt the Season will provide your sister with all she desires—more's the pity." With that, he had expressed his need to be going and quit Lady

Brook, appearing as thunderous as when he had arrived an hour earlier.

Constance thought of his love for Marianne as she turned back into the house. She was not looking forward to the London Season. Marianne's ambitions, in her opinion, far outweighed her countrified connections and breeding.

To be sure, as the sister-in-law of Viscount Ramsdell, she was assured of *entrée* into many of the finest town houses and mansions in Mayfair, but the poverty of the Pamberley ladies prior to her own marriage was well and widely known. If Marianne succeeded in her ambitions and outshone some of the far better connected and dowered young ladies, Constance had little doubt the ensuing jealousy would soon give her sister a nasty tumble.

She knew well the barbed nature of the tongues of Mayfair. Her own Season had taught her as much, as it did every young lady who aspired to cut a dash among the *beau monde*.

Constance shuddered. She had seen enough machinations in her first Season to be well prepared for the onslaught which would ensue once the scope of Marianne's intentions became known. Due to her sister's lack of guile, whatever Marianne purposed would not be withheld from scrutiny by anyone. Marianne, for all her beauty, lacked discretion.

She wished her sister every happiness, but how was she to convince her that a brilliant match for the sake of making such an alliance would never bring her true contentment? Unless Marianne was very wise, she might end up a miserable peeress.

As she moved back into the house, she recalled an incident from last summer which still disturbed her. She and her family had resided at The Priory, Sir Jaspar's home, while Lady Brook was being rebuilt.

One evening she had been enjoying a private moment with Lord Ramsdell in Sir Jaspar's gardens.

Jaspar and Marianne had suddenly emerged from the house, brangling as they were wont to do. Jaspar had actually drawn her quarrelsome sister into his arms and kissed her quite thoroughly. Constance had been shocked but delighted, for it was obvious that after an initial effort to repulse his advances, Marianne had actually enjoyed being kissed by Sir Jaspar. Constance had fully expected Marianne and Jaspar to quickly follow herself and Ramsdell to the altar.

Instead, however, Marianne had become absolutely belligerent in her conduct toward the newly created knight. She had, upon more than one occasion, said Jaspar was an encroaching mushroom and any other man in his situation would have known better than to insinuate his presence among the local gentry.

"Everyone has been taken in!" she exclaimed after finding Sir Jaspar at yet another mutual social event. "And all because he is a nabob and as rich as Croesus. Well, I will never accept him. He will always be my father's stable boy and nothing more!"

Constance had tried to open Marianne's mind to the possibility that Jaspar had done as many gentlemen and ladies were able to do—risen above his birth and earned a right to enter polite society, both by his acquisition of a fortune as well as by his studied efforts to educate himself, reform his speech, and learn the many graces required by the *ton*. Certainly it was the rare person who could accomplish such a feat in only one generation. Did not that lend credence to Jaspar's claims, rather than repudiate them?

Marianne had laughed at her and countered with, "I see you have been taken in, as well!"

Poor Jaspar, Constance thought.

Poor Marianne, as well. She was convinced her sister

was indeed in love with the knight who had once pinched her nose as a child.

Constance paused in the entrance hall, her mind remaining fixed on Sir Jaspar. There was still so much to do in order to be ready to journey to London on the morrow, yet she believed she had yet another task to perform, this one a great deal more serious than advising the housekeeper to settle holland covers over the new furniture while she was away.

So it was that Constance donned a serviceable pelisse and bonnet, ordered her curricle brought round, and, once aboard, headed to The Priory.

Half an hour later, she found Jaspar in The Priory's morning room in his shirtsleeves, with several large black ledgers scattered over the table. He held a pen and his fingers were ink stained.

"Do I disturb you, my friend?" she inquired, smiling as she entered the room.

"You could never disturb me. But what are you doing away from Lady Brook, when you must have a thousand tasks yet unattended in anticipation of your journey?"

"I had to come," she said, "for there is something of great importance I must show you before I go. Will you come with me?"

"Something of great importance? How intriguing. Will you give me a hint?"

"No, but I promise you will find it of considerable interest. I would have waited until I returned to Berkshire in three months' time, but I have the strong impression what I wish you to see will not exist then."

"Now you have made me curious. Of course I will come. I would do anything for you, as you very well know."

"Come, then, for I have the curricle waiting."

"You seem in high gig," he commented, settling his pen on a tray near the ledgers.

"I am, indeed. It has been a very long time since I have handled the ribbons. I had forgotten how much I enjoy driving." She cast a glance over his ledgers. "Though I am myself fond of keeping careful records, I do know one reaches a point when a diversion is greatly appreciated."

"You have read my mind exactly."

A few minutes later, seated beside her, Jaspar said, "Then we are headed to the village."

"Yes."

"Is it the village you wish me to see?"

"No, not by half. Merely an event occurring there which I am convinced will bring you much pleasure."

The lane opened up, and Constance took the whip in hand and sent the thin strop of leather singing through the air. The horses immediately picked up their strides, digging their hooves into the cold gravel bed of the road.

In due course, the tall spire of the church appeared, and another bend in the road brought the village into view. The alehouse sign had been recently painted in a bold blue and red and stood out among the tall green elms in which it was framed.

From the edge of the village, Constance could see a number of children gathered in the yard of the alehouse, grouped, as she had hoped, around Marianne. She drew her curricle to a stop near the blacksmith's, which was at least a hundred yards away, for she did not want Marianne to see Sir Jaspar just yet.

Jaspar's attention was caught immediately as the group of children parted slightly and Marianne's beautiful face came into view. At the same time, her voice rose into the air as she sang "London Bridge Is Falling Down." The children began to play the accompanying game, and Marianne actually joined them.

"She came to say good-bye to her many friends," Constance explained.

"This is what you wanted me to see?" he asked, slightly bowled over.

"Yes," she said. "Dear Marianne has many faults, as you well know, but I believe the greatest is she does not know her own mind or even her own heart. I am persuaded only a life in the country will do for her, not the glittering tonnish life to which she so desperately aspires. I know to some degree her ambitions appall you; however, I want you to understand the source of all her schoolgirlish schemes.

"You see, from the time my father died and my mother suffered a fit of apoplexy, each of us soothed our grief in a different way. I believe Marianne, especially given that she is extraordinarily pretty, concocted an elaborate daydream about how one day she would venture to London during the Season and make a marvelous match that would rescue the rest of us from our poverty and suffering. I even suspect she resents me a little for having married Ramsdell, for it has been through our union that her dreams have been realized. Yes, yes, I know it must sound ridiculous, even childish . . ."

"Not ridiculous," he countered quickly. "Not by half. I begin to understand."

She turned to face him squarely. "I brought you here in the hope of encouraging you to take up your sword, as it were. I fear Marianne views my opinions as quite worthless, for I am but her elder sister. For that reason, she refuses to listen to my arguments concerning any aspect of her life. I am convinced that, if left to her own devices, she will make her brilliant match and doom herself to a lifetime of misery.

"Jaspar, I fear for her. I am asking . . . no, I am begging you to come to London this spring and make a push to win her." She turned toward the inn and watched as Marianne lifted one of the youngest Applegate children into her arms and whirled her about in a circle.

Marianne had never looked prettier in her life than at this moment, with the ribbons of her bonnet streaming behind her and her cheeks aglow with the gentle exercise attendant with the play of children.

"She would make a lovely countess or marchioness," Constance added, "but I do not for a moment believe she would be happy in anything other than a small community of gentlefolk. What you see before you is Marianne's true heart, her true desires."

Jaspar was touched beyond words, first by the sight of Marianne kissing a village child on the cheek before she lowered her to the ground, then by Constance's sweetness in placing his own dilemma in an entirely new light.

"I had given her up," he said. "At least, I was trying to reconcile myself to losing her to London forever. She was most convincing when she refused me."

"She cannot find it in her heart to relinquish her dreams, because for so many years they were her entire hope, her reason for living. She does not know how far she has outgrown them."

He gestured for her to move the team forward. "Bring me adjacent to the inn. There is something I would say to her."

"You will be kind?" she asked hurriedly.

"I am always kind." He smiled rather crookedly.

Constance chuckled and encouraged the horses forward.

Once the curricle came into view, the children ceased their games and ran to the low white fence which fronted the alehouse. Constance waved to them and called out each of their names.

Several of the younger children began begging to be taken up for a turn in the curricle, but she said, "No, no, my dears, we do not have time to take even one of you up the street and back, for as you know we are leaving for London on the morrow. However, I promise to return in June, and each of you shall have a turn then."

A rousing cheer rent the air. Marianne moved forward, now holding a toddler in her arms.

Constance called to her, "Young Tom is growing more each day, is he not?"

Marianne was apparently not of a mind to engage in conversation, for she merely glared at Constance, then addressed Jaspar. "Whatever are *you* doing here?"

Jaspar lifted a brow, mirroring her hauteur. "I came to inform you, Miss Marianne, that I have decided the country has become quite dull of late. I am in need of some diversion and fully intend to go to London for the Season after all—the entire Season."

Marianne looked so horrified, her complexion paling, that for a moment Jaspar feared she might faint.

"You cannot be serious!" she cried. "Constance! You must prevail on him not to make a cake of himself. Do you not understand, Sir Jaspar, that you will be given the cut direct wherever you go? What person of consequence would be willing to receive a stable boy?"

Sir Jaspar narrowed his eyes. "The Regent has invited me to Carlton House for a fete Friday next. I daresay *he* will not give me the cut direct. I trust others will follow suit."

"C-Carlton House?" Marianne cried, stunned.

Sir Jaspar nodded. "Perhaps I will see you there."

"P-perhaps," Marianne murmured.

"I think we should return now, Lady Ramsdell, don't you?"

"Indeed," Constance murmured. She waved to the children and bid them all another farewell, then set the horses at a spanking pace up the High Street. Once there, she turned about at the crossroads and headed back. Since this was the usual method for maneuvering a cart or carriage, Marianne and the children were still at the fence waiting for the curricle to pass by again.

Constance did not disappoint them, but cracked her whip grandly once she neared the alehouse. Jaspar told her he was quite impressed with her abilities and had the pleasure of hearing the children set up a loud cheer once more as the horses lengthened their stride.

"I had forgot you were called 'the gentleman,' once upon a time," he said. "You are handy with the ribbons."

"Thank you."

"And you were right to have brought me here just now. I enjoyed seeing the shocked expression on Marianne's face."

"I am sure you took great delight in putting her out of countenance. But tell me, is it true you have been invited to Carlton House?"

He smiled ruefully. "I suppose it does seem impossible, but I would never lie to Marianne, nor would I invoke the Regent's name without being able to substantiate his interest in me. As it happens, the invitation rests on my shaving stand. I can hardly credit it myself."

"Would this have something to do with your knighthood? You never told me how it came about you received it."

"And I never shall," he said quietly. "The entire matter was quite embarrassing."

"But it did involve the Regent."

"Yes, that much I will tell you, but I trust you will say nothing. Prinny requested I keep my peace."

"How provoking," Constance responded. "But if His Royal Highness insists on your silence, I suppose I will never know the particulars."

Jaspar only laughed.

Three

The next day, Marianne stood by the window of her bedchamber, which overlooked Grosvenor Square. She sighed with delight as she pushed back a length of finely woven muslin in order to peer to her heart's content out the window.

The Ramsdell town house was neatly situated in the heart of Mayfair. Very soon she would be known to as many ladies and gentlemen of consequence as her heart could desire. She gazed out with satisfaction at the various conveyances flowing about the square.

An elegant landau released two ladies of fashion, a young gentleman hopped into the seat of a quick-paced Stanhope gig most dashingly, and a traveling chariot, muddied about the wheels, deposited a man and a woman, stiff with the common aches of travel, at an elegant door on the opposite side of the square.

The general traffic of the square in every way expressed the life of the city. Marianne felt entirely overcome with gratitude. Never once in the past seven years had she believed she would ever see London in this most wonderful fashion, with exquisitely dressed young ladies and matrons, gentlemen, and even a dandy or two laid before her eyes like a scrumptious feast.

The circumstances of the Pamberley ladies had been so wretchedly unhappy since her father's death that until this moment she had only dreamed of a London Season. Now here she was, her heart in her throat as she watched a large barouche turn into the square, all four horses matched to a shade.

How had it become possible, after so many years of yearning, hoping, and dreaming, that Grosvenor Square would be her home for the next three months? How had it been possible that a crooked lane in Berkshire had brought Constance's future husband tumbling heroically before the front door of Lady Brook Cottage, in turn affording Miss Marianne Pamberley the opportunity of fulfilling every childhood fantasy?

She heard a scratching on her door, followed by Constance's voice. "Marianne, may I come in?"

"Oh, yes, indeed!" She turned to smile at her sister as Constance crossed the threshold. Surprisingly, she saw her through a mist of tears.

"Whatever is the matter?" Constance cried, moving forward quickly.

Marianne sniffed and swiped at the unexpected tears. "I—it is just that I am so very happy! Dear Constance, you cannot imagine how I have longed to be in London. And look, even the sun is shining!"

Constance drew near, joining her by the window. She, too, pushed back part of the sheer muslin and glanced down into the square. "It is lovely, is it not? I daresay there is not a finer aspect in all of London."

"Even my sweetest dreams were not so pretty or elegant."

"I was only in Grosvenor Square once or twice during my Season. The personages we will be meeting as our neighbors are quite exalted."

The barouche passed by and drew to a stop two doors down. "Do you know to whom that fine conveyance belongs?"

"I believe to the countess of Bray, a family of ancient

origins—rather high sticklers, though. I recall the eldest son from my first Season. Quite dashing, though
rather rigid in his opinions."

"Given the perfection of their horses and carriage,
I am of a mind that the family has every right to be
as particular as they wish."

"You cannot mean that, Marianne," Constance said
softly.

Marianne turned toward her. "What an odd thing
to say," she countered. "I do not comprehend your
meaning in the least. If a family has a strong tradition
of elegance and exceptional deportment, why should
they not demand such conduct in others?"

Constance let the curtains fall back into place. She
met Marianne's gaze and said, "I value what is honest
and true. To be puffed up in one's conceit because of
a fine carriage is not what I consider worthy."

"Well, I did not mean that the owner ought to be
proud in a disagreeable manner, merely holding dear
the standards of several generations."

"Ah," Constance offered in just such a manner that
did not at all satisfy Marianne. "Perhaps we are talking
at cross-purposes, then."

"Perhaps." Already, Marianne was bored with the
conversation. She rarely understood what her elder sister said, and she had the worst sensation Constance
was moralizing with her. She decided to change the
subject.

"Is our cousin settled in her room?" She had long
since decided to call Miss Theale her cousin. For the
purposes of taking her about London, it seemed so
much better than having to say *my friend, Miss Theale,*
or *my acquaintance,* or *my brother-in-law's cousin.* How
much better *my cousin, Miss Theale.*

"Annabelle seems quite content, only . . . ah, well,

I am certain the situation will right itself soon enough."

"What do you mean?"

Constance seemed rather distressed. "Her gown of yesterday," she began uneasily. "Did it not strike you as odd in some manner?"

"Quite countrified," Marianne remarked. She had noted the faded quality and style of the gown, but had decided Annabelle's intention of appearing a perfect dowd in London was entirely her own affair. In truth, given the knowledge that Annabelle's mother was quite wealthy, she had greatly feared her new cousin would be dressed to such magnificence that she might outshine Marianne entirely, and that would have been completely unbearable.

As it was, she decided Annabelle's choice of traveling costume to be perfection itself. No one in the establishments from Berkshire to London had paid the least notice to Annabelle. Marianne had therefore enjoyed all the attention she had wished for on the brief journey from Lady Brook to Grosvenor Square.

She smiled wistfully at how lovely her own costume had been this morning, for it was a new creation made especially for the Season. Her poke bonnet was a finely decorated apple green silk which matched to perfection her elegant pelisse. In marked contrast, Annabelle had worn a gray shawl over a gray round gown of a worn woolen fabric.

Yes, in her opinion, Annabelle had dressed to perfection.

To Constance, she observed, "I would say my cousin's gown was nearly ten years past in style. Would not you?"

"Precisely. Ramsdell gave me to understand that her mother has taken very little interest in her. I fear she may have nothing suitable to wear."

"Perhaps you should speak with her."

"I was hoping you might be able to do that. She seems to have taken to you, and you were indeed solicitous of her the entire journey from Lady Brook. Ramsdell was grateful for your attentions. Indeed, we both were."

Marianne had the good grace to blush, for she had merely been practicing her role with Miss Theale for the coming Season. Her hope that Annabelle might form an adoring part of her court as a lady-in-waiting seemed destined to come true.

Annabelle was precisely what she needed. She was neither pretty nor plain, her fashion was wretched, and her light red curly hair was quite abominable. She was just what a prospective reigning beauty required to establish her place in the *beau monde*.

"I was trying to be helpful," she offered lamely.

"You were more than kindness itself," Constance said. "Miss Theale—Annabelle—has asked after you. Once you are settled, perhaps you might go to her. She seems quite nervous—just as she ought to be, since this is her first trip to the metropolis."

"She is our family now," Marianne responded, again rehearsing her role as the beautiful, anointed one, "and we must make certain she knows every happiness. Was that what you wished to tell me?"

Constance smiled broadly and handed a sheaf of papers to her sister. "Not precisely. Though I had intended to speak with you about Annabelle from the first, the actual reason I came to you was that I thought you might want to see these."

"Oh, my!" Marianne's heart skipped a beat. "N-not invitations?"

Constance nodded and smiled. "Once it was known Ramsdell meant to be in town for several weeks, the housekeeper informed me these have not ceased arriving. There must be twenty more, but I thought you might enjoy reviewing the ones Ramsdell indicated we must accept."

Marianne felt as though her joy could know no bounds. She held the cards in her hands like a miser counting his gold coins.

"Oh," she breathed. "I should like nothing better. Now I can become acquainted with the names of my brother-in-law's friends." She smiled at Constance and held the invitations to her breast.

"You are here at last," Constance murmured, a smile of understanding suffusing her features.

"Indeed, I am." Marianne's heart burgeoned with every happy sentiment.

"Well," Constance mused, "pray enjoy your perusal of our invitations, but when you are able, see to Annabelle that she might be made more comfortable. I myself am not feeling at all the thing—no, no it is nothing; I have a very slight headache—and I mean to have a lie down for a little while. I daresay traveling this morning did not agree with me."

Marianne wished her sister would leave. "You must rest, then, Constance, for it seems to me we shall be very busy in the coming weeks."

"Indeed, we shall." Constance again expressed her hope that Marianne would find the Season everything she had always dreamed it would be, then at last quit the chamber.

Marianne threw herself on her bed and splayed the invitations in front of her. She examined each one with great care and tenderness. The names were soon familiar to her tongue, the addresses were quickly burned into her mind, and the vellum became a delicacy to her fingers as she reviewed the invitations over and over.

She belonged to Mayfair now, and she felt within

her soul that she always would. Her future was here, and here she would complete the fantasies of nearly a decade.

She knew her attractions were numerous. She was the prettiest of her sisters, for she had been told as much ever since she could remember. Her hair was the color of spun gold—or so she liked to think—and no matter what anyone said, fair hair was much more likely to attract notice than mousy brown, reddish, or deathly black.

She was fully aware of precisely what happened when she entered any drawing room. All eyes were immediately riveted to her. She welcomed the attention, yet at the same time she knew how not to disappoint her admirers.

Ever since she had become aware of her charms, she had practiced the arts of deportment and manners. She knew how to hold her shawl and her fan, how to tease with a fair showing of her beautiful small white teeth, how and when to bat her lashes, and how to dance to perfection. She had a fine array of anecdotes for the telling, and no lady could hold a glass with so elegant a turn of wrist as she. She was, in essence, highly accomplished in the artful dance of the genteel drawing room.

As she regarded the invitations before her, she wondered just who, among all the gentlemen represented by the fair copperplates before her, would fall victim to her charms.

She rolled onto her back and stared up at a lovely rosette in the center of a fine chintz canopy. "All of them," she murmured, smiling with deep satisfaction to herself.

And why not? She was Marianne Pamberley of Lady Brook Cottage, sister-in-law to Viscount Ramsdell, and a diamond of the first stare.

* * *

Three days later, Marianne stood at the top of Lady Donnington's ballroom, quivering from head to foot with nothing short of excitement. Before her was an array of elegance.

Lord Ramsdell, who had hooked her arm and was holding her upright, leaned down to her and whispered, "I am seeing this ball through new eyes this evening. You are putting me in mind of my own early experiences in London. I had forgotten how enchanting a ball could be."

"How could anyone not be thrilled by this?" With her free hand, she gestured to the throng of dancers who were presently going down a very beautiful *contredanse,* the music a familiar Handel melody. The orchestra, seated in an alcove above, spilled the sedate tunes over the befeathered and bejeweled heads of the revelers below. Three enormous chandeliers sent a sparkling of light off every crafted prism. The ballroom was alive with motion, the scents of heady perfume, and the glittering candlelight.

Marianne would remember this moment as long as she lived.

Ramsdell guided all three of the ladies to chairs by the wall, but prevented Marianne from being seated. "My wife insists I escort you onto the floor for your first dance. Will you do me the honor of standing up with me?"

Marianne turned to her sister, who had already taken a seat. "Oh, but, Constance, you must desire above all things to dance with your husband just now. On no account will I deprive you of such a pleasure on your first London ball together. Besides, what of Miss Theale?"

Annabelle, who was looking ghastly in a low-waisted

round gown of white silk, took up Constance's hand in her own. "It is all settled, Marianne. We know how much this means to you. Pray accept my cousin's offer."

Marianne felt the gesture deeply and promised herself she would soon find a string of partners for Annabelle. She turned toward Ramsdell and laid her hand on his arm, dimpling. "I should be more than delighted, my lord," she said sweetly, "to go down the next dance with you."

Ramsdell merely laughed at her and, once he had turned her away from Constance, whispered, "Try not to be too much of a baggage this evening, my dear sister-in-law."

Since his expression was full of good humor, Marianne could only giggle and wait at the edge of the ballroom for the *contredanse* to end. She held her head high, her spirits soaring.

She was already the object of much interest and scrutiny all about the long, rectangular chamber. Indeed, upon her entrance to Lady Donnington's impressive town house in Berkeley Square, all eyes had become quickly fastened upon her, just as she had expected them to.

She was exquisitely gowned in pale-gold figured silk, over which a layer of gold-embroidered tulle floated. Her hair was dressed in the Grecian mode and her blond curls cascaded behind from three tiered gold bands. She wore pearl eardrops and a matching pearl necklace of a simple design, as befitted her maidenly state. She had no need for rouge for her lips or her cheeks, since her excitement kept a perpetual rosy glow upon her complexion.

She let her gaze drift slowly about the ballroom and noted several handsome young gentlemen whose eyes were fixed quite purposefully upon her. She observed each with interest, yet was careful not to encourage any of the dashing smiles she received. Time enough, upon proper introduction, to offer an appropriate degree of enthusiasm for each of the men she would soon meet.

At last, she took up her place for the waltz and met the gaze of her brother-in-law, who was eyeing her with some amusement. She knew the nature of his thoughts—that he, too, had witnessed the general interest in her.

She gave him a soft, demure answering smile and prepared herself for the pleasure of the dance. She had already experienced Lord Ramsdell's prowess on the ballroom floor at the local Berkshire assemblies and knew him to be a fine dancer, indeed.

"You are a baggage," he murmured as the first chords of the waltz were struck. "However, you will do well this Season."

She blushed happily at his compliment. He drew her into his arms and, with expertise, guided her into her first London waltz.

Marianne performed the steps to perfection, enjoying every twist and turn of the dance as he moved her up and back, around and around. She gave herself completely to the delight of whirling about Lady Donnington's ballroom. She was not in the least anxious, for she was an accomplished dancer herself. Nor did she give a fig that the gabblemongers would already be bandying her name about like a cricket ball in a heated match.

She understood clearly the rules of her society. Before the dance ended, the precise size of her dowry, as well as her relationship to Lord Ramsdell, would be known from one end of the ballroom to the other. She had nothing to fear from the revelation of such knowledge and knew, in particular, that her dowry would easily double the size of the court which she fully expected to swell around her within the next hour.

Sir Jaspar Vernham arrived in time to watch Marianne take the ballroom floor with all the ability and aplomb of an army presenting on the battlefield its oldest and most seasoned veterans. He could only smile in delight, for she was a vision to behold not just because she was far and away the most beautiful lady present, but because it was evident even to a sapskull that she was enjoying herself hugely.

She made the entire ball appear fresh and new, as though such an occasion had never occurred in the history of society. If he had had any doubts about her success, one glance about the perimeter of the ballroom allayed them all. She was the object of nearly every observer, and by the time the waltz ended, Marianne would be inundated with requests for future sets.

Desiring to hear for himself what was being passed from lip to lip about the beautiful, unknown young woman who was floating about the ballroom on gold silk slippers, he began a slow progress around the elegant chamber.

A severe matron inquired of the lady next to her, "Is she Ramsdell's wife? I had heard Lady Ramsdell was a very tall woman."

"No, no, you are quite mistaken. The lady he is partnering is Miss Marianne, Lady Ramsdell's sister."

He took a few more steps. A young man spoke. "By J-Jove, I might be w-willing to live on f-five hundred a year with such a b-beauty by m'side."

"She would never have the likes of you," his friend discouraged him.

"Wh-why not?"

"You've no lands, no title, and no fortune. She would be a complete simpleton to accept less than a man with all three."

Very true, Jaspar thought, and moved on.

A young woman whispered bitterly, "Mama, I told you I could wear the gold silk! Do but look at her, parading about in a gown like that."

"You'd look like a witch with your black hair. No, no, you are perfectly arrayed in white." A long-suffering sigh ensued.

Jaspar took a few more steps. A gentleman's deep voice intoned, "Ramsdell's sister-in-law? I shall marry her before the end of May, for I vow I have been waiting all these years for just such a one to come to London."

He shot a quick glance at the man who had spoken and met the sharp gaze of Lord Crowthorne, heir to the earl of Bray. Something turned in him, dark and wary. The instinct of challenge was so strong he suddenly found his fists clenched and the muscles of his arms flexing unaccountably.

He withdrew his gaze abruptly, for he was unacquainted with Lord Crowthorne and had no true knowledge of either his disposition or his worthiness to pursue the woman Jaspar loved. However, he could not help but wonder why the son of an earl, with every social advantage already in his possession, would so quickly determine to wed Marianne.

The waltz ended. Because he had hoped to engage her for at least one dance, Jaspar began a quick progress in her direction. By the time he was halfway across the floor, he was beaten on all suits by a score of gentlemen already begging to stand up with her. Ramsdell took charge of her instantly and began making all the appropriate introductions. Undoubtedly, all her dances would be given away before he could so much as speak her name.

He was forced to be content with merely watching his beloved. When she caught sight of him, he could only offer her a smile of resignation as she in turn flashed him an expression of supreme triumph. Marianne had been in London precisely three days and six hours and had already conquered the *beau monde*. He wondered suddenly whether he had lost her already.

Spying Constance across the ballroom floor, he immediately crossed the room to her, at which time she introduced him to the young lady seated beside her.

"How do you do, Miss Theale," he responded gently, for he could see her color was high and she was quite nervous. "Is this your first Season?"

She nodded vigorously. "Why, yes, though I am three and twenty. Mama had no wish to venture to London. She insists the climate is adverse to her health. You can imagine, therefore, how grateful I am that my cousin, Lord Ramsdell, was willing to take me up in his coach. He is not precisely my cousin—his mother and my mother were cousins—so, here I am."

He had listened intently throughout this speech and saw within the young lady's stammering an unfortunate inexperience in society generally. Her features were quite excellent, but her hair appeared rumpled and her gown less than flattering. With just a little Town bronze, however, he believed Miss Theale could become a delightful creature to behold. "May I beseech a dance of you, Miss Theale? That is, if you wish to dance."

She rose abruptly to her feet. "Oh, yes, very much so. I dearly love to dance, and before I quit Hertfordshire Mama hired a dancing master for me."

He chuckled. "Then we ought to take full advantage of every note, thereby justifying her expenditure."

Miss Theale smiled broadly at this nonsense. "You are perfectly correct!"

"Will the quadrille suit you?"

"Indeed, yes. It was my favorite, though we had to force my three brothers, one of their friends, and three of mine to make up the proper numbers. It soon became a romp and we all fell into a fit of the giggles. Eventually, however, we learned the patterns quite well."

He guided her onto the floor and together they took their places among three other couples. He felt a certain qualm in doing so, given Miss Theale's lack of experience. However, before long he found he could relax. Not only could the young lady recall all her steps, her movements had a certain pleasing air which captured the attention of more than one future partner.

The glow of her complexion following the dance gave her countenance precisely the right aspect. When he began making introductions to the several young men clustered at her elbow, her confidence began to grow and much of her nervous chatter softened. He left her in the capable hands of Sir Giles Chalfont, a friend of Lord Crowthorne's.

Returning to Constance's side, he found her just quitting the ballroom floor, having danced with Henry Speen. He begged to bring her a cup of iced champagne, an offer which she immediately accepted.

"I find myself greatly heated from the dancing. Are you warm as well, Sir Jaspar?" She fanned herself with a lovely lace fan, her color high.

"Not overly much. But come, I am certain we shall find a footman bearing a tray of cups once we leave the ballroom, and I daresay another chamber will not be nearly so stuffy."

He guided her into an antechamber, which was

crowded with revelers. "Oh, my," she murmured, her fan moving more swiftly still.

Two young gentlemen, caught up in an intense conversation, blocked the entrance to the hallway beyond. He felt Constance's hand grip his arm. "You must make them move. I—I am not feeling at all the thing."

He turned to discover she had suddenly grown quite pale. "Dear Constance." He slid an arm swiftly about her waist, just barely preventing her from falling into a faint.

"Please, Jaspar, help me to a chair. I—I am so mortified!"

He drew her steadily toward the arguing gentlemen. "Stand aside, if you please! There must be a dozen souls in need of departing the ballroom."

The gentlemen quickly obeyed him, as much from the obviously inconsiderate nature of their positions as the authoritative tone in his voice.

Once they entered the hallway, a cool stream of air swept through, since the front door had just been opened to admit a large party.

"Oh, thank heavens!" Constance said. "Now, if I can just sit down for a time. The chair near the end of the hall looks quite inviting." She moved swiftly in the direction of the conservatory and, upon reaching the chair, sank down onto the soft red velvet cushion. "I do not know why I was so overcome," she said, drawing in several deep breaths, "except that the ballroom was so very hot."

Jaspar watched her in some concern for a moment. Then, spying a footman carrying a tray of iced champagne, Jaspar signaled for his approach. He handed Constance a cup.

She took several sips. "Jaspar, I am beyond grateful to you," she said, turning toward him. "Thank you for attending me. I would have swooned had you not caught me."

"Tell me you are not truly ill and I shall be content."

Constance smiled, her complexion still pale. "Indeed, I am not. Except for a trifling dizziness, I am as right as rain. Only—would you fetch Ramsdell for me?"

"Of course, if you are well enough that I might leave your side without danger of your again succumbing to the heat."

"I am perfectly well now. I merely wish to speak with my husband."

"As you wish."

Sir Jaspar found Ramsdell readily enough, for he was standing at the perimeter of the ballroom floor watching Marianne and Miss Theale in turns as each went through the movements of another country dance. "Your wife," he murmured, drawing close, "awaits you in the hall beyond. She nearly fainted."

The terror which jumped into Ramsdell's eyes seemed entirely out of proportion to a mere swooning in a ballroom, which was a common enough occurrence. Jaspar smiled as he watched Ramsdell's retreating back, noting his lordship's former reputation as a rather bored bachelor had been entirely supplanted by the more amusing one of devoted husband.

Once Ramsdell disappeared into the antechamber, Jaspar turned his attention to Marianne and Miss Theale. He was struck at once by the disparity between the two ladies. Marianne was smiling and chattering as she went through her steps. Miss Theale was listening attentively to her partner. Marianne's steps were as lively as those of a foal in an open pasture. Miss Theale conducted herself with grace and elegance. Marianne knew she was being ogled by a dozen eligible beaux. Miss Theale was presently blushing acutely because her partner had just complimented her on how well she danced.

He smiled to himself and shook his head. Poor Miss Theale would be naught but a shadow beside the flame of Marianne's beauty and flirtatious propensities. He made a sudden decision, therefore, to champion Miss Theale, to form one of her court, and to do all he could to make her season a pleasant one. Besides, his chivalrous devotion to Miss Theale would undoubtedly provide him ample opportunity to keep a close watch on Marianne.

Four

An hour later, Marianne was exceedingly content with her success, save for one nagging remission. She had learned through the usual avenues of gossip that the most desirable gentleman on the Marriage Mart was none other than her neighbor, Lord Edgar Hurst, known more commonly as Lord Crowthorne. As the eldest son of the earl of Bray, he would one day inherit a fine, well-established peerage, extensive lands including one of the largest county seats in Hampshire, and an income in excess of twenty-five thousand pounds a year.

Ramsdell had only eight thousand.

When she had first learned of Lord Crowthorne's worth, a profound dizziness had overtaken her. For the longest moment, she feared she might fall into a swoon and forever disgrace herself. With a stamp of her foot, however, she forced the dizziness to pass.

Recovering swiftly, she heard the rather dampening news that the future Lord Bray was quite unattainable. Over the years, the most beautiful heiresses and eligible ladies of the *haut ton* had attempted every manner of flirtation in the hope of enticing the viscount to the altar, but none had come close to the mark. How was she, then—a mere country miss—to succeed where so many ladies had failed?

Regardless, Marianne set about gaining Lord Crowthorne's interest through a method she had found tended to work quite well—she ignored him, particularly since she could see he was already observing her closely. She concentrated instead on the happy task of gathering her court about her. She wanted not only gentlemen clustered about her, but young ladies as well, so she spent a great deal of her time begging the young men who fawned over her to introduce her to their sisters, which they did quite willingly.

After a time, she found herself surrounded by several charming courtiers, each of whom had clearly spent many Seasons in London acquiring the Town bronze even a whipster could see shone on each countenance. She fanned herself, smiled and smiled a little more, offered a compliment here, an attentive listening ear there, a giggle at just the right moment of an expressed anecdote, and accepted every gentleman's request for a dance, no matter his general style or the beauty of his features.

In the subtle moods of a ballroom, an appearance of magnanimity was worth at least three critical beaux who would be watching her conduct most scrupulously, like hunting dogs after a fox. In the same way that a man who snubbed a worthy young woman in a ballroom was unfit for company of any kind, so must a young lady take great care to refrain from offering insult to the gentlemen around her.

"She is behaving just as she ought," one imperious matron stated boldly as she passed by on the arm of a spotted young man, preparing to go down a set with him, "though I must say I do not like to see so much gold upon unmarried females."

Marianne could only smile. She would wear as much gold as she wished, a compromise she felt to be eminently suitable for the torture she would now endure in dancing with the unhappy, nervous youth whose arm trembled as he escorted her onto the ballroom floor. By the time the dance ended, her toes were bruised, as well as at least three of her fingers, yet she continued to smile graciously long after the good man had released her.

"Someone should have warned you," a masculine voice whispered. "Freddy Shiplake is a fine fellow, admirable in many respects, but he does not know his left foot from his right."

Warmth suffused her cheeks, for Lord Crowthorne had quite improperly addressed her.

"Sir," she murmured softly, "we are not at all acquainted. You should not be speaking with me."

Since at that moment Sir Giles Chalfont was passing by, Lord Crowthorne hooked him with his arm and drew him to an abrupt stop. Sir Giles weaved on his feet. "Lord Edgar—what the deuce?"

"You are already acquainted with Miss Pamberley, are you not?"

"Indeed I am," Sir Giles said.

"Then you must perform a much needed service for me. Will you not present me to Miss Pamberley?"

Marianne felt such a sparkle of excitement explode in her stomach at the knowledge he had taken the time to learn her name that she hiccuped. She covered her lips quickly with her fan, feeling her blush deepen.

Lord Crowthorne, to his good credit, pretended not to notice.

Sir Giles bowed formally, and Marianne could see at once that he was nearly disguised. Clearly he had imbibed far too much of Lady Donnington's most excellent champagne. "It would be my honor," he gushed, again bowing to her. "Miss Marianne Pamberley, permit me to present to you one of our most esteemed and honorable gentlemen, a member of Brook's fine establishment, the boldest horseman in all of Albion, heir to the Earl of Bray, the most eminent, the—"

"Do stubble it, Giles. You are making me sound like a veritable coxcomb. The lady requires nothing but my name. And if you do not make haste, I shan't be able to secure the next waltz with her."

Marianne was fairly trembling from head to foot, even though Sir Giles's foxed state was making her giggle.

"Lord Crowthorne, my dear lady. Lord Crowthorne, may I present Miss Marianne Pamberley of Berkshire?"

Lord Crowthorne smiled broadly at his friend and gave him a shove toward the doorway. "Take some air, Giles. I believe you are in great need of it at present."

Marianne was caught by the warm, playful friendship between the men, as well as by the smile which had softened much of Lord Crowthorne's habitual hauteur. He had a great deal of countenance generally, but seeing him smile in this youthful manner made him seem more human and therefore more accessible.

When Sir Giles had disappeared into the antechamber leading to the entrance hall, Lord Crowthorne turned to her and bowed formally. Marianne, in turn, dipped an elegant curtsy.

"I am very happy to make your acquaintance," she began, "for we are neighbors in Grosvenor Square. I met your mother earlier. She is a very fine lady."

His brows rose in some degree of surprise. "Indeed, she is," he responded, watching her carefully. "I must say, you are not in the usual style."

"Oh? Pray tell me, what is the usual style?"

"All simperings and artifice. Do I offend you if I tell you I had expected much of the same from you?"

She laughed. "This may be my first London Season, m'lord, but I enjoyed my first come-out ball many years ago. I hope I know how to conduct a conversation with

a man without resorting to schoolgirlish absurdities."
Oh, but she was pleased with the degree of composure
she was exhibiting. How could Lord Crowthorne fail
to be impressed by her?

"You are a fresh breeze in a very stultified room,
and I do not refer only to our hostess's ballroom."

"But to the larger society in which we move. How
unfortunate you would find so many lively personages
disagreeable in that fashion. I suppose I have the advantage of not having been to London before."

"I believe you do."

Sir Jaspar Vernham had been near enough to hear
and to observe the entire exchange. Marianne had
never appeared so confident and attractive. *She has chosen him already,* he thought, his soul sinking, for he
could hear echoing in his mind Lord Crowthorne's
earlier declared intention of making Marianne his wife
if he could. He wondered suddenly if she had been
right after all in her assessment that she was destined
to make a brilliant match.

He moved slowly to the opposite end of the ballroom, where Miss Theale was straining to sustain a
halting conversation with a young, spotted man by
the name of Freddy Shiplake. He was grateful he had
already determined to champion Miss Theale. Had
nothing diverted his mind from the sight of Lord
Crowthorne leading Marianne so elegantly onto the
ballroom floor, he rather thought he might have
fallen into a brown study.

As it was, the immense relief on Miss Theale's face
as he detached her from Mr. Shiplake was the precise
diversion he needed to mend his drooping spirits.

Miss Theale took his arm and gave it a squeeze. "I
was never more grateful," she whispered. "He began

to stammer, telling me of his bay mare, and the more involved the story became, the worse he tripped over his words. I pitied him so, but there was nothing for it. Believe me, Sir Jaspar, when I tell you that not only did you come to my rescue, but to Mr. Shiplake's, as well. I only wish I might do something for him, because otherwise he seemed an intelligent sort of person, and not once did I have the sensation he had begged for a dance in order to bring himself within Marianne's orbit."

Her gaze shifted down the ballroom. "Oh, do but look at her! I vow she is the most beautiful young woman I have ever seen. It is no wonder . . . oh. I see she is dancing with Lord Crowthorne."

"Are you acquainted with his lordship?" he inquired, intrigued by her sudden disquiet.

"As it happens, I am. I know him very well, for his mother was used to be acquainted with my mother at Miss Lightwater's Seminary for Young Ladies. He has been a frequent guest in our home."

"Ah," he murmured in response. "And what is your general opinion of Lord Crowthorne? Is he a man of information, of kindness and generosity? I have not met him myself, nor do we share a mutual acquaintance, and I should like to know a little about him."

"I have always admired him," Miss Theale stated frankly. "Whenever we were in company, which was quite often, he made every effort to converse with me, an act I attribute solely to his kind nature. He is ten years my senior, and unless he sought me out, I confess I was far too conscious of the disparity in our ages to be comfortable in his presence. Even now, though it has been years since I left the schoolroom, I find I never quite feel I am his equal when we are together. I daresay the fault is mine entirely. When I am with him, I feel very shy for no particular reason. Although you have already observed I am on occasion stupid in company."

"I have noticed no such thing," he responded warmly.

She lifted her gaze to his and much of the tension deserted her small face. "You are very kind to say so, and I am deeply appreciative of your attentions to me. Otherwise I believe I should be all at sea. Lady Ramsdell is not well tonight and Marianne . . . need I say more?" She gestured toward the dancers with an elegant sweep of her fan.

Jaspar turned in the direction of her fan and could not help but laugh, for at that moment Marianne was spinning past them in the arms of Lord Crowthorne, smiling as though she was filled with sunshine.

He caught his breath. Faith, he wished he had not tumbled in love with her summer last. There was no greater torture than watching the woman he loved flirting with a gentleman whose birth, breeding, and fortune could fulfill her every schoolgirl's dream.

He tore his gaze from her and led Miss Theale from the ballroom, changing the subject completely. "When you say Lady Ramsdell is not well, I trust she is in no danger?"

"N-no," Miss Theale murmured. "That is, I should not have said anything. I only suspect . . . pray forget that I have spoken." Her blush was fiery.

"Oh, I see!" He guided her through the antechamber and into the entrance hall. "Yes, of course, you must be right. How very perceptive. However, I will say nothing more, for all your freckles have now become blended together." He was afraid she might be offended by his reference to her complexion. Instead, she emitted a laughter that warmed his heart.

"It is the most abominable circumstance that I blush so readily. You would think a woman of my age would have long since learned to command her complexion."

He nodded in mock solemnity. "Yes, of course, a woman of *your age*. I daresay another year or two and you risk many of the usual declines of advancing years—the gout, a powerful need for very thick spectacles, perhaps a cane."

She giggled a little more. "How you make me laugh!" she cried, glancing up at him as together they moved into a high-ceilinged drawing room of blue and gilt.

"Do you know, when you smile I vow you are as pretty as Marianne. No, I will listen to none of your protests—though I wonder if I might make a suggestion?"

"Oh, yes, if you please. I would like it above all things."

"It concerns your hair," he said, lowering his voice.

She sighed deeply. "The greatest trial of my existence. Edgar was used to tell me that I appeared like a flame gone wild."

"Edgar?"

"Lord Crowthorne," she said dismally.

"Ah. Well, perhaps he was not as tactful as he ought to have been."

"He never is," she stated simply, with all the appearance of one who had long since accepted the matter entirely. "Tell me what you think."

"Only that Miss Marianne's abigail is known to be adept with a pair of shears and curling irons."

"And how do you know this?" Miss Theale queried with a smile.

He leaned toward her rather conspiratorially. "Winter last, Miss Marianne told me so, though I must say she need not have said a word. I had already witnessed the transformation. Her new abigail arrived in October, and by early November I was bowled over by her improved appearance."

"What gammon!" she cried. "As though anything could improve Marianne's beauty even the slightest."

He found he had to agree with her. Even drenched from a heavy rain, he doubted Marianne would appear anything but exquisite. However, he did not feel his companion needed to hear such an admission. "I must disagree, for I know one thing which would improve her appearance even as we speak."

Miss Theale turned surprised eyes upon him. "And what could that possibly be?"

"A disposition as sweet as yours."

Miss Theale began to blush anew. "Now you are trying to turn me up sweet, but to what purpose I cannot begin to imagine, unless . . . Sir Jaspar, are you hoping to ingratiate yourself in my company in order that you might be nearer the object of your heart's desire?"

"Only a little," he admitted, "for I am certain by now you have guessed the state of my heart—"

"You are in love with her," she whispered.

"Hopelessly," he admitted, maneuvering her among dozens of guests crowded into the long, rectangular chamber. "However, I wish to assure you that my strongest desire is to be of service to you. I know very well what it is to be at odds in society."

She seemed anxious suddenly. "Would it be impertinent of me to inquire about something Marianne told me this morning?"

"Not in the least. I believe in being forthright—about *nearly* everything."

She chewed on her lip, then asked, "Is it true you served in her father's stables?"

"She said as much?" he asked, much surprised.

"Yes," she responded slowly. "She was in a bad temper this morning because one of the undermaids had scorched a piece of lace she had wished to wear this evening. When the conversation at breakfast turned to you, she blurted out that she did not know how you had come to be in London when you were naught but a stable boy in satin breeches. I must say Ramsdell stared very hard at her, and she soon fell into a fit of the blushes and begged pardon just as she should have. She is a puzzle to me, I confess. At the very moment one begins to think badly of her, she redeems herself, for she was contrite for the remainder of the meal."

"I know precisely what you mean. I can never think too harshly of her. She has suffered, I believe, from the want of a father. Simon Pamberley was one of those unfortunate creatures who lost his fortune gaming, then perished unexpectedly, leaving his daughters penniless."

"Lady Ramsdell was kind enough to share her history with me, though I must say it is a wondrous miracle that Mrs. Pamberley is recovering so well."

"A miracle, indeed."

"I enjoy your company very much, Sir Jaspar. I find I can speak quite easily with you, and that is something I treasure beyond words. I shall take your suggestion— with Marianne's permission, of course—and apply to her maid for assistance. My abigail is not in the least talented besides, being far too old to tend a young lady with even the pretense of enthusiasm. She has been here only three days, and already I can see she detests London. She complains constantly of the ill effects of the nightly fog."

He murmured the appropriate responses, intending then and there to bring Miss Theale's misfortunes to Marianne's notice as soon as he was able. He was certain under her auspices Miss Theale would bloom appreciably. He could only hope Marianne was not so sunk in her own vanity that she would refuse to help her new cousin.

Settling Miss Theale in a comfortable chair near the fireplace, he went in search of some refreshment for her. When he found Freddy Shiplake ogling her from across the room with every appearance of working up his nerve to descend upon her, he reminded him several young ladies had not yet been asked to dance.

"I s-say!" Freddy cried. "N-never one to f-f-forget m'duty!" He blushed scarlet and turned in the direction of the ballroom.

When Jaspar returned to Miss Theale with a chilled glass of champagne in hand, he watched with delight as she smiled up at him and bid him take a seat, for she believed Miss Caversham meant to play. "She is widely acknowledged as an exemplary pianofortist. I have heard nothing else since I crossed the threshold this evening. Ah, here she is now."

At that moment, a young woman dressed in an elegant gown of blue satin approached the pianoforte amidst a gentle round of applause.

"I understand you play, as well," he whispered. "Marianne spoke of your having made use of Ramsdell's instrument with great fervor one morning."

At that, Miss Theale giggled. "I am afraid I woke her, but it was well past eleven and I had been given to understand that everyone was astir. I was deeply mortified."

Sir Jaspar grunted in an undignified manner and leaned back into the sofa. He understood Miss Theale perfectly. Marianne, it would seem, had taken to tonnish life like a fish to water, and was already sleeping until nearly noon. He was not at all pleased.

Since Miss Caversham struck the first notes of a Mozart sonata, he was able to forget for a time his ignoble thoughts concerning Marianne's frivolous choices. In the end, however, he could only conclude that a great deal of his irritation was due to the fact that even while the lovely sonata rang through the air, Marianne was probably still in the company of Lord Crowthorne.

When Miss Caversham completed her excellent performance, he noticed Miss Theale was eyeing the instrument with great longing. He did not hesitate, but turned to her and said, in a carrying voice, "Will you play for us, Miss Theale?"

She was startled by his request. Since several listeners nearby turned her direction, she hesitated only briefly before inclining her head. "I would be happy to oblige you, Sir Jaspar."

Miss Caversham relinquished the pianoforte graciously but took up a seat nearby, intent on observing the lady who had been chosen to succeed her.

To his delight, Jaspar watched the rather mousy young woman with her hair—how had Crowthorne described it?—like a flame gone wild confidently approach the pianoforte. She took a full minute to adjust the bench to her liking, holding her fingers above the keys each time in order to ascertain her relationship to the instrument. When she was satisfied, she began a work by Beethoven.

Jaspar wondered if he had erred in pushing forward a young lady so unaccustomed to society, yet some instinct had told him Miss Theale was longing for the chance to play. He was not disappointed in her performance.

She played brilliantly and with great feeling, to the effect that the same audience which had attended solicitously to Miss Caversham now lent their ears and hearts to Miss Theale, as well.

He could not help but watch Miss Caversham's expression now and again. She went from stunned aggravation that so accomplished a musician had succeeded her to a true admiration of Miss Theale's abilities and finally to a complete involvement in the music. She was the first to rise to her feet and applaud her successor when the sonata came to an end.

Miss Theale was startled by the applause which rose around her, even more so when a number of her audience hurried to her side and congratulated her on her superior performance.

Jaspar stepped aside and felt himself smiling with perhaps more self-congratulation than he should have as he watched his young protégé receive the praise of her new admirers.

His instincts had always been excellent, for they had won him both a fortune and a knighthood. Yet in the course of his career, he had to admit that this small triumph, directed also by his instincts, had been worth a hundred others which the world might have deemed of far greater value.

Marianne held Lord Crowthorne's arm the entire distance from the ballroom to the drawing room and the far wall where the pianoforte was positioned. She was aware her "cousin" had just played magnificently and was too shocked to register anything except a growing indignation that she had been supplanted by a mere Miss Theale. At the same time, her gaze was fixed upon Sir Jaspar Vernham, for somehow she knew he had been involved in this wretched debacle. He was presently explaining to a rather tall woman in a sapphire blue gown his relationship to Miss Theale as a mere friend.

Her gaze drifted to Annabelle.

Annabelle had eclipsed her!

How was it possible?

Earlier, when the waltz had ended, she had remained on Lord Crowthorne's arm at his insistence. He had procured her some refreshment while the strains of a Mozart sonata were being played quite nicely in the drawing room. She was fully engaged in a delightful conversation with his lordship about his childhood in Hampshire when Beethoven replaced Mozart.

She watched as his attention drifted away, slowly at first and then quite suddenly. "If that is not Miss Theale playing," he exclaimed, "I shall give a guinea to the first fool who smiles at me."

She thought it an odd thing to say, yet it would be an even odder circumstance were her cousin actually performing for the *beau monde* without even the smallest preparation. "I do not believe it is Miss Theale," she explained. "Dear Annabelle is very shy of company. She would not put herself forward in this manner."

"Then you do not know Annabelle as I do. She cannot resist displaying her musical abilities."

"You are acquainted with my cousin?"

"She is your cousin?" A frown creased his brow. "I thought I knew all her family."

Marianne dimpled. "She is not precisely a relation of mine. She is Ramsdell's cousin, and I have adopted the relationship because it seemed to make everything simpler for us."

He did not seem in the least interested in her explanations. "Come," he said, still frowning. "I am persuaded Miss Theale is playing. I must see for myself."

"Of course, my lord, if you wish it." She pouted to show her disapproval of the scheme, but he did not glance down to discover her wishes. Instead, he took her arm most forcefully and guided her quickly to the drawing room.

She had been shocked to find Annabelle was indeed playing, not only with a great deal of composure but with so much ability that her audience was entirely enraptured. What was worse, though, was finding that she lost Lord Crowthorne's attention entirely. He soon became equally enamored of her performance.

Now, as she watched Annabelle surrounded by an appreciative audience, she heard her say, "Sir Jaspar was so kind as to recommend that I play. I was happy to oblige him."

So it was true! Jaspar had done this! Well, if he thought to cast her in the shade with such antics, he was much mistaken. She quickly devised a scheme to overcome the situation.

She disengaged her arm from about Crowthorne's, fully intending to win the day. Slipping deftly through the crowd, she quickly made her way to Annabelle's side. She embraced her cousin and praised her performance to the skies. "You have shown us all how the pianoforte ought to be played!" she exclaimed.

Annabelle blushed to the roots of her hair. "Oh, Marianne, how can you say so, when Miss Caversham preceded me? I only followed her lead and her example."

Marianne did not comprehend the error she had just made, but the general whispering and tittering which resulted in her proclamation concerning Annabelle's performance convinced her she had stumbled into a wasp's nest. She did not even know, of the many personages surrounding the pianoforte, which lady was Miss Caversham.

"You are far too modest, Miss Theale," the young woman in the blue gown stated. "I fear I must agree with, er, Miss Pamberley. You are by far the superior performer."

Miss Theale lifted her chin and declared most forcefully, "I am no such thing. However, I am beyond grateful to think you have admired my skills even a little. Perhaps we could discuss our mutual enjoyment of music at some point in the future?"

Miss Caversham's spine slackened a trifle. "I should be happy to do so," she returned with an elegant bow of her head. She cast a scathing glance at Marianne, however, and afterward strolled toward a corner of the room where her particular circle of admirers and friends waited.

When much of the crowd dissipated, Annabelle drew near to Marianne and took her arm in a conspiratorial fashion. "You were so kind to champion me," she whispered. "You have no idea how happy you have made me this evening. Even though Miss Caversham was miffed by your words, I was entirely overjoyed. You see, though I have three brothers, I have never had a sister with whom to advance on society as I have seen other siblings do."

Marianne blinked at Annabelle. Though she had been put out of countenance at having committed the *faux pas* against Miss Caversham, Annabelle's praises were presently putting her to the blush. Her own motives had been wholly self-interested. She had not thought of Annabelle's feelings even once.

"You are being too generous," she responded, "especially when I behaved in such a ridiculous manner."

"You do yourself an injustice. Sir Jaspar will bear me out." Before Marianne could prevent her, she called Sir Jaspar forward and said, "Do you not agree Marianne has supported me wonderfully?" She turned her sweet countenance toward the aggravating knight.

Sir Jaspar appeared to be pondering her supplication, but Marianne could see the irony in every sun-baked line beside his twitching lips and devilish brown eyes. "Of course I will agree with you, Miss Theale. Only a nodcock would do otherwise. Miss Marianne showed a remarkable amount of loyalty in rushing to praise you as she did. After all, you are cousins."

Miss Theale trilled her delicate laughter. "Yes!" she cried, "because we are cousins!"

Marianne did not know which person she wished to strangle more—Sir Jaspar for smiling in that sardonic manner of his, gloating as he was at having caught her in a predicament of her own making, or her cousin for the manner in which she was holding Jaspar's arm and looking up at him as though he was a god.

She searched about in her mind for some perfect retort, but Lord Crowthorne was suddenly at her side. He addressed his remarks, however, to Annabelle. "Well done, Miss Theale. I vow it has been an age since I heard you play, but I could not fail to recognize your skill even from the hallway beyond."

"Oh . . . hallo, Edgar," she responded softly, the joy leaving her face. "I saw you dancing earlier."

Marianne regarded her in some surprise, for she had called Lord Crowthorne by his Christian name, a cir-cumstance which indicated a relationship of long standing. She stared at Annabelle, aware that had her words not indicated some distress, the paling of her complexion most certainly bespoke the current state of her sentiments. Did Annabelle not approve of Lord Crowthorne? Did she know him so well that she found much in him to dislike?

The viscount smiled, apparently unaware of Anna-belle's sudden disquiet. "How happy I am to see your mother finally permitted you to come to London," he said. "I thought she never would."

"My aunt, the dowager Lady Ramsdell, finally persuaded her to allow me to come, which she did primarily because I would be residing in Ramsdell's home."

"His patronage will assure your success. In that regard, your mother was very wise. I trust you will find London everything you hoped it would be."

"Thank you," Annabelle murmured, a faint blush touching her cheeks.

Marianne glanced from Crowthorne to Annabelle, aware that something inexplicable lay beneath the surface of their relationship. The words each spoke were inconsequential, the usual polite verbiage of old friends greeting one another. However, the meaning of it all seemed fraught with an old history, one which obviously did not entirely satisfy Annabelle.

She could only conclude her cousin did not favor Lord Crowthorne—which was just as well, since Marianne intended his lordship to form the largest ornament in her court. She certainly had no interest in sharing him with Annabelle.

Five

"So you made a push to see that Annabelle performed last night," Marianne stated coolly, glancing at the large bouquet of flowers Sir Jaspar held. He had come to call upon the Ramsdell household the day after Lady Donnington's ball, but, as chance would have it, Constance had just retired to her bedchamber to rest and Annabelle had not yet returned from a trip to Hookham's library.

Marianne received him anyway, for she felt she ought to give him a hint about taking greater care with Annabelle. In her opinion, he had jeopardized what little confidence her cousin possessed by putting her forward last night as he did.

"Yes, she seemed to wish it." He smiled in that maddening fashion of his, as though he understood her perfectly.

"Were you not concerned that she might have faltered, as nervous as she is in company? I believe you did her a great disservice."

"No, you do not. You would have been happy had she stumbled through her piece. Then you might have rescued her and appeared noble in front of the *beau monde*."

Marianne ground her teeth and glared at Sir Jaspar. How dare he read her mind so clearly! Was nothing to be hidden from him?

She lifted her chin, "What a simpleton you are!"
She turned away from him, moving to stand before
the fireplace, above which was suspended a gilt-edged
looking glass. While pretending to gaze at a charming
ormolu clock on the mantel, she perused her reflection.

She was always slightly stunned by the image which
returned to her. Where had she gotten her large,
round green eyes and the thick fringe of lashes which
fluttered so beautifully? How had the small delicate
retroussé shape of her nose come into existence? None
of her sisters had her particular nose.

And from whence had such a delightful chin
emerged, sculpted so delicately with its charming cleft,
a kiss of the angels? She smiled faintly and her dimples
appeared. The angels had kissed her not once, not
twice, but thrice.

She was indeed blessed, but not just by her natural
beauty. Presently, she was in possession of an extraordinary maid who daily performed miracles with her
blond locks. Her abigail, Angelique, had studied all
the most recent issues of *La Belle Assemblée* and had
promised to create a dozen coiffures, each prettier
than the last, with which to dazzle the *ton*. This morning, she had labored for over an hour on Marianne's
hair, the curling tongs kept hot on a plate in the fireplace.

The result was perfection itself, for her hair was a
mass of ringlets caught up high on her head and cas-
cading in long rivulets almost to her shoulders. Inter-
spersed among her curls were nearly a score of small
pink star-like artificial flowers. She wore pearl eardrops
and a necklet of gold which held a small ivory cameo.

In the reflection, she could see only the top of her
gown, which was cut fashionably *décolleté* but softened
with a narrow length of Brussels lace. Her morning

gown was of a simple pink gingham, a homey confection meant to be worn only to receive visitors in her sister's drawing room. The high-waisted skirt of the dress had been designed to sustain a small bustle in the back, which meant nearly twice the quantity of fabric had been used to give the gown a full, fashionable appearance. On her feet she wore decadent slippers of pink silk embroidered with seed pearls. Even thinking about her slippers made her giddy with happiness.

She wondered if Jaspar thought her pretty this morning.

"At all events, *sir knight*," she continued, "might I suggest you take greater care in just how you force Annabelle into society? Perhaps next time you will overstep the bounds and find her flailing in rough seas."

"How kind of you to be so concerned for her well-being, Marianne," he returned.

She did not have to look at him to know he was being sarcastic.

"You may leave the flowers on the table by the door," she returned tersely. "I suppose I must thank you for them."

"I do not see why you should. I brought them for Miss Theale."

At that she turned to glare at him. "How noble of you," she said haughtily, resuming her pretense of admiring the clock.

"What is the hour?" he asked, advancing toward her.

She glanced down swiftly and saw that it was half twelve.

"Just as I thought," he murmured. He came up behind her and, because he was tall, he could see her quite well over the top of her head. Meeting her gaze in the looking glass, he said, "In case you needed such an assurance, yes, you are beyond beautiful this morning. I hesitate to mention it, however, since you were besieged with admirers last night following your waltz with Ramsdell. I fear puffing you up in your own conceit by offering you even one compliment."

"I—I do not take your meaning."

He merely smiled and shook his head. "My lovely Marianne, what pleased me more than the vision you presented in your gold silk gown last night—and, yes, of course I noticed—was how kindly you agreed to dance with even Freddy Shiplake."

"It would have been unconscionable not to have done so, even though he looks like a frog."

"And that is what I value most about you. Your generous spirit toward Freddy will be remembered by him for a long time. Now, what have I said to have brought such a stricken look to your eye?"

"I do not wish you to think more highly of me than you ought, and the compliment you've just paid me is more than I deserve. You—you know it is!"

"I see," he murmured, narrowing his eyes. "Is everything a design with you, then?"

"N-no," she responded quietly. "Perhaps . . . oh, I do not know. It is merely that I wish to enjoy every success during my first Season. I desire it more than anything else in the entire world, and if that means I must dance with Freddy Shiplake when I had much rather not, well . . ."

"You do not see yourself clearly, Marianne. You do not do yourself justice. Mr. Shiplake was refused by a dozen young ladies."

"He was?" she asked. "But that is so unkind!"

"There, you see?"

Marianne was thoughtful for a moment. "Maybe I am not so bad after all," she mused, "although I was fully aware of how any kindness to Mr. Shiplake would appear to the high sticklers. I do so long to be given vouchers to the assemblies at Almack's."

"I have no doubt you soon will."

"Do you think so, indeed?"

He smiled broadly. "Yes. Who could possibly disapprove of you?"

"Indeed, I do not know. I am striving to behave properly and to mind my tongue. If you must know, I find it a great relief to converse with you, for I do not have to guard my words. You already know my many deficiencies, and so I cannot shock you if I say something untoward." She was silent, then said, "Annabelle said you were very kind to her last night."

"I was happy to have a distraction. I did not like to see you surrounded by so many beaux, as you may well imagine. When I saw Miss Theale struggling to sustain a conversation with Mr. Shiplake after having danced with him, I did not hesitate to be of service to her. I even prevented him from asking her a second time. He seemed much struck with her, even though she is hardly the beauty she could be."

She chuckled at that.

"Why do you laugh?"

"Annabelle? A beauty?" She tugged at a ringlet near her ear and settled it in a better position relative to her cheekbone. "I think not. She has a very nice smile and even teeth, but what is there to admire beyond these meager attributes? I do not mean to be ungenerous, but I hope you were not encouraging her last night to think otherwise."

"As it happens, I was." He again met her gaze in the mirror. "I am convinced, given her natural grace, her love of dancing and music, and the sweet charm of her temperament that, with a proper wardrobe and coiffure, many will account her pretty, if not beautiful."

Marianne stared at him, believing he had gone mad. She did not comprehend in the least how Sir Jaspar could have come to such a conclusion. "We are speaking of Annabelle, whose hair curls riotously at the mere hint of a raindrop?"

"The very one." His smile was crooked.

"You have gone mad, and I daresay you have given my cousin hopes that are beyond false. Again I say you have done her a disservice."

"And I say you do her one by not helping her."

"Not helping her! Whatever do you mean?"

"Last night I suggested she apply to you for the services of your abigail. From the evidence of the past several months, your maid is obviously quite talented. Would not Miss Theale enjoy at least some improvement under her auspices?"

Marianne rolled her eyes. Jaspar could be such a nodcock, and he was not in the least aware how ridiculous he was being—and that over a mere Annabelle Theale! "What you are proposing is absurd and, yes, even hurtful. Annabelle will begin to have hopes far beyond any reasonable expectation."

Jaspar frowned slightly. "I do not see what great evil could result from a new coiffure and one or two more fashionable gowns."

"Now we are speaking of gowns?" she asked archly. "Faith, but you have taken a great interest in Annabelle. Are you, perchance, tumbling in love with her?"

She watched him carefully as he weighed his response, a niggling doubt within her at the possibility he could be in love with her plain cousin.

"No," Jaspar responded sincerely. "I am not in love with her."

"So you say, yet I vow you take a greater interest in her than in me, and you profess to be wildly in love with me."

He gently caught her elbow and turned her toward him, away from the looking glass. "Of course I am in love with you." He met her gaze boldly. "I fear, however, that were I again to declare my love with any degree of force, you would box my ears."

She should not have pressed him, for now he was speaking his heart all over again, making her smile and staring down at her with that look of his, as though he knew the world's secrets and meant by a kiss to tell them all to her. Her knees were trembling as they always did when he was about to . . .

Now he *was* kissing her. The beast! How sweet his lips felt. She should not permit this assault. But he had been too full of talk of Annabelle, and she wanted to know he was still hers to command. Yet to what purpose?

His arm slid about her waist as he drew her close. She touched his arms, feeling their strength. For this moment, she became a different woman, with different ideas about her life and her future. What these were precisely she could not say, except that the High Street in Wraythorne came suddenly to mind. She was playing with Mrs. Applegate's children and the sun was in her hair.

"Why do you let me kiss you?" he murmured into her ear. Gooseflesh traveled the length of her neck and her side. His breath was moist and warm.

"I do not know," she replied against his shoulder. "I do not know."

He drew back. "I know," he murmured, "and I shall tell you why. You are in love with me, Marianne. Admit it."

She shook her head and frowned. Her gaze fell to his neatly tied neckcloth. "I am very wicked."

He laughed softly. "That you could never be. So, tell

me, will you be of service to Annabelle? She needs your help."

Marianne compressed her lips. "I will not. I stand firmly by what I told you earlier, that changing her would be a dreadful mistake."

He was silent, watching her closely. She began to fear he would read her mind again. A blush inadvertently stole into her cheeks.

"I see what it is!" he cried at last. "Oh, Marianne, this is beneath you, truly it is. Why must she play the role of handmaiden to your queenly presence?"

To be thus exposed rankled deeply. "How dare you say such a thing to me?"

"Tell me it is not true."

"I will not justify such a horrid accusation by refuting anything."

"I thought as much. Well, if you will not help her, I shall."

He turned around and marched toward the door.

"And how shall you do that?"

"I shall beg Constance to permit me to take her shopping in New Bond Street. Once there, I have little doubt one of the shopkeepers will be able to recommend a new maid for her, which I will undertake to provide for her until the end of the season."

"I do not understand!" She stamped her foot. "Why do you give a fig for Annabelle Theale? What is she to you?"

He opened the door. "Someone who needs my assistance, that is all." Then he was gone.

Marianne stared at the flowers, which were for her dear cousin, and would have screamed with vexation had she not feared frightening the servants. Instead, she stamped her foot several times and muttered vile things about Sir Jaspar beneath her breath until some of her frustration departed.

When she was calmer, she sat down near the fire-place to review the entire dreadful interview, including the wretched kiss he had placed on her lips yet again. How was it he had such command of her, and why had she allowed him to kiss her—except that all his interest in Annabelle had undermined her confidence, and now he meant to transform her?

She did not understand. Surely a man who professed an undying love would never involve himself so nearly with another female. Perhaps he did not love her after all, but only believed he did.

Her heart began to ache in an unfamiliar manner. She chewed on her lower lip and hiccupped. Oh, why was everything so complicated?

After several minutes of entirely useless ponderings, she rose from her chair, intending to go in search of Constance. For some reason, she felt compelled to lay the dilemma before her elder sister, even though she would not wish to hear her sister's opinions. The thought, however, of having to live with so much turmoil was beyond bearing.

She had taken but two steps when the butler entered the room and ceremoniously announced Lord Crowthorne, Sir Giles Chalfont, and the Honorable Henry Speen.

Marianne, though stunned, composed herself quickly, and requested that Spencer inform Lady Ramsdell of her guests. He said quietly, "I do beg your pardon, miss, but I was given to understand all the ladies were within."

"We shall be very comfortable until my sister arrives, for Lord Crowthorne and I are fast friends."

"Very good, Miss."

Once the butler had quit the room, Marianne turned to her admirers, a wonderful sensation of joy pervading her heart. To think that three of London's most fashionable young gentlemen had come to call the day after the Donnington ball was beyond her expectations. Of course, she had hoped she might be able to gather them into her court, but such immediate attention bespoke a prosperous Season.

"How happy I am to see all of you," she said magnanimously. "For was not Lady Donnington's ball a delight?"

She took up her seat by the fireplace, and the men followed suit, gathering, just as she had hoped, about her in a half circle.

When she had first arrived in Grosvenor Square, she had spent nearly an hour rearranging the drawing room for just this purpose—every queen must have her throne, and hers was to be the forest green wing chair by the fireplace. An elegant screen of handsome needlework was situated just behind the chair and further gave the impression of a throne. Next to her, on an inlaid table, sat a small brass globe of the world.

Across from her, Lord Crowthorne took up his seat on a sofa of white-and-beige striped silk. She smiled at him, acutely aware that he was watching her closely. *Ah,* she mused, *he is weighing my merits to discover whether or not I am worthy of his future title, but is he worthy to become my husband?*

The thought that she would do the choosing tickled her heart with pleasure. She observed him in kind. He was not so tall as Sir Jaspar, but he had a great deal of air about him which gave him by far the better countenance. His features were pleasing, even handsome, though his nose was thin and rather hawkish. His eyes were an unusual gray which presently, because he was scrutinizing her, seemed less than compassionate.

He was dressed to perfection, just as he ought to be, in dove gray small clothes, a well-fitting coat of charcoal gray superfine, and glossy black shoes. A single fob hung from a white silk waistcoat. His hair was raven's-wing black and cut *a la Brutus*. His presence, she decided, was nothing short of formidable.

She was not entirely content to be so closely scrutinized and decided to give him a shock. She turned to Sir Giles and said, "I know you were in attendance last night, but I daresay you have little memory of the ball—or am I much mistaken?"

Mr. Speen burst out laughing, and Sir Giles stared at her dumbly. He then smiled rather sheepishly. "Was I so very indiscreet?"

"Yes, you were. But a gentleman, nonetheless."

He dropped his elbow onto the arm of the chair, and lowered his chin into his waiting hand. "Faith, but I believe I have tumbled in love," he murmured nonsensically. "At last, a lady who understands me."

Lord Crowthorne chuckled. "She said nothing of understanding you," he stated, "merely that you apparently behaved in a gentlemanly fashion even though you were foxed."

"In his altitudes," Mr. Speen added.

"Completely disguised," Sir Giles said, "for after so many years on the *ton*, I find it is the only manner in which I can endure yet another insipid night of a London Season."

"Sir Giles!" Marianne cried. "How can you speak so? I was never happier in my life than last night."

"Then you must be from the country," he retorted, pretending to yawn.

"Can only country folk truly enjoy London?" she asked gently, eyeing him with great innocence and permitting him a single long bat of her thickly fringed lashes.

He swallowed visibly, then said, "In your company, Miss Marianne, I begin to feel as though I have just arrived from a long sojourn in my home in Surrey."

Marianne offered him a warm, inviting smile, which further reduced his expression to one of bliss. She would have continued her assault on his sensibilities, except at that moment the door opened and Constance and Annabelle entered the chamber.

Annabelle's hair had been gathered up into a long braid and wound at the nape of her neck. Tendrils stuck up oddly all over her head. Oh, dear! Jaspar was right. Poor Annabelle was greatly in need of assistance. She wore a brown wool gown which served only to whiten her complexion. Worse followed, when, upon greeting each gentleman in turn, two bright spots of color appeared upon each cheek.

Marianne felt stricken with sudden remorse. How was it possible she had ever determined not to help her new friend?

She hiccupped softly and went forward to take Annabelle's hand. "Is it not marvelous that Lord Crowthorne and his friends have come to make us feel easy in our first London season?"

Annabelle cast a shy smile toward the viscount. "Indeed, so very kind. However, having known Lord Crowthorne since I was a child, I am not at all surprised by his having called upon us today. How did you enjoy the ball last night?"

Lord Crowthorne, now standing, approached them both. "Prodigiously, for I had the pleasure of hearing you play again. How long has it been since I last saw you in Hertfordshire? It must be over a year—"

"Fifteen months," Annabelle returned swiftly. "That is, I believe it has been fifteen, perhaps longer. You had come to us at Christmas with your mother. Do you recall that you and I joined the carolers and went about the countryside for hours with none the wiser as to your identity?"

Marianne shifted her attention fully to Lord Crowthorne and addressed him. "Did you do so, indeed? What delight. I love Christmastime and all the special songs of the season. Imagine, though, caroling with perfect strangers?"

Annabelle nodded. "A few were known to us, but they kept mum."

"You fell in the snowbank," he stated, smiling.

Annabelle giggled. Marianne looked at her and recalled Jaspar's remarks concerning her cousin. She did appear uncommonly fetching when she smiled. If only her hair was not so unruly and her gown so very brown.

The conversation became more general for a time, until Sir Giles begged Annabelle to perform a little of the sonata about which Crowthorne had been exclaiming. Constance, who also had not heard the performance, joined them at the pianoforte, along with Mr. Speen.

Lord Crowthorne drew Marianne toward the window. She was pleased beyond words at the intimate attention—less so, however, when he brought Annabelle forward as the principal subject. "I have known her since she was a child and I a student at Harrow. Even then she was gifted in her abilities on the pianoforte. I only wish—"

Marianne pressed him. "What do you wish?"

"You see how it is with her. She has come to London after all this time, and yet her mother apparently took not the smallest interest in promoting her success."

Marianne felt a sudden bolt of pique shoot right through her. Why did *both* the principal gentlemen in her existence concern themselves with *poor* Annabelle? What would he say next? That Marianne ought to concern herself with Annabelle, reform her fashion, change her coiffure, give her lessons in deportment? Her nerves prickled with irritation.

She turned her gaze toward the far end of the elegant rose chamber so Lord Crowthorne might not see the certain glitter in her eyes. He fell silent as Annabelle's sonata began to dominate the room.

The music had a curiously soothing effect upon her, and very soon she was not nearly so agitated. Her mind reviewed the dilemma from every facet, until a sudden inspiration dawned on her. She stole a glance at Lord Crowthorne and realized he was almost fatherly in his affection for Annabelle.

The entire situation could be turned to her advantage in the simplest manner possible. She drew closer to him and said, in a soft voice, "Ever since her arrival I have been pondering how I might help her. I am so grateful you brought forward your own concerns, for now I am determined to take Annabelle under my wing."

His attention immediately reverted to her, just as she hoped it would. "You would do this for her? But you scarcely know her."

Marianne opened her eyes very wide and let her lashes fall every so slowly. "She is my cousin now. Why would I not be of service to her if I might?"

His expression filled with something very close to wonder. "You are a fresh breeze, Miss Marianne." He suddenly possessed himself of her hand. "And I am beyond happy you have come to London. If this is indeed your purpose, you will have my devotion, my gratitude, even my admiration, forever."

His lips were on her hand and sparkles of triumph popped in her head.

She would have a proposal of marriage from him before the first of May!

Six

Much to Marianne's surprise, the next few days were some of the happiest of her existence. She was making excellent progress with Lord Crowthorne, but that was not what was bringing her such contentment. Instead, the transformation of Annabelle was daily becoming so extraordinary she could only congratulate herself on the wonders she was performing.

She had bid her abigail take Annabelle's hair under her masterful fingers and her clever eye. The result was a much shorter coiffure. Though her red locks still dangled past her shoulders, they could be much more easily managed.

With the use of heated curling tongs, the frizzy curl of her hair could be sufficiently smoothed away with enough left to form pretty ringlets of varying lengths and sizes. Gold bands fastened in her hair in the Greek fashion also served to keep the natural curl in check.

Grudgingly, she had admitted to Jaspar that his perceptions were far more incisive than her own. Not only was Annabelle thriving and gaining more confidence with her new look, but she had become a very pretty woman, and when she smiled, yes, even beautiful. Jaspar had merely laughed at her, calling her a peagoose for feeling even the mildest threat that Annabelle might eclipse her.

Marianne had retorted, "Now you are being absurd!

All I said was that she is become quite pretty. I did not say I thought she might steal all my beaux."

"No, you did not. However, you were chewing on your lip just now, and . . . there, you hiccupped again!"

She had been outraged that he was accusing her of feeling insecure and flounced from the drawing room, leaving him in the company of her sister, Annabelle, and Sir Giles Chalfont.

Lord Crowthorne, upon witnessing Annabelle's daily improvements, complimented Marianne prodigiously. Among the many epithets he showered upon her included a worker of miracles, an angel most high, and a lady of exalted compassion.

Marianne accepted these accolades quite graciously, always with a lowering of her chin, a dipping of her forehead, and a protest that she fell quite short of his praises. "I assure you," she demurred softly, wafting her lashes up at Crowthorne in humble flirtation, "I am none of these things. I merely wished to be of assistance to a new friend."

"If Annabelle had more friends as devoted as you, her future would be all but secured."

Her lashes paused in mid bat. *Why must all her gentlemen friends be so devilishly concerned with Annabelle's future?* She was sick to death of Jaspar's fawning over her day and night, and now it seemed Lord Crowthorne held Annabelle in his thoughts more often than he ought, given that he formed the most prominent jewel in her London crown.

She changed the subject abruptly. "Do you mean to attend the opera this evening?"

"Of course, for you will be there," he said softly, "and I shall visit Ramsdell's box during intermission, if that would please you."

Marianne drew in a deep breath of satisfaction. Finally, the subject had become dear to her heart. "Oh, yes, very much so. I have come to think of you as one of my most trusted friends."

"And I you," he murmured in perfect response.

That evening, Marianne descended the stairs arrayed in a light blue silk gown, a matching cape lined with soft white cashmere, and a small diamond necklet Constance had loaned her. She found her cousin standing in front of the round table which graced the entrance hall and upon which were arranged several beautiful bouquets. Annabelle bent over a cluster of violets. She appeared to be smelling them, but to what purpose? Violets had little fragrance.

"Who are they from?" she called down to Annabelle.

"Oh!" her cousin cried, drawing upright immediately. A blush formed quickly upon her cheeks. "You gave me a start. I did not hear you on the stairs."

"I never meant to frighten you," Marianne said, smiling, "but how pretty you look in your lilac silk. It's a lovely complement to your complexion and your hair. My pearls appear to great advantage, as well."

She reached the bottom of the stairs and Annabelle moved toward her with tears in her eyes, her hands outstretched. "How will I ever be able to thank you for helping me as you have? You are the kindest person I have ever known. You cannot know how happy you have made me."

Marianne took Annabelle's hands in her own and gave them a squeeze. Her conscience, however, smote her greatly, for in no manner had she entered into the project of recreating Annabelle with the smallest purpose of being of use to her.

Indeed, her motives were entirely selfish on all counts. For one thing, she did not want Jaspar to think so badly of her. For another, she knew she would have Lord Crowthorne's approval and gratitude were she to help his old friend. She had the good grace to blush in turn.

"I am certain you have a number of friends who would have taken such an interest in you had they been under the same roof. Why, even Lord Crowthorne expressed his concern."

Annabelle withdrew her hands, her mouth falling slightly agape. "He did?"

"Why, yes, but surely I told you as much." When Annabelle shook her head, she continued, "It would seem he is well enough acquainted with your mother to comprehend your sufferings, and he expressed his sadness that you were so poorly gowned. Pray do not be mortified. His words indicated the strongest, most sincere concern for you and for the success he wished you to have this Season."

Annabelle seemed dumbstruck, and her gaze shifted from one object to another about the small entrance hall as though she were trying to gain her bearings. Her color seemed much heightened, as well.

"I—I do not know what to say. I have known Edgar forever, but he always treated me as an annoying gnat he had trouble batting away. Not that I blame him. For many years before my first come-out ball, I did tend to dog his heels. He seemed much like a god to me, especially because I was a mere child when I met him and he a young man preparing for university."

Marianne had already grown bored with a conversation which had become centered exclusively on Annabelle. She smiled politely, however, and once her cousin fell silent, said, "Who are the violets from? What an elegant little bouquet. Would they not fit into a tuzzy-muzzy?"

"I believe they should, though I daresay they would not at all complement your blue silk."

"I was not thinking of me, but of you. Do you care to take them to the opera tonight?"

"I should like it above all things," she cried, smiling. "However, you should know they are for you. Lord Crowthorne's card is here." She gestured to the table.

Marianne felt a swell of happiness rise up within her. There were several bouquets present—roses, carnations, even tulips. However, the violets were exquisite, and she could see very well his lordship had meant for them to be carried to the opera.

"You shall carry them!" she cried at once. She could increase the impact of them were Annabelle to bring them to the opera. "They suit your gown to perfection and I am fully persuaded Lord Crowthorne would want us to share his gift."

Annabelle smiled ruefully. "There you are out. I am certain he thought only of pleasing you. He is greatly taken with you, but of that you must be aware."

Marianne picked up the violets and began carrying them toward the nether regions with the purpose of securing a posy holder from the kitchens. "I would like to think so, for I fully intend to marry him, if I can."

Annabelle watched Marianne disappear down the hall, but did not follow after her. The impetuous words which had slipped from Marianne's lips were daggers to her own heart.

Of course Edgar had formed an attachment to Marianne. What gentleman of any sense would not? She was by far the kindest young woman Annabelle had ever met, besides being as beautiful as Aphrodite.

Yet from the moment the dowager Lady Ramsdell

had succeeded in persuading Mrs. Theale to permit Annabelle to accompany Lord Ramsdell and his new bride to London, Annabelle's thoughts had been fixed on only one aim—to enter Edgar's society and see if she might arouse his interest in her as he had so quickly commanded her interest in him so many, many years ago.

To hear Marianne's intentions, so similar to her own yet with a profoundly greater chance for success, brought an ache to her throat and tears to her eyes. Even with the lovely transformation Marianne had secured for her, she was no match for the beautiful Miss Pamberley.

Withdrawing a kerchief from the beaded silk reticule dangling from her wrist, she dabbed at her eyes and willed her sadness away. From the start she had known she had only the barest chance of succeeding. If she must lose Edgar to another lady, she had to admit nothing would make her happier than to see the man she loved wed to her new and dearest friend.

With that, she straightened her shoulders and finally followed in Marianne's wake.

Marianne had taken too much wine at dinner, for she felt giddy and strange, besides stumbling over her words now and then. However, nothing would stop her from enjoying the champagne Lord Crowthorne offered her during intermission at the opera. When Jaspar leaned over to her and suggested she had had quite enough, she merely laughed and had yet another glass handed to her by her favorite beau.

She beamed up into Lord Crowthorne's face—at least she tried to. For the oddest reason, sometimes two or three of him swirled about happily. Since he attentively served the rest of Lord Ramsdell's guests, she did not have to continue trying to focus. Instead, she could relax and enjoy the sight of so many fashionable personages crammed into one enormous building and ogling one another with complete abandon.

Since these images had begun to swirl rather strangely, too, she closed her eyes, hoping they might stop. She felt sleepy and wonderful and perhaps would have drifted off had not a commotion in the box brought her attention round.

She turned to find Constance had risen to her feet and Lord Ramsdell was supporting her from the box. Annabelle was with her as well, holding her elbow and whispering to her. Lord Crowthorne was nowhere to be seen. On stage, the performers had once more begun singing to the rafters.

"What is happening?" She turned toward Jaspar.

"I believe your sister has been taken ill. Remain here. I shall find out what is going forward."

"Thank you. I—I admit I would prefer to remain in my seat at least for the present. I—I am a trifle dizzy."

"I cannot imagine why," he mused facetiously, passing by her.

She neither knew the cause of her dizziness, nor why he was smiling at her in that ridiculous manner, as though to say he really did understand and could not she divine the reason herself? Well, no. She could not!

She sighed deeply and found she was better able to see now, though she felt overheated. She fanned herself and hummed along with the music, enchanted by the sight of several dandies parading near the front of the stage. She had never seen such affectations before and was vastly amused by one in particular dressed entirely in green.

When Jaspar returned, she inquired, "Is that the

Green Man of whom I have heard so much?" She inclined her head toward the stage.

Jaspar, who had resumed his seat, lifted his quizzing glass to search the numerous personages below and finally drew back laughing. "The very one. What a quiz of a fellow, would not you agree?"

Marianne giggled, then recalled suddenly that Jaspar had returned from a mission of no small import. "How does my sister fare?"

"I fear she is not at all well. Ramsdell and Miss Theale have accompanied her home. I was instructed to bring you along when you wished for it."

"Indeed," Marianne murmured, not certain precisely what Jaspar had said to her. She felt sleepy again, and once more closed her eyes.

What seemed like a moment later, Jaspar was urging her, "Come, m'dear. Time to return you to Grosvenor Square."

Marianne looked around, a trifle confused. "But the opera is not yet finished."

"But you are. Come." He rose and extended his hand to her.

She took it readily and weaved on her feet as he took a strong hold of her elbow and drew her close to him. She would have protested his arm, which was suddenly about her waist, except that she could no longer feel her feet.

"Oh, dear," she murmured. "I feel quite odd, Jaspar. Whatever is the matter with me? Perhaps I have the same illness which has afflicted Constance."

"I certainly hope not."

She thought his remark strange, but her mind was unable to center itself on just why, so she remained silent. He guided her firmly from the opera house and, within a scant few minutes, handed her up into his ge. He sat very close to her and arranged her cape solicitously about her shoulders, then settled a warm carriage rug across her knees.

"How very cozy," she murmured.

"Too cozy, I begin to think," he responded, again nonsensically to her ears. He called for the coachman to start.

After a few minutes, the gentle bouncing and swaying of the vehicle was once more lulling her asleep. She leaned her head into Jaspar's shoulder and was grateful when he took up her hint and slipped his arm about her. She sighed, feeling happier than ever.

Her hand found Jaspar's neckcloth and the show of lace above his waistcoat. She began fingering the lace and sighing, then fingering the lace a little more. Jaspar was so warm next to her, and she was so happy. They would marry one day and have perhaps a dozen children.

"Would you like to have a score of children, Jaspar?"

"Perhaps not quite a score, but several, yes."

"I, too. We shall have at least a dozen, you and I. Does not that sound positively delightful?"

When there was no response save an awkward clearing of Jaspar's throat, she looked up at him. "Do you not wish to give me a dozen children?"

He looked down at her, his eyes glittering in the darkness of the coach. "You should not say such things to me," he said. "We are not betrothed."

She held his gaze steadily. "Then we should be betrothed. I wish to marry you more than life itself and have a dozen children with you and kiss you now."

She caught his neck and lifted her mouth to his. He hesitated, but only for a moment. Then he crushed her lips with his own, kissing her boldly, just as he always did. Oh, why were they in London when they could be back at the Priory and married and having children together? Did not Jaspar know how terribly she loved him?

The kiss made her dizzier still, especially when she parted her lips and he took possession of her tender mouth. Her body caught fire in the most extraordinary way, and engulfed her in flames that teased and tormented her with pleasure.

She felt born anew as his tongue played within her mouth. Her every sense was heightened in a manner she had never known. She could go on kissing him forever and ever. Yes, a dozen children would be lovely!

"Oh, Jaspar," she murmured throatily against his lips, "take me to bed."

A sudden and surprising darkness followed . . .

Marianne awoke the following morning feeling as though something sharp had been crammed into her brain. She had never known such pain, and she could barely open her eyes. The dim light filtering through the closed draperies seemed like the brightest July sunshine.

Worse, however, was the terrible knowledge that she could not recall a single moment of her trip to the opera the night before. She felt utterly horrified. She felt something untoward, unexpected, and entirely unwelcome had occurred—but what?

After several minutes spent calming her panic, she struggled to scoot herself up in bed. Her eyes remained closed and the pounding in her head had grown worse with the effort. She drew in deep breaths as she leaned against her pillows.

Opening one eye, she glanced at the clock over the fireplace and saw that the hour was half eleven, time to be rising. Constance had made it known the ladies of Ramsdell's town house would be receiving morning

callers at one o'clock that afternoon. Marianne would
need at least an hour just to be ready to receive her
maid and, oh, she did not want to think about breakfast. "Oh," she groaned aloud, her stomach suddenly
flip-flopping violently.

She wished the entire day to the devil.

Oh, dear, what an ungracious thought. But her head
hurt her so and her tongue felt as thick as the pillow
beneath her head. She wondered if she could even
speak properly.

She had heard many times of the notorious effects
of too much wine upon the frail human physique, yet
she had never experienced the subject of many hilari-
ous anecdotes. She found nothing amusing in how she
felt and believed with all her heart she never would.

More to the point, how was she to conduct herself
with even a semblance of dignity throughout the day
if these vicious symptoms continued? She must make
a monumental effort. She had no inclination to beg
off from the day's proposed entertainments because
she had been indiscreet last night, especially since
Lord Crowthorne would be among the callers today.

A memory returned to her. Lord Crowthorne had
come to Ramsdell's box last night bringing—oh,
dear!—a great deal of champagne with him for everyone's general pleasure.

She slid her legs over the edge of the bed. Nausea
poured over her. She clutched at her stomach and
again took several deep breaths.

After a time, she was able to ring for her maid. After
an even longer interval, she was able to take her bath
and sip some coffee, which seemed to steady her
nerves considerably.

A slice of dry toast was the only accompaniment to
the beverage she felt she could endure, and she sent
word to Constance she would not be joining the others

for nuncheon. Even the word made her stomach boil unhappily.

Angelique encouraged her with soft words and gentle brushings of her hair, admitting she had been foxed a time or two herself and knew the pain her mistress was presently enduring. Marianne was grateful for her maid's understanding.

At last, gowned in a summery calico frock of tiny daisies on a white background and her hair dressed with thin yellow ribbons, she descended the stairs slowly to the drawing room. She heard a great deal of chatter as she approached the doors, and Annabelle's voice suddenly filled the air with laughter. The sound of so much good humor nearly knocked her backward. She winced and slowly edged her way into the room.

Lord Crowthorne was present, along with his two constant companions, Sir Giles Chalfont and Henry Speen. Freddy Shiplake was, oddly enough, performing puppets for Annabelle's amusement, and even Constance was laughing riotously. Lord Ramsdell stood behind his wife, smiling in a great deal of amusement.

Marianne was grateful that the attention was removed from her, for she could become better accustomed to all the dreadful noise. Lord Crowthorne spied her and at once his face reflected concern. Oh, dear. He knew already she was unwell, and she was trying so very hard to appear as she normally did, apparently without effect.

He approached her and smiled ruefully down into her face. "I should have not brought the champagne to your box," he said quietly.

She smiled in return. "Then you can see I am suffering."

"Perhaps you should have remained in bed. I blame myself. Will you ever forgive me?"

"There is nothing to forgive." She patted his arm,

which she now realized was supporting her own. "How can you be to blame? You could not have known I had stupidly partaken of five glasses of wine at dinner. Somehow I thought that so long as I was enjoying the fine meal I would be able to drink as much as I wished. Was any female ever so stupid?"

He smiled and drew her toward a chair as far from Freddy's silly antics as the size of the drawing room permitted. Once he saw her settled, he took up a seat beside her. "You were ignorant only," he said. "I am fully persuaded had you been conversant with the nature of, er, *too much wine*, you would not have been so imprudent."

"Indeed, I would not. I suppose it comes from having grown up with only sisters. Had I had a brother or two . . . and Papa, as you know, perished many years ago. Well, there it is. I have had no example from which to learn."

He shook his head. "In one innocent phrase you have completely condemned my sex. Do we all appear to be libertines and drunkards?"

"Oh, no!" she cried, horrified. "How can you misconstrue what I am saying? It is merely that gentlemen tend to launch themselves into all manner of physical sensation—riding to hounds at every opportunity, hunting so many brace of fowl that the meat must be shared with a score of neighborhood families, swimming in every manner of pool, lake, or river. If a young man must take a drink, he plunges in as he does everything else. Oh, I must stop speaking. My head is pounding again."

"You certainly are not in the usual style. How glad I am you finally came to London, Miss Marianne."

At that she turned to him. "Are you, truly?" she inquired. "You are in every respect a gentleman to say so, especially in this moment when the results of my

foolishness are so very evident. I feared you would con-
demn me. Instead you have been compassionate and
gracious. I thank you for that, Lord Crowthorne, from
the bottom of my heart."

He caught up her fingers gently in his and placed
a soft kiss on the back of her gloved hand.

What he might have said at that moment was lost in
Ramsdell's approach. "Are you feeling better?" her
brother-in-law asked. "Sir Jaspar told me when he
brought you home that he rather thought you would
not feel entirely well this morning."

His expression was full of understanding, and because she was surrounded by so much goodwill, tears
rose to her eyes. "You are very kind, but I shall do,
thank you."

Ramsdell's gaze shifted to Crowthorne, and Marianne was a little startled to see a coolness in her
brother-in-law's expression, which she suddenly realized often characterized his discourse with Lord Crowthorne. She felt rather than saw Crowthorne shift in
his seat.

The entire exchange was subtle, yet so full of meaning that she could not concentrate in the least on what
they were saying to one another, though she caught
words here and there, like *Tattersall's* and *a fine bit of
flesh and bone,* which gave her the impression they were
speaking of a recent purchase of horses.

Did Ramsdell in some manner not approve of Lord
Crowthorne? If not, what was the basis for his dislike
of a man she found perfectly unexceptionable in manner, fashion, and conduct?

Freddy Shiplake's performance came to an end. She
found herself surrounded by all the support anyone
would require, for it was obvious her condition had
been previously discussed by one and all. She was
about to take Constance's and Annabelle's combined

suggestion that she return to her bedchamber until she was entirely well when a disturbance in the doorway drew her notice.

Since she was seated and everyone else save Lord Crowthorne was standing, she could not see the newcomer.

"Sir Jaspar!" Constance cried. "Come. You must add your voice to ours and help us coax Marianne to retire until she feels better."

Marianne did not know she was rising to her feet. Her heart had begun beating so fast that she felt as though it had been replaced by a hummingbird. Her head filled with stars.

As the small crowd about her parted to bring Jaspar fully into view, the memories of having shared a coach ride home with him dominated her mind. He had kissed her—or, rather, she had kissed him so forcefully that he had responded in kind until she had been on fire.

The fire even now blazed up from her slippers, traveling along her silk stockings, up her legs, rising past her belly, taunting the hummingbird in her chest, and exploding the stars into a thousand fireworks in her brain.

"Oh, dear," she murmured, and promptly fell into a faint.

Seven

Lord Crowthorne watched Miss Marianne crumple into a heap almost at his feet. He was so stunned that for a long moment he merely stared at her prostrate form, unable to credit that she had actually fainted. Before he could command himself to take charge of the situation, Sir Jaspar had scooped her up and whisked her away.

In truth, he only left his seat when the crowd about Sir Jaspar, with Marianne cradled in his arms, moved out of the drawing room and into the entrance hall. Even then, he felt as though he were a spectator at a play.

No one turned to him for assistance or advice, not even to express shock at the unexpected swooning of the beautiful Miss Pamberley—not that he would have had anything of extraordinary value to add to the many suggestions and decisions which were occuring at lightning speed, for he had never been of any use in a sickroom.

His attention was not even fixed upon Marianne, precisely. He was more struck by the simple and quite stunning truth that Jaspar Vernham, who was mounting the stairs with Marianne in his arms, was a familiar, welcome, and intimate member of the Ramsdells' home. The very thing he had wished for since time out of mind Sir Jaspar had accomplished in a matter of months, apparently from the time he returned from his sojourn in India.

The remaining three young men returned to the drawing room. Sir Giles remarked dryly, "Rather eclipsed all of us, wouldn't you say?"

"Yes," Crowthorne acknowledged quietly.

Henry Speen drew close and addressed the more pertinent question. "Who the devil is he? I've never seen the fellow m'self before this season."

Freddy Shiplake offered his vast store of knowledge. "N-nabob," he stammered. "R-returned from In-india, summer l-last. Rich as Cr-croesus!"

Sir Giles stared at Freddy. "Yes, but *who* is he? Who are his parents, his connections?"

"N-neighbor, I s'pose. Miss Theale said he's kn-known the f-family for years."

"A second son, perhaps?" Lord Crowthorne mused, almost to himself. "I've never heard of the Vern-hams—of Berkshire? Very odd."

"In-in-indeed!" Freddy agreed, appearing quite pleased with himself.

Ramsdell returned at that moment and graciously requested that the gentlemen proceed to their next destination. "For the ladies have retired, as you may well imagine."

With that, all four men quit the town house and decided to return to Lord Crowthorne's family home two doors away. Once there, Crowthorne led them to the billiard room, where Sir Giles and Freddy quickly engaged in a competitive game. Freddy Shiplake, for all his stammering and spots, was an accomplished player.

For himself, he could not keep his mind from dwelling on the image of Sir Jaspar carrying Miss Marianne up the stairs. He felt decidedly uneasy. He could recall now, in vivid detail, precisely how Marianne had looked when she had recognized Sir Jaspar. Her expression had been one of horror.

At the opera, she had been pleasantly situated beside the knight and had been engaged in a light banter which he had found unexceptionable. That Miss Marianne seemed to be a trifle disguised did not occur to him until he was about to depart her box and she waved good-bye to him, calling his name loudly. He had at that point regretted bringing the champagne to Ramsdell's box, for he could see she was half foxed.

The question which rose now was what precisely had occurred between last night and this morning to have given Marianne such a fright? Had he done something to her, perhaps taken sore advantage of her when she had been in her altitudes? The very thought of it made his fingers clench into a tight fist.

What else could it have been?

The notion of calling him out raced through his mind. Every nerve in his being demanded some sort of satisfaction, yet he had no claim on Marianne Pamberley—at least, not yet. Perhaps he should lay his concerns before Ramsdell.

He sank back into his chair. This line of attack he dismissed readily. He had only vague suspicions that something untoward had happened, and from what he could tell, Sir Jaspar had become something of a favorite of Ramsdell's. There were even rumors that Ramsdell was putting him up for White's.

There the entire scenario began to rankle. Who was Jaspar Vernham that he had suddenly appeared in London and gained the obvious respect and favor of a man who, from all Lord Crowthorne apprehended, had known Vernham but a brief time? And a nabob as well!

The more he mused upon Sir Jaspar Vernham, the more thoughts of him formed a boil in his mind. Nabobs generally were viewed with as much respect as a man of trade, sometimes less so. Yet this fellow had dined at Carlton House only a few days past. *Carlton House!*

Here was a mystery, he decided, that seemed to be having an effect on his own plans. Not only had he noticed Marianne's expression when she had swooned, but not less so Sir Jaspar's. The knight's face went white as he uttered a shocked, "Dear God," spoken in a manner that betrayed his particular interest in her.

How deep was his interest, though? Was he merely a good friend of the family, of Ramsdell's, or did he have designs on Marianne, as well?

"What do you say, Crowthorne? Shall we?"

Lord Crowthorne shifted his attention to his friends, who were all staring at him. "I beg your pardon? Shall we what?"

"Air dreaming?" Sir Giles murmured.

"I was pondering Miss Marianne's illness. I admit to some concern. You will forgive me if I was not attending to your conversation."

"You did not appear as though your thoughts were at all kind," Sir Giles pressed. "If anything, I would say you were scowling. Would not you agree, Henry? Was not Edgar scowling?"

"Most definitely."

"Sc-scowling, I say!" Mr. Shiplake intoned.

Lord Crowthorne rose to his feet. "If you must know, it rankled to see Sir Jaspar carrying the woman I mean to make my wife up the stairs."

At that, all the gentlemen fell silent.

"M-marry M-miss M-marianne?" Freddy cried, stricken.

"Sorry, old chap," Crowthorne stated. "I confess it is so. I have fallen deeply in love with her and intend to begin my pursuit in earnest. I trust your objection is not too profound?" He was smiling as he drew on his gloves. What could Freddy Shiplake object to?

"N-no! Of course not! I—I just hoped—but never mind th-that. I wish you every h-happiness."

"And I wish it were that simple," he returned. "The lady has not yet heard my proposals. I refuse to believe winning her hand will be a simple matter, but I thank you anyway. And now, what is it you were all discussing earlier? Shall we what?"

Henry Speen also rose to his feet. "Hyde Park, of course. I have my eye on a certain bird of paradise who promised to be there today."

"Ah, then we must ready ourselves. Speen, has your black mount arrived from Lincolnshire?"

"Only this morning."

"Then you must ride him. I must see for myself this extraordinary hack you purchased for a mere fifty pounds!"

Marianne was propped up on her bed against several pillows and sipping a very mild dose of laudanum in a tall glass of water. She was beyond humiliated that she had actually swooned in front of Lord Crowthorne and his friends. Worse yet, however, was having come to the horrifying awareness of why she had swooned.

She closed her eyes and groaned softly. Constance was with her immediately. "Marianne, ought I to send for the doctor? Dr. Kent, as you well know, is a gifted physician. He will be able to help you in a trice."

Marianne looked into Constance's face. Her sister was gravely concerned.

Marianne laughed, though not happily. "There is nothing greatly wrong with me, I assure you. I was, indeed, rather foxed when I arrived home last night.

In fact, so badly was I inebriated that until Jaspar arrived in the drawing room I had no memory of the evening save that Lord Crowthorne had brought some champagne to our box. I am merely suffering the ill effects of too much wine and I am deeply, deeply embarrassed." Tears trickled down her cheeks.

"Dearest," Constance murmured, "I am so sorry, but whatever possessed you to drink so very much?"

"I do not know," Marianne said. "I suppose I thought I could, so I did."

Constance's gaze drifted away, and she appeared at once sad and contemplative.

"Now, whatever is the matter? Tell me you do not blame yourself for my foolishness."

"No, not precisely. It's just that—Marianne, you will not like my saying this, but in some ways you are such a child."

Marianne stared at her and felt her lower lip tremble anew as more tears seeped from her eyes. "I take it very unkindly in you to say as much when I am feeling very miserable and thinking the very same thing."

"Oh-h-h, dearest." Constance leaned forward and gathered Marianne up in her arms.

Marianne leaned her head against her sister's shoulder and wept a little more. The position was entirely uncomfortable, for the angle was all wrong and her own neck felt badly tweaked, besides the fact that she was struggling to keep the glass of laudanum upright. Still, the sisterly comfort was precisely what she needed, as miserable as she was.

After a moment, she released Constance and queried. "Is Jaspar still here? There is—that is, I need to speak with him. I feel I ought to, since he was so kind as to carry me up the stairs."

"Are you certain you wish it? I know he can raise

your hackles with scarcely a lift of a brow when he is so inclined."

"Yes, I know." She nodded. "However, I must speak with him. I fear I may have said something last night that I ought to put right."

"Ah, I see. Did your temper get the best of you again?"

Marianne chuckled. "Not precisely my temper," she said, her cheeks beginning to burn.

"Very well, if you truly wish to see him."

"I do."

A few minutes later, Jaspar was ushered into her bed-chamber. Constance glanced from one to the other, then addressed Sir Jaspar. "Were we at Lady Brook, I should not hesitate to say you could remain with Marianne for as long as you wished. Here in London, however, where the servants are unknown to us—and servants' gossip being what it is—pray restrict your conversation to five minutes. I shall be in the hallway."

"Thank you, Constance." Marianne felt drowsy but much improved.

Jaspar drew forward to stand at the end of the bed, smiling ruefully. "Your color is much better," he commented.

"I imagine it must be." She returned his smile.

Jaspar rounded the bed and sat on the edge near her.

Marianne continued, "I swooned because I remembered what happened last night. Jaspar, I am utterly ashamed of what I did and said. Will you ever forgive me?"

"Forgive you? No, I do not think so."

Marianne was puzzled. "Why ever not?"

"Because, goose, I enjoyed myself thoroughly. Not only did you assault me in the most fiery and pleasant manner possible, but you confessed the true state of your heart to me."

"I was utterly foxed, as well you know! I—I am persuaded I thought you were someone else. You cannot truly believe I knew what I was doing or saying."

He lowered his gaze, as though weighing what he ought to say next. "You've been ill," he said at last. "And for that reason I do not mean to argue with you. I will only say I disagree entirely with what you have just said. No, pray do not say anything more. We shall merely quarrel, and then I truly will be distressed. If you wish, you may attempt to argue me into your position sometime tomorrow. In fact, let me take you and Miss Theale to Astley's."

"Astley's?" She brightened quickly. "Oh, Jaspar I should like that above all things. Constance does not wish to go, and I would not impose something so ridiculous upon Ramsdell. Only—do you think we could keep the excursion very, er, *discreet*?"

Sir Jaspar laughed and rose to his feet. "Of course, if that is what you wish. I suppose it would not do at all for Lord Crowthorne to learn you had gone to Astley's. One does not hear of *high sticklers* attending such a riotous event."

Marianne pouted and scowled. "Why must you always put me in the worst light?"

"Not you, dearest," he said, heading toward the door. "Merely Crowthorne. Imagine being such a simpleton that he would not cross the portals of Astley's merely for appearances' sake."

"Oh, do go away. You are giving me the headache again."

"Astley's tomorrow," he reiterated, smiling as he stepped into the hallway.

When Constance entered the chamber, Marianne

cried, "Jaspar has invited Annabelle and me to go to Astley's tomorrow. Is it not marvelous?"

"I am very happy for you. I am only sorry I was unable to oblige you by taking you myself."

"Do you wish to go with us?" She yawned, for the laudanum was having a happy effect on her.

"No, I thank you. I am still unwell myself, though not nearly so much as last night."

"Did you also imbibe too much champagne?"

"No," she confessed.

"Well, then," Marianne added, yawning again, "we do not share the same affliction after all, just as Sir Jaspar said."

She closed her eyes. As she drifted off to sleep, she heard Constance murmur, "I should hope not, indeed."

Over the next sennight, Marianne conducted a secret life with Sir Jaspar and Annabelle which gave each day the air of an adventure. Jaspar took them everywhere—to Astley's famous and exciting amphitheatre where every manner of horsemanship was on exhibit, to the Tower of London to see the lions, even to Bartholomew Fair, which was quite beyond the pale but oh, so delightful!

These excursions were conducted in the strictest secrecy, which made them all the more fascinating and enjoyable. Besides, Jaspar quite excelled at keeping both Annabelle and herself in perfect comfort.

He seemed to divine when either of them was hungry or chilled or fatigued. An umbrella always appeared the moment it began to rain. When her feet began to hurt or Annabelle's stomach began to rumble in a most unladylike manner, suddenly a chair would be brought forward in which to sit or a stall would appear just around the next corner from which an array of quite edible delicacies might be procured.

Every day which took them into less exalted parts of the city saw them return to Grosvenor Square laden with packages of all manner of frippery—ribbons, bits of lace, unusual wooden toys which Marianne was collecting for the Applegate children, along with mechanical automatons, whistles, and large hoops and sticks. She also had a growing collection of copper rings which quickly turned green when placed upon the finger and every bauble imaginable to please the sensibilities of ladies escaping the strict bounds of their society.

Marianne confessed she had not been happier. In the evenings she would find Lord Crowthorne waiting to take Jaspar's place and guide her into all the delights of society. She learned to play and love silver loo, she danced until her feet ached at every ball, she rode beside him in Hyde Park every day, and enjoyed immensely the sensation she caused. It would seem Lord Crowthorne had never singled a lady out in such a manner before, and he introduced her to many famous personages, including the Duke of Wellington and the Green Man.

Wellington she found to be as noble as she had expected in bearing and in conduct, while the Green Man was as absurd as his chosen costume. Gradually she was taking on her own patina of Town bronze, and only occasionally stumbled while in Lord Crowthorne's presence.

One day at Hyde Park, she had insisted upon being introduced to a fashionable woman who was riding with Sir Giles. How shocked she was when his lordship presented her to Harriet Wilson. *Harriet Wilson!* The most infamous of all the tonnish courtesans.

She was never more mortified, and wondered that

Crowthorne had actually done so. However, he seemed to take it all in stride. "You were so eager to meet Sir Giles's friend that I felt I could do naught else but make the introductions."

When she told Jaspar of the circumstance later, he was oddly horrified. "He introduced you? Why the devil—I mean, why did he not simply order the coachman to drive on? Miss Wilson would certainly have understood. He had no business exposing you as he did!"

However, Marianne merely lifted a brow to him and retorted, "This from a man who took me to see the bearded lady at Bartholomew Fair?"

She had silenced him, at least for the present.

A fortnight after her dreadful fainting spell, Lord Crowthorne took Marianne on a private excursion to Richmond Park on the southern side of the Thames.

"So," he mused gently, "you have been longing to come to London these seven years and more?"

Marianne, who found herself in the happy circumstance of a *tête-à-tête* with her chosen beau, nodded slowly. She fairly kept her gaze pinned to his, her heart thrumming with excitement in her breast. She knew Crowthorne had singled her out and had been doing so more each day. She could not be in doubt of his intentions—only the night before at Drury Lane, she had overheard two rather foxed bucks boasting of having laid odds at Boodle's to the effect that Crowthorne would wed the Pamberley chit before the end of May.

May!

Oh, that it could be true!

She knew with every feminine instinct she possessed he was within a hairbreadth of offering for her. He had arranged to be alone with her today, which led her to believe he might even perform the feat while they were at the park.

He had taken her to Richmond Park to view the extensive gardens, which covered an area over two and a half miles wide and contained herds of fallow and red deer. The rain which began to fall just after they crossed the Thames had not deterred the excursion in the least, since Crowthorne had wisely chosen to transport her in his family's coachman driven barouche.

Marianne was quite comfortable inside the vehicle. When the rain showed a hint of letting up, she suggested they wait to see if in a little while the gravel walks might be suitable for at least a brief stroll. "For of course I have never been to the gardens before, and everyone has told me I must pay several visits in order to see everything. Is it true the gardens once belonged to Charles II?"

Lord Crowthorne had been pleased to reveal his knowledge of the gardens, including a recounting of the tug-of-war waged against George II for the purpose of obtaining public right of way so that anyone who wished to see the gardens might do so.

Marianne quickly grew bored of the subject, but he seemed content to prattle on. She used the opportunity to study his face and determine, if she could, which of his features she would wish her children to display combined with which particular aspects of her own countenance. She had just decided she would rather none of her children possess his somewhat sharp nose when he asked her if she had been longing to come to London forever.

Finally she could take part in the conversation. She spoke in a low voice "Papa was used to tell me he looked forward to the day he might bring me, in particular, to London. He felt I, even more than my sisters, would take great pleasure in all the various entertainments the metropolis provided."

"You have taken to silver loo, I will admit to that."

"Oh, very much so," she gushed. "You have no idea. I have already won twenty pounds, which I keep locked up in a music box in my bedchamber and from which I take only a small portion with me each evening for card play."

"You must not let the game overtake you. Did not your father succumb to the vice?"

How very unkind of him to say so. She kept her features impassive. "I have been given to understand that, yes, he was a gamester."

He lifted his hand and gently pushed aside a curl that was touching her cheek. "I was very sorry to learn of the troubles you and your sisters endured. You must have been greatly relieved when your eldest sister wed Lord Ramsdell."

She looked at him and chose her words carefully. "Will you think me entirely ridiculous if I tell you I was never more chagrined—though I said nothing to Constance, of course. I had always hoped that one day I would form an alliance which would restore my family's fortunes. I suppose I am being absurd."

His fingers caught her chin. "You are being the noble creature you are. I am not surprised in the least that you had hoped to save your sisters from their disgrace—"

"Not disgrace," she interrupted. "Surely."

"Unhappiness, then," he corrected.

"Much better." She smiled and knew her dimples had appeared beside her lips. She batted her lashes slowly.

"You are so beautiful," he murmured, leaning toward her.

Marianne had been kissed a dozen times before, perhaps even a score. This kiss, however, was the one she had awaited her entire life. She felt dizzy and exhilarated all at once. She drew in a deep breath and waited for his lips to touch hers. She closed her eyes and tilted her head back a little.

When his lips were pressed against hers, she waited for the fireworks to explode in her head, for her heart to create the most exquisite melody ever before composed, for the day to turn to night and the night to day.

She waited and waited, hoping the magic of their first kiss would transport her to places previously unimagined. Her hope blossomed when his arm slid about her shoulders and he drew her in a close embrace. She hoped and hoped and waited a little more.

She waited in vain. The fireworks did not appear, her heart was completely silent, and the day remained cloudy and rainy, just as it had been before his lips touched hers.

Her thoughts drifted most aggravatingly to Jaspar and how she felt when she was in his arms—as though the world had begun spinning faster and faster.

She shivered suddenly and Lord Crowthorne drew back from her. "You are chilled? Or have I frightened you?"

Marianne looked into his eyes and blinked.

"I was too precipitous," Crowthorne said.

"N-no," she murmured, then hiccupped. "That is, I fear I am grown quite cold. Oh! Do but look," she cried hurriedly. "It no longer rains, and I see patches of sunshine everywhere! Shall we walk about for a while?"

Eight

Hours later, when Marianne returned to Ramsdell's home in Grosvenor Square, she stood before the round table in the entrance hall, untying the ribbons of her bonnet slowly, as one caught in a trance.

Her thoughts were dull and stupid, her spirits so dampened by the experience of having kissed Lord Crowthorne that she felt as though she had aged five years since she first set out with him to Richmond Park. Whatever did it mean that she had not enjoyed kissing the man she intended to marry?

She could not fathom the implications of it, not one whit. Her throat began to ache. When the butler approached her, begging to know if he could serve her in some manner, she merely shook her head and headed up the stairs. Halfway to the first landing, she turned and inquired, "Is my sister in her bedchamber?"

"I believe so, miss."

Constance kept to her bedchamber a great deal these days, Marianne realized suddenly. She was not surprised, however, for Constance dearly loved the country and probably took little delight in tonnish festivities. No doubt she was wishing to be home even now.

Entering her sister's room, upon Constance's warm command, she found her reclining in a chaise longue near the window. She was reading quietly. A glass of milk sat on a table at her elbow, and a shawl was draped over her legs, for even though the sun had permitted Marianne to stroll about Richmond Park for a time, the clouds had rolled in more thickly still, and a steady rain was now drenching London. A fire burned in the grate, but the fringes of the chamber were nippy.

"Did you enjoy your excursion to Richmond?" Constance closed her book and settled it on her lap.

"Very much so," Marianne replied. This was not the entire truth, but she had found the gardens quite lovely and the deer an enchanting sight.

"You were gone so long that I began to fear some accident might have befallen you, especially since it has been raining for the past hour."

Yes, an accident has befallen me, Marianne thought, much depressed.

To Constance, she said, "Returning across Richmond Bridge on our way home, a cart lost a wheel and an entire load of cabbages was sent sprawling everywhere. It would have been quite amusing, except that I became chilled."

"Are you now? Perhaps you should come stand by the fire."

Marianne removed her bonnet and sighed heavily as she settled it on a chair by the door. She unbuttoned her pelisse, which was damp from the rain, and removed it as well.

"You may hang your pelisse on one of the hooks in my wardrobe, if you like."

"Thank you," Marianne murmured. Her feet felt heavy as she moved to obey her sister.

When the pelisse was draped on the hook, she found her sister watching her carefully.

"Marianne," Constance began, "what is troubling

you? Your spirits are decidedly low. Was Lord Crowthorne all a gentleman ought to be during your journey?"

"Of course," Marianne responded with a shrug.
Maybe that was what was troubling her. Perhaps Lord
Crowthorne had been too much of a gentleman. Perhaps he should have dragged her roughly into his arms
and kissed her wildly, instead of so carefully as he had.
"His lordship was kind and attentive—and he kissed
me, but I was very willing."

Taking a chair opposite her sister, she watched in
some amusement as Constance bit her lip. She chuckled, for her sister suddenly appeared ten years younger.

"Pray do not concern yourself," Marianne added. "I
wanted him to kiss me, for I am persuaded he means
to offer for me very soon."

"Indeed?" Constance queried. "But you have known
him such a short time—just a few weeks."

Marianne stared down at her hands and nodded.
She suddenly felt very young, as well. "Four weeks, two
days, and six hours."

"You desire to marry him, then?"

"Yes," she said softly, still staring at her hands.

"And do you love him?"

"Of course I love him. I would never marry a man
I did not love."

"Then what is amiss, dearest? You do not seem at
all happy that the man you hope to marry, whom you
believe wishes to marry you, may very well soon beg
for your hand in marriage. Is it possible—Marianne,
did you not like being kissed by Lord Crowthorne?"

At her sister's amazing perceptiveness, Marianne
lifted her gaze and blurted out, "I did not like it at
all! I was never more shocked! I expected to hear
church bells suddenly pealing over the countryside. In-

stead—" She pressed her fingers to her lips, as though fearing to speak the truth aloud.

"Instead—what?"

Marianne sighed yet again. "His lips were hard. Constance, have you ever heard of anything so ridiculous? How can a man's lips, his manner of kissing, be *hard?*"

"I do not know." Constance shook her head in bewilderment.

"Ramsdell does not kiss in such a ridiculous manner, does he?" Marianne leaned forward expectantly.

Constance shook her head. "Not by half."

Marianne nodded quickly several times. "I thought not. Even Jaspar does not and I *detest* him!"

"You do? I had thought you had made a sort of peace with him. Did he not take you and Annabelle to Bartholomew Fair?"

"Yes, but then he said something quite wretched about Lord Crowthorne, or at least of something he did—for, if you must know, he introduced me to Harriet Wilson."

"I know," Constance said, frowning a little. "Lady Donnington was so kind as to inform me that she saw him perform the offices. I must admit I was a little shocked."

"Lady Donnington is one of the worst gabblemongers I have ever known, besides being platter-faced. I have no opinion of her!"

Constance merely smiled and sipped her milk.

Marianne watched her curiously for a moment. "I did not know you enjoyed milk so much."

"There was a time when I did not." Constance smiled a little more broadly. "Presently, I cannot seem to drink enough of it."

Marianne frowned as she watched her sister take another swig. Constance drinking milk! Marriage to Ramsdell had certainly altered her sister. She was not nearly so lively as she was used to be, and recently she had swooned at the Donnington ball and nearly cast up her accounts at the opera and had to be taken home.

"Are you feeling well?" she asked. "You are not falling into a decline, are you?"

Constance shook her head.

Marianne frowned. "I must say, Constance, I begin to think being married does not at all suit you. You lie abed for hours every morning, you do not attend half the balls or soirees which Annabelle and I do, and now you are drinking milk, which I do not think a healthy habit at all. This is merely a suggestion, for I am becoming rather concerned for you, but perhaps you should consider seeking Dr. Kent's advice about these odd symptoms of yours."

"I have," Constance admitted. "The good doctor was here only this morning."

"Oh, excellent. Does he give you cause for alarm?"

"Not one whit. He says I am perfectly well for a lady in my condition."

"What condition?" As the words left her mouth, enlightment flooded her mind. "You are increasing!" she cried, rising from her seat.

"And you are to become an aunt."

"When?"

"Sometime in November."

A glow of warmth suddenly flowed through Marianne as she stared at her sister in wonder. Constance would be having a baby—in November, before Christmas. She could hardly credit it was true. First Augusta, and now Constance. She would be an aunt twice over before the year was out. What glorious news!

She crossed the room swiftly and embraced her sister tenderly, kissing her on each cheek in turn. Her eyes were moist with tears, and when she met Constance's gaze she discovered her sister's were, also. "Why did you not tell me the moment I entered the chamber?"

"You seemed too sad for words, dearest."

Marianne nodded and sighed once more. "I was . . . I am." She suddenly dropped to her knees and took hold of Constance's hands. "I am in the worst predicament of not knowing my own mind. I mean"—she hesitated, for she felt foolish in laying her troubles before anyone. Yet she needed another woman's opinion, and though she did not always agree with Constance—that is, she hardly ever agreed with Constance—still, her sister was a very sensible sort of female and might have an opinion that would set her heart at ease. "Constance, you must tell me what I am to think! I feel so terribly confused."

Constance's brow puckered. "About what, precisely?"

Marianne rolled her eyebrows and glowered at her sister. "About Crowthorne's kissing, of course. What else would worry me so? What do you think it means that I did not enjoy kissing him?"

"I cannot say."

Marianne released her sister's hands and rose at once to her feet. "How is that possible? You have an opinion on everything."

"Too much so, I fear."

Marianne met her gaze forcefully. "Do you have an opinion now, and are you merely withholding it from me?"

"Not precisely. I mean, you already know what I think of you and Jaspar and the nature of the kisses you have shared with him. If I have an opinion at all, it is that your distress confirms my suspicions about the true state of your heart. I do not believe that is what you wish to hear."

Marianne should have guessed Constance would

take up sides with Jaspar once more. "Well, that is pure nonsense," she retorted, "for you are suggesting I should judge my heart by the way I feel when I am kissed."

"I am not saying that the experience is a sole predictor, merely a cause for alarm or justification. I think your own distress confirms this. However, you must judge the matter. Begging an opinion of me or anyone else is essentially of little value. Were I to proclaim that you love Jaspar Vernham and you could never love Lord Crowthorne, I would do you a disservice. I no more desire to persuade you toward one man or the other than urge you to crop your hair as short as Caroline Lamb's. You alone must judge of your heart— and apparently your kissing, as well. No, no, I am not poking fun at you, though it is ironical, do not you think? Particularly when you have been kissed so many times that the one man you earnestly wish to marry is the only man about whose kissing you have ever complained."

At that, Marianne began to smile. "You are right!" she cried. "I must have been kissed a score of times and never . . . oh. Perhaps, I should not have confessed as much to you."

Constance laughed outright. "You have confessed yourself so violently in love with so many young gentlemen that I would have been a perfect peagoose not to understand your lips had been trespassed more than once."

Marianne brought her fingers to her lips absently. "You are right, and it is very ironical. Do you . . . do you think a man might improve with practice?"

At that Constance wagged her finger at Marianne. "Pray do not engage in any such experiment."

Marianne blushed warmly. "Of course I will not. I

was merely wondering if, with a little practice, a man might kiss better."

"I should think it likely."

"Like the pianoforte," Marianne stated with growing confidence. "Oh, I am so glad I told you. I was perfectly desolate earlier and now—yes, like the pianoforte. Well, with that settled, tell me, have you been thinking of names for the baby? *Marianne*, perhaps, if it is a girl?"

Constance smiled. "A perfectly lovely name. However, Ramsdell desires, should the child be born a girl, to name her Mary, after his mother."

"Oh, of course. That would be lovely. Perhaps if you have a dozen children, you will have more daughters and one of them you could name after me. I promise I would become her most favorite aunt and would purchase her all manner of trumpery until she was properly spoilt."

"I can think of nothing more charming."

"Will you attend the masquerade tonight at Vauxhall?"

"Of course. I am feeling better and better, and one reason I have been resting today is to make certain I am fit for this evening's festivities—so long as the rain ceases."

"It will. I am convinced of it, particularly since I have been longing to go to Vauxhall and taste the wafer-thin slices of ham and hear the orchestra and see the Grand Cascade."

"Will Lord Crowthorne be attending?"

"Yes, he said he would escort us. Jaspar as well, which shall make the numbers perfect, for then he can attend to Miss Theale."

"Yesterday in the park, I invited Mr. Speen to join us, as well as Sir Giles, to make certain you and Annabelle would never lack for a partner."

"How very foresightful of you, Constance. I vow in this moment I do not understand how we ever quarreled."

"Nor do I."

She turned to leave with her bonnet swinging on one arm and her pelisse draped over the other, but just before she crossed the threshold, she whirled around and queried brightly, "Do you think I *should* crop my hair short like Caro Lamb's?"

At that Constance laughed heartily. "On no account!"

Marianne laughed as well, and left the bedchamber.

That evening, however, one member was absent from the party, which completely dashed part of Marianne's schemes for the evening's entertainment. Contrary to her promise, she meant to encourage Lord Crowthorne down one of the darkened pathways—about which any number of her friends had been telling her since her arrival in London—and see if practice might improve his kissing.

Unfortunately, he had sent word he could not attend her to Vauxhall after all. In his letter, he apologized profusely for having become slightly feverish subsequent to their excursion to Richmond Park, but assured her he would call upon her as soon as his doctor pronounced him well, which he firmly believed would be in but a day or two.

Marianne was supremely disappointed. Not only could she not commence her plans for improving Lord Crowthorne's kissing techniques, but she would be bereft of one of her dancing partners. After a quarter of an hour of contemplating her disappointments, however, she remembered that this would be no ordinary ball or masquerade, but rather the Vauxhall Pleasure

Gardens, and her spirits quickly rose. After all, she would be attending the famous gardens for the first time in her life, and what could be more exciting than that?

For the masquerade, she donned a simple gold domino over a white muslin gown embroidered with gold thread. A half mask of black silk completed her ensemble. Annabelle wore a similar costume, with her hair dressed beautifully atop her head in a cascade of proper ringlets and threaded throughout with a dark green satin ribbon. Her gown was of a pale green satin over which a lovely half robe of embroidered pink roses on white silk flowed from the high waist. She was a vision, especially wearing a mask covered in seed pearls. For all her loveliness, though, she did not seem in high gig.

Marianne inquired if something was amiss, and Annabelle drew her away from the assembled revelers just before they climbed into the several carriages arranged for the excursion. She said in a low voice, "It is just that I am truly concerned for Lord Crowthorne. Did you say he was caught in the rain today?"

"Yes, I told you as much, just as I was."

"Once, when he was much younger, he suffered a terrible inflammation of the lungs after becoming wet through. For several days we did not know if"—she paused before composing herself sufficiently to continue—"if he should survive. It seems to me that frequently when one has been severely ill, the tendency toward future illness is more marked than in those who have never suffered. Are you certain the letter he sent you is a true reflection of his condition?"

Marianne stared at Annabelle and began to share her fears. "He did sneeze at least three times on the journey from Richmond, once while we were on the bridge and the cabbages prevented us from returning home and twice as we turned into Grosvenor Square. Oh, dear. Do you suppose—I mean, what if he has become wretchedly ill?"

Sir Jaspar called from the lead carriage, "The horses are ready, Miss Marianne. Let me assist you within, and you as well, Miss Theale."

Marianne begged Jaspar to wait. She then addressed Sir Giles, who had just opened the door of the second coach and four. "I have an office I wish you to perform, if you would, Sir Giles."

"I am at your service!" he cried, readily. "Whatever is amiss? I can see the pair of you are distressed."

She beckoned him near. "We wish you to escort us to Lady Bray's front door and to inquire of the butler of Lord Crowthorne's health."

"I am certain he is perfectly well . . . no, no, say no more. I see by both your expressions that I must and will oblige you even now."

Marianne then informed the remainder of the party, in particular her sister, who had just emerged from the doorway, of their intended mission. Sir Giles offered an arm to each lady. Within a minute, he had guided them to Lady Bray's front door, where he made liberal use of the knocker. A moment more and the three of them were standing in the entrance hall.

The magnificence of the house outshone Lord Ramsdell's abode in almost every detail. Marianne caught her breath as she lifted her gaze to the massive, spiraled staircase which rose upward to the first floor and an arched ceiling painted an elegant royal blue. Gilt trimmed the edges of the extensive stucco relief work surrounding a number of extraordinary paintings by the Dutch masters.

The butler disappeared into the drawing room. After a scant few minutes, Lady Bray emerged, gowned elegantly in purple silk accented by carefully chosen gold necklaces, bracelets, and rings.

"How kind of you to call!" She smiled as she approached Annabelle first, then Marianne, and finally Sir Giles.

Marianne began, "I hope we are not intruding, my lady, but Annabelle expressed a deep concern for your son's health, knowing he had been ill some years ago with a like complaint. His missive was informative, yet we wished to hear how he fares. Is he much worsened?"

"No, not at all," Lady Bray proclaimed firmly. "A trifling fit of the ague, which will pass swiftly I am sure." Turning to Annabelle, she added, "He exhibits none of the terrible symptoms of that wretched time, my dear, I assure you."

Annabelle released a deep sigh of relief. "I am so grateful to hear you say so. I have been alarmed the entire afternoon since having heard of his illness. Perhaps I am being ridiculous, but I recall those weeks with abhorrent clarity. They were some of the most frightening of my existence."

"Mine as well," Lady Bray murmured. "Be assured, however, that my son is perfectly well except for—well, he shall not like my saying so, but I shall say it anyway—a slightly reddened nose."

At that, the small party chuckled and much of the tension deserted everyone.

Lady Bray wished them every pleasure on their forthcoming excursion, then addressed Annabelle. "I admire the style of your hair. I always thought with just a little Town bronze you could be rigged out in style, and now you are. Do we have Lady Ramsdell to thank for this?"

"No," Annabelle responded, hooking Marianne's arm. "Miss Marianne loaned me her abigail for the season and also has taken me shopping in New Bond Street nearly every day for the past three weeks."

The countess turned to Marianne. "Then we are all indebted to you. Mrs. Theale is as dear a friend as I could wish for, but as a parent there have been many times I could have simply strangled her."

Marianne did not know what to say to this ingenuous, frank speech.

Fortunately, her ladyship again addressed Annabelle. "And are you enjoying your Season?"

"More than I ever dreamed possible."

"I am glad for you, my dear. As much as I love your dear mother, I honestly cannot account for her dislike of London, nor her disinterest in giving you a proper Season or two."

Marianne watched the exchange with some interest, and realized Annabelle was far better acquainted with Lord Crowthorne and his family than she had previously comprehended. She knew their friendship was of long standing, yet until this moment she had not understood the degree of intimacy between the two families. She felt an odd uneasiness in this knowledge, as though she was in some inexplicable manner trespassing on something which belonged to Annabelle.

Not given to a great deal of contemplative moments, however, she shrugged off the quirky sensation, then suggested they had taken up enough of her ladyship's time.

Annabelle was quick to agree, as was Sir Giles. A moment later, they returned to the carriages.

"You seem to be on easy terms with Lady Bray," Marianne observed as Annabelle climbed into the lead carriage.

"I have always thought her one of the kindest ladies I know. She frequently argued with Mama about permitting me to come to London, even offering to launch me when I was eighteen. Mama, however, did not wish to be under such an obligation to her dear friend, who was of no relation to her. So it was not until your brother-in-law offered that I ever believed I would see London."

"Now you are here," Marianne responded happily as she climbed in and took a seat beside Annabelle, facing forward. "You know, it seems to me we share the same background. Though I, too, dreamed of coming to London, until Lord Ramsdell married Constance, I had given up all hope of ever seeing the metropolis, not to mention enjoying such a wonderful Season."

Annabelle slipped her arm about Marianne's. "We are like sisters, are we not, sharing the same fate and the same rescuer in dear Ramsdell?"

"Indeed, we are," Marianne responded. She enjoyed nothing so much as the camaraderie she was at present sharing with Annabelle. Their mutual concern for Lord Crowthorne had given her one more reason to feel a certain happy bond to Annabelle.

Nine

She was being foolish, dreadfully so, running down path after path, hiding from Sir Jaspar in a game which closely resembled hide-and-seek, except that she was so happy.

Vauxhall was all she had been led to expect and more. The nearness of the supper boxes to the orchestra affected her so magically that her every sense reeled with pleasure and excitement. She had danced several dances already with each of the gentlemen present, a quadrille and two country dances with Mr. Speen, an old-fashioned minuet, a waltz, and a country dance with Sir Giles, and a quadrille and—heaven forbid!—a Scottish reel with Sir Jaspar. Her slippers were nearly worn through, and the bits of gravel along the path promised sore toes in the morning.

For the present, however, she was dizzy with being chased.

The evening was very fine and the gardens were crowded with thousands of masqueraders. She would not be known in her domino and half mask and so felt at liberty to behave as a child, with great abandon, laughter, and enjoyment.

Twice Jaspar almost caught her, but each time she was able to wiggle out of his grasp, slide past several revelers, and lose him down yet another darkened path. The shrubberies were lit by the glow of Chinese lanterns swaying in an occasional breeze, but emitting so dim a light that the gardens were rife with hundreds of places to hide.

She glanced behind her and saw he was but a few yards away. She squealed, picked up her skirts a trifle, and dashed down another path. The crowds had thinned a little, and the longer she engaged in the silly game, the farther afield she went. With so few obstacles now, she was able to run faster than before. She glanced behind her again and realized with a start that Jaspar was nowhere to be seen. She had lost him! Hurray!

She stopped suddenly. The gardens in this area were quite dark. Scarcely a handful of lanterns illuminated the paths.

Oh, my! She placed a hand on her stomach. She was breathing very hard. "Jaspar?" she called out softly.

A breeze answered, tipping the lanterns twenty feet away, shifting the shadows about in an eerie manner. Her heart pounded with fear. "Jaspar?" she called again. In the distance, she could barely hear the orchestra, so far away had she flown.

"Jaspar, I am frightened," she whispered.

Suddenly, someone twirled her about and grasped her hard about her waist. She screamed, and a hand covered her mouth.

She met familiar, laughing eyes through the slits of a mask.

"Oh, you beast!" she cried, as Jaspar smiled at her and removed his hand from her mouth. Somehow he had stolen up on her and won the day.

"You are my prize, now," he murmured, not releasing her. "Were you indeed afraid?"

"Yes, for we have ventured so far from my sister."

"You must know, however, that I would never let harm come to you."

She believed him. He was very determined and his arm about her waist was strong.

"I know," she said, "which I believe is the reason I let you chase me and did not care where the paths led me." She smiled and felt rather silly. "We are being very ridiculous, you know."

He nodded. "Do you wish to see the Grand Cascade? I will take you there, though I believe it will be a walk of some few minutes. It is on the opposite side of the gardens."

She would have responded, but a sharp whistling rent the air, followed by a loud explosion.

"Do but look!" She whirled in his arms and leaned against him as she stared up into the night sky. "The fireworks have begun."

"So they have," he murmured against her ear, settling his arms about her—just to support her, mind!

Marianne knew she should not let him do so. However, she was far too caught up in the sight of the fireworks to care. Besides, she was beginning to feel the chill of the night air as moisture from the nearby river drifted across the gardens. She had been quite heated from running, but now she felt particularly susceptible to the damp air.

The boom, hiss, and crackle of the fireworks seemed particularly fitting after such a long and exhilarating chase. Marianne watched each climbing rocket with great appreciation and sighed deeply.

"Are you happy, my dear?" he asked.

"Immeasurably," she responded, and gave another heartfelt sigh.

A large series of fireworks exploded into the sky, the smoke from the previous ones drifting away from the gardens.

"Have you ever seen anything prettier?"

"Yes. The woman in my arms."

Marianne giggled, feeling very safe in Jaspar's embrace.

"London pleases you?" he asked.

"Beyond words!"

The fireworks continued for several minutes, and from every corner of the garden, applause and squeals of delight could be heard.

When at last they drew to a close, Marianne shivered. "We ought to return, for I forgot my cape in all the excitement." She glanced up at him over her shoulder and caught his eye. He seemed rather intense suddenly.

"What is it, Jaspar? Whatever is the matter? I have not offended you, have I?" She turned to face him.

He shook his head. "Not by half, but there is something I would ask you, though I daresay you will think the question impertinent."

She was in such a happy state that she did not hesitate to show her dimples. "You may ask me anything tonight, for you have made me very happy. You have not scolded me in the least, you danced so delightfully with me, especially during that riotous reel, and you have made Annabelle at ease in company. I vow I would grant you nearly anything at this moment. You have but to ask." She felt warm, wonderful, and magnanimous.

Sir Jaspar hesitated, but only for a moment. "Are you to be married?"

She was so much taken aback by the unexpected question that her mouth dropped open. "Am I to be married?"

"Yes, to Lord Crowthorne. Has he offered for you?"

She felt herself blush and averted her gaze. She had not been thinking about Lord Crowthorne at all, nor of her hopes of one day wedding him. She wished Jaspar had not put her in mind of his lordship, for she suddenly felt guilty she was allowing herself so much enjoyment in Jaspar's company.

She wondered if she had been at all wise in permitting him to chase her about the gardens. Of course she had not. By doing so, surely she had encouraged him to hope she might experience a change of heart.

"I wish you had not asked me," she admitted. "I know I said you might ask me anything, but I had no notion you meant to ask about Lord Crowthorne. Please, let us return to Constance and Ramsdell. I—I do not wish to think about the future right now, just the present and how much I am enjoying your company tonight."

"You could enjoy my company every night," he whispered, sliding his arms about her waist very gently and leaning down to let his breath touch her ear.

She shivered, but it had nothing to do with the cold night air. She should tell him to release her at once, but she did not want to. "Are you flirting with me?" she whispered.

"Yes." Again his breath was on her ear.

"It is most improper," she stated, still failing to command him to release her.

"Most improper," he agreed.

His breath was so warm. She drew in a quivering breath and felt oddly frozen to the spot where she stood. Her skin tingled all over. He leaned down again and kissed her very lightly, yet quite near her ear. She blinked, feeling like a small, stunned animal. Still, she did not move or object to his advances.

"You are very beautiful, even in your half mask." His voice was a low, masculine rumble in her ear. She closed her eyes and sighed as he continued, "Your lips are like sweet cherries."

"Are they indeed?" she whispered, smiling faintly.

His lips brushed her own. "And they taste as sweet."

"That is impossible!" She giggled.

"I would spend my days tasting of your sweet cherry lips and at night something more."

"Oh." She was scandalized in the most exciting way. She did not even know what to say in response, for her mind was suddenly full of too many images to allow her to form an answer. Days and nights with Sir Jaspar! Oh, my!

She was no longer in the least chilled. Even the exposed parts of her arms above her long gloves felt warm, as though a summer's breeze had enveloped her. She lifted her gaze to him, completely mesmerized, but could see only shadows of his eyes through the slits in his mask.

He reached up and untied her mask and drew it away from her. Still no objection passed her lips. She even quite brazenly untied his mask, but she did not catch it in time and it fell to the gravel walk.

"I shall retrieve them both in a moment." He let her mask flutter on top of his and gathered her up in his arms. "I would apprehend that you are not yet betrothed," he whispered.

"I am not yet betrothed."

She closed her eyes and his lips were on hers. She laid her hand upon his shoulder. His arm slid about her waist and he drew her against him roughly. She wondered how it was she fit so perfectly against him when he was so tall and she not nearly so.

He kissed her fiercely, and she could feel all his love for her in every subtle movement of his body against her, of the way he entered her mouth and ran his tongue the length of hers, the way his hands were restless about her waist. Of all the men she had kissed over the years, Jaspar outkissed them all, yet she could not say precisely why. She had known softer lips, gentler hands, more skilled embraces. Why did she prefer his touch to anyone else's?

The mystery of her desire for him, of her delight in his kisses, swept her up in a whirlwind of passion. She could no longer think, only feel. Her mind spun with all the days and nights of which he had spoken. He would love her so well and so completely. She could feel it in how involved he was in just kissing her. She would be happy with him.

The thought pierced her pleasure.

She did not want Jaspar Vernham. He had been her father's stable boy and, in her mind, even though he was a knight in possession of a grand fortune as well as The Priory, he would forever be the boy who pulled her braids.

She drew back, a strange lethargy keeping her from jerking from his arms. She saw him as one in a fog. "You should not be kissing me, Jaspar. Nothing will come of this. I have told you as much."

He took hold of her arms. "How can you be so blind, Marianne?" he cried. "Do you truly believe these kisses we share have no meaning for you, for your future, *for our future?*"

"They are just kisses, Jaspar. Why must we argue about this each time—" Her senses were returning to her in full and she pulled away from him. "You are the fool to keep assaulting me in this manner. I shall answer the question, however. I do not know why your kisses, the way you hold me and, yes, the way you love me, seem to cast a spell over me, but I vow to you I will never think of this as anything but some sort of stable boy's magic which you must have learned from the gypsies who used to camp near Lady Brook each summer!"

At that, he laughed. "You are such a simpleton! Can you think of nothing more than to remind me of my origins? You must do better if you hope to convince me or yourself you will not one day become my wife, take your place in my bed, and bear me a dozen children."

His words felt like a knife in her breast. They were base and cruel in a way she could not explain. She felt as though he had reached inside her soul and exposed to her the very things she most longed for in the entire world—to live with a man in loving simplicity and to let her womb speak the joys of her heart. She gave a small cry and immediately headed back to the orchestra.

The following morning, Lord Crowthorne sat in the library of his father's town house, making liberal use of one handkerchief after another. He sneezed and regarded Henry and Sir Giles over a neatly embroidered kerchief. "How long was she gone with him among the paths?"

"Half an hour. Even Lady Ramsdel became concerned."

"And when she returned, was she overset or in any manner aggravated?"

His friends glanced at one another.

"No," Sir Giles said, "but Sir Jaspar was in a temper. Whatever occurred in the shrubberies did not please him."

"And are you certain you heard correct, Giles, when you were dancing with her? Did she indeed say Sir Jaspar had been her father's stable boy?"

"I had not imbibed even half a bottle of champagne," Sir Giles returned earnestly, "when she told me. I promise you, I could not have misunderstood her, particularly since I requested she repeat the information twice before I was willing to credit it."

Crowthorne fell silent and blew his nose. The news of Marianne's jaunt with Sir Jaspar among the darkened pathways of Vauxhall Gardens was mixed, or so it would seem. The pair had been absent from the general party for an intolerable length of time, and yet whatever had occurred had not resulted in the knight's triumph.

He raised a brow. From the first, he had thought Sir Jaspar Vernham an odd personage to be so nearly connected to the Pamberley ladies. Except for Prinney's attentions, the newly created knight would have long since been given the cut direct by half the members of the *haut ton,* because his origins were as low as could be.

A stable boy! The mere thought that Marianne had been in his company in questionable circumstances made Lord Crowthorne as mad as fire. He wanted no scandal attached to the lady who would one day replace his mother as the countess of Bray, and he certainly did not want her connected with a stable boy.

Besides, something about Sir Jaspar made him uneasy. There was an intelligence in his eye, in the way he surveyed an assembled group of people, which put Crowthorne in mind of Wellington. Did the man possess such abilities? If so, had he set his sights on Marianne?

Vernham had certainly ingratiated himself into the Ramsdell household, for the two men were often seen together—at White's in St. James's Street, at the cock fights, escorting Lady Ramsdell and Annabelle to Hyde Park, at Manton's and at Jackson's Saloon, even at the Royal Gallery.

He felt his face grow flushed, a sensation which had nothing at all to do with his cold. Thoughts of Sir Jaspar's connection to Ramsdell rankled sorely. For years, Lord Crowthorne had attempted to enter

Ramsdell's exalted circle, but had failed—for what reason he could not say. His birth, his breeding, his education and status as heir to an earldom should have been all the *entreé* he needed.

He had made a number of overtures to Ramsdell himself, addressing him in private moments at a ball or soiree, exhibiting politeness and interest in his family, and paying particular attention to his mother and to his cousin, Charles Kidmarsh, by making certain they were invited to every fete his parents arranged.

To no avail. Ramsdell had been as elusive as snow in July and equally cool. Lord Crowthorne could not imagine having offended Ramsdell, yet for the life of him he could not comprehend why the viscount, so inferior to his own future station, should have snubbed him. Even his interest in Marianne had not brought the smallest warmth to Ramsdell's demeanor upon being addressed. Ramsdell merely cast him a level glance, as though he understood him completely, and moved on to the next person who addressed him.

Lord Crowthorne shook his head, blowing his nose soundly again. He was entirely perplexed. How could Ramsdell host a stable boy at White's, yet affect not the smallest interest in his own proferred friendship? Lord Crowthorne was dumbfounded.

He looked up at his friends, who had remained politely silent while he contemplated the news they had brought him. Finally, he said, "Would you be so good as to continue calling at Ramsdell's while I am laid up? I should like to know your observations not so much of Sir Jaspar's interest in Marianne but whether you believe she reciprocates his marked attentions."

"Happy to," Mr. Speen responded immediately.

"We intended to call after speaking with you," Sir Giles added.

Lord Crowthorne smiled ruefully. "She is devilishly pretty, is she not?"

Both men sighed gustily. What was it about a beautiful woman that eased an ache in every man's heart? Curious.

When the gentlemen left, Lord Crowthorne sent for his private secretary and he spent an hour arranging a number of gifts, missives, and flowers to be sent to Marianne in a strict succession over the forthcoming days so that while he was recovering, she should be kept constantly aware his suit was not in any manner diminishing.

He rather thought, especially since Sir Jaspar had kept her in the shrubberies for half an hour, he had best make his intentions clear to her as soon as possible so this sort of conduct would never happen again. He would not share the attentions of his future wife with anyone!

Marianne took every offering of Lord Crowthorne's into her bedchamber, where she could glory in them. The quiet message he was sending in his presents and the less subtle hints of his increasingly amorous missives led her to understand she was near to accomplishing what had been her sweetest dream from childhood.

She was tumbling in love with him, as well, of that she was certain, for every night she lay awake for a long time imagining being his wife, all the balls she would give, as well as soirees and musicales, how she would preside at his country seat once she became Lady Bray, and how jealous so many young ladies would be once they learned she had stolen a march on them all and made what she believed would long be remembered as the match of the decade.

Oh, yes, her dreams were coming true, just as she had known they would, were she to come to London begowned as a future countess ought to be—which, thanks to Lord Ramsdell's generosity, she had been.

Her heart was aflutter day and night. She thought of little else than what she knew in the depths of her bones to be Lord Crowthorne's approaching offer of marriage. His last missive, sent with a charming bouquet of lilies of the valley mixed with bluebells, indicated he had something of great importance to ask her once he had made a complete recovery, and would she be willing to receive him in private in two days' time?

She had spent three hours penning her response, copying her assent to his request at least a dozen times until every letter was perfectly shaped and every word chosen to show the very best portrait of her many abilities. She had shown Lord Crowthorne's final letter to Constance, who had seemed rather stunned, but who had agreed he must be desirous of making her an offer of marriage.

"Now you must read my letter of response, over which I have been laboring these past several hours. I believe Sir Jaspar will be pleased when he reads it."

Constance had stared at her, for Marianne had not realized the error she had made. "What do you mean, when Sir Jaspar reads it? Do you intend him to see the letter you are sending to Lord Crowthorne?"

Marianne had been horrified at her *faux pas* and had pressed a hand to her breast. "I cannot have said Sir Jaspar. I cannot. I have been thinking only of Lord Crowthorne these three hours and more."

"You said *Sir Jaspar.*"

"Well, I cannot imagine why I might have done so."

Yes, she could, she realized with a start. As she had approached Constance's door, for some reason her experience with Sir Jaspar several days ago, of being chased by him about the gardens at Vauxhall, had come suddenly and vividly to mind. She had thought, *Will Crowthorne be inclined to chase me, were I to suggest such a game?* Then her mind had rushed on to the wicked kiss she had shared with Jaspar in the darkened walkways, her mask lying atop his as he played his lips over hers in such a marvelous way.

Constance had not pursued the mistake, but instead had read the final copy of Marianne's response to Lord Crowthorne. She had said all that would be expected of an older sister—admired the penmanship, her sister's choice of words, the playfulness of the style, even the brevity of the response.

However, when Marianne returned to her bedchamber, she felt a distinct oppression of spirits. Constance had not shown a particle of true enthusiasm for the most brilliant match of the season. She stood in the center of her room, turning slowly to observe the numerous bouquets and gifts of glass hummingbirds, ceramic bowls, and even a beautifully crafted gold cross. The barrage of gifts struck her suddenly as having occurred by design.

She shook her head, unwilling to believe she had attributed Lord Crowthorne's lovely courtship to anything so calculating. Yet she had to admit that had she been in his shoes and wished to marry, she would have done precisely the same thing, for then she would have been assured of success.

She dropped onto her bed, her spirits drooping even further. She had always thought she would value just this manner of courtship above all things, a pursuit marked by a careful attentiveness visible to all.

Now, however, as she stared up into the knotted chintz canopy overhead, all she could think was how much fun she had had at Vauxhall while being chased by Sir Jaspar. If there had been a design in his pursuit, she knew it would have been in order to make her laugh, to shower her with his obvious affection for her, and in the end to kiss her passionately.

Ten

On the following evening, Marianne stood in the elegant space which separated a very grand split staircase, making the acquaintance of one of the five patronesses of Almack's Assembly Rooms, Lady Cowper.

Emily Cowper had the countenance of an angel and so much laughter in her eyes that Marianne could not help but be charmed by her, as were so many of the *beau monde*. When she but entered a drawing room, she was instantly besieged by admirers and her numerous acquaintance.

Marianne made a pretty curtsy and hoped beyond hope that the beautiful woman would find her manners, her breeding, and her conduct all that was agreeable in order that she might be approved to attend the elegant and quite exalted rooms. Not everyone was granted vouchers, and the rules were so strict that any personage who arrived even a minute past the final hour for admittance was turned summarily away from the doors. The five patronesses held complete dominion over the *haut ton* in this way and to some degree kept the high spirits of many young ladies and gentlemen in check.

"And how do you find London, Miss Marianne?" her ladyship asked in a gentle voice.

"Extraordinary. Wonderful. Fully beyond my expectations."

Lady Cowper fanned herself slowly and nodded. "I am so glad you were able-to finally come to the metropolis. I was used to know your father many years ago. He boasted he had the prettiest daughters in all of England. Between you and your sister"—here she nodded to Constance—"I am inclined to agree with him. I was very sorry to learn of his passing and that his untimely death prevented your journeying to London sooner. He was very proud of his family."

Marianne felt a sudden lump swell in her throat as tears touched her eyes. "He wanted me to come to London very much. He knew I would be enchanted by the Season, and so I am. I am very grateful you have spoken of him to me. I believe your words are some of the kindest I have ever received." She drew in a halting breath and felt Annabelle's hand slip into her own.

Lady Cowper nodded gracefully, then gestured with her fan to the stairs which rose to the first floor. "Have you seen Lady Hurley's ballroom?" she asked. "No? Then I promise you, you have never seen a ballroom before! Let me join your party. We shall all ascend and then descend together—if that would suit you, Lord Ramsdell?"

"Well you know it, my lady." He took her proferred hand and settled it on his arm. Constance took his other arm. Marianne walked behind them, feeling her cup was full to overflowing.

The ballroom was indeed like nothing she had ever seen before. The Hurley mansion was a large house in an old part of Mayfair which had not yet given way to rows of town houses. Inset into the walls were a number of enormous statues of Greek gods and goddesses. The orchestra was high above the floor in a recessed alcove, and it seemed to Marianne the elevated chamber could easily manage thirty-five or forty musicians.

The descent into the ballroom was an exact replica of the original stairs. One could not help but make a grand entrance, even if one were as shy as a church mouse. Several enormous chandeliers cast the ballroom into a glitter of light so bright that were she to close her eyes, she would vow the sun was shining.

Sir Jaspar, who walked beside her on her left, leaned close. "You appear as though you have been transported to Olympus."

"I have. Indeed, I have! Oh, Jaspar, you must waltz with me, for I wish to spin and spin beneath so many lights and let the full sound of the orchestra bring me fully into the abode of Zeus."

"I shall be happy to oblige you."

As if Marianne's most secret desires had been contemplated by the heavens and granted without a word having been spoken, the waltz was the next dance to be enjoyed.

Jaspar led her in his elegant, polished manner to an appropriate place upon the floor. As the musicians struck the first few chords, he deftly guided her into the sway, pause, and sway of the dance.

"We have not waltzed together before," she said.

"No, we have not."

"How is that possible?" she asked, as he turned her and turned her again.

Jaspar chuckled. "From the first—Lady Donnington's ball, I believe—you have been so beset by hopeful young men that I could never so much as draw near, let alone hope to acquire your hand for the waltz."

Marianne smiled dreamily. "You dance perfectly," she admitted, giving herself fully to the marked three-quarter rhythm of the music.

"Thank you. I will confess it is not only your beauty

which brings all the men to your side begging to dance with you. You are as light on your feet as feathers tossed in the air."

She giggled. "What a delightful image! Do you truly think me so ethereal? I am not convinced. I believe the talent is all yours. Generally, I must mind my steps a great deal more, but there is something in the way you hold me that keeps me spinning just so."

At the extreme happiness on her face, Jaspar felt a stillness deep within his heart. He wanted to hold this image of her forever in his mind, to recall with perfect perception in years to come the Season Marianne Pamberley took London by storm.

The joy writ on her features was precisely how he knew her best. For some reason, of all of her wonderful qualities, this was what he loved most about her, that she knew how to enjoy life. She possessed a true *joie de vivre* which, from his vast experience of cultures, few were able to realize.

His own life had been marked with difficulty and heartache for he had come to Lady Brook as an orphan. His father had been a vicar in a small hamlet in Yorkshire and his mother the daughter of a sheep farmer. Both had perished in the same year of a terrible fever which had ravaged the entire countryside.

He had no work, no relatives to whom he could turn for assistance, only a friend of his father's of many years' standing, John Stiveley, who had migrated south to Kent, where his own brother lived in the village of Wraythorne. Mr. Stiveley had been head groom of Lady Brook for three years. Jaspar's father on his deathbed had recommended his son apply to Mr. Stiveley for employment. "For I know he was quite fond of you,

Jaspar, and he would do anything for me. He will honor your request, make no mistake."

As the son of a vicar, even though his mother had been a farmer's daughter, he could have gone to a fine school and perhaps himself entered the clergy. Without connections, however, his only course was to make the suggested request to Mr. Stiveley.

In truth, he had never regretted this particular turn of fortune, for Fate had brought him to Lady Brook. The beautiful brick walls of that charming country house held the girl who was now the woman twirling safely in his arms as he turned her about the ballroom floor.

Faith, but he loved her more than life itself. If only there might be some way to reach her. Perhaps he should tell her his father had been a vicar in Yorkshire. Perhaps then she might not despise his past so vehemently.

Yet even as this thought passed through his mind, he knew he would never do so. He wanted her on his terms, to have her heart so fully given to him that she would not give a fig if he had been a balloonist or a collier or even a gypsy.

"I love you," he murmured softly, drawing her more closely to him as he turned her vigorously at the edge of the ballroom floor.

"W-what?" Her attention suddenly snapped to his eyes.

"I love you," he repeated. "We were made for each other. Can you not feel it even in the manner in which we move about the floor together? You say it is my ability, but I refuse to believe it is so. When I countered it is your lightness on your feet which makes our movements about the floor so idyllic, I was only partially right. Now I believe it is because we were made for each other in every particular."

"You should not say such things, nor speak to me in this manner," she urged him.

"I have not finished what I wished to say."

"Do not say it!" Her eyes were enormous with emotion.

"I will say it. We dance together so well because we are meant to be together. We are like pieces of a puzzle which fit exactly and make the whole picture have shape and meaning. A sennight past, at Vauxhall, the very same phenomenon occurred. Admit it is so."

She appeared rather frightened, her green eyes luminous in the bold light from the chandeliers above. "I will admit to nothing except that you should not have kissed me as you did!"

"You did nothing to prevent me. You wished for it." He held her gaze forcefully. He would not permit her to look away.

"I—I was behaving foolishly again, as I am wont to do in your base and unfortunate company. You are, after all, merely a stable boy who learned some manners and is now passing himself off—"

"Hush," he murmured, silencing her. She always threw his past in his face whenever she felt threatened by the emotions coursing through her breast. He knew now were they alone he could easily take her into his arms and ravish her lips with the kisses she enjoyed as much as he. "You love me," he whispered. "You know you do."

"I—I think you have gone mad to address me in this fashion while we are dancing."

"I can think of no better moment."

"I am dizzy from all the spinning and turning. There, you have twirled me again, and I feel as though I might swoon."

"You feel as though you might swoon because you are nearly engulfed in your true feelings for me. Come,

Marianne, enough of this pretense. Admit you are nearly delirious with loving me."

Marianne stared into his brown eyes. They seemed to be lakes of fire. She was dizzy and delirious and exhilarated. The music drew to a close, the final chord echoed through the ballroom, and she and Jaspar were no longer moving. He was merely holding her in his arms, releasing her ever so slowly.

Still, she stared into his eyes, utterly mesmerized. How had he done this magical thing to her? What trickery had he used? She felt like that old fable about a flute player and the passel of rats who followed blindly after him.

"Oh, Jaspar," she whispered, her heart flooding suddenly with a wave of something so wonderful she could hardly contain the joy which began to well up within her.

"Yes, my sweet?" he whispered next to her ear. "Say what is in your heart. Speak the words."

"Jaspar, I—I—"

"Miss Marianne!" a strong masculine voice suddenly called out.

The spell shattered about her feet like a thin bowl of glass she had suddenly dropped. Sir Giles and Henry Speen approached her rapidly from the nearby figure of Cupid, looming tall in the niche behind them.

"Oh, hallo," she said stupidly, her mind not seeming to function very well.

"You promised the quadrille to me," Mr. Speen said hurriedly, taking up her arm on her left.

Sir Giles possessed himself of her right arm and cried, "And a country dance to me, which I believe will be the next dance. May I say you look lovely tonight? Prettier than even Aphrodite who—oh, yes, I see her now—resides near Artemis on the other side of the chamber."

Marianne let herself be carried away by Lord Crowthorne's friends. Indeed, she could do naught else. The dance with Sir Jaspar and the subsequent conversation with him had depleted her of the ability to do anything but acquiesce to their lively conversation and the hold each had upon her arms.

She glanced back only once at Jaspar and saw him still standing on the ballroom floor. He seemed surrounded by a halo of light, and she knew the most pressing need to return to him, to tell him something of extreme importance, yet she could not move. She could only be carried away by Sir Giles and Mr. Speen.

The following morning, Jaspar awoke early, his mind whirring to life with a sudden burst of awareness that Marianne was slipping from him as surely as the sun rose and set each day.

He did not understand all that was happening either between them or with her. Sometimes when he kissed her—or last night, when he had danced with her—he was so certain she loved him, so certain she was coming to comprehend her love for him, that he felt assured of victory. Yet the moment she quit his side, some other force beyond his comprehension seemed at work to keep her from him forever.

He was completely bemused by the situation and frustrated intensely by the fact that he seemed to have not the smallest effect upon her once she was beyond the length of his arms or his voice or his lips. Was it not love, then, that existed between them? Had he misunderstood or misinterpreted the powerful sensations he experienced whenever he was near her?

He paced his bedchamber, the floor creaking with each pass he made at the foot of his bed. He slapped the bed rail when he passed by, the smooth wood soothing beneath his palm. He shook his head. No. He would never cease to believe that the strong pull between himself and Marianne was anything other than love, whether she admitted it or not.

Yet he knew he would lose her—he felt it in his bones—if he did not do something now!

He summoned his valet and began the tedious process of dressing for the day. The entire time his mind worked and travailed over the difficulty before him. He must speak with her today, before she forgot entirely that for a moment last night at Lady Hurley's ball, she had nearly confessed her love for him.

He did not know when Lord Crowthorne meant to beg for her hand in marriage, but if the actions of his friends following the waltz were any indication, his lordship meant to place his proposals before her very soon. He must reach her, and quickly, before she made the greatest mistake of her life and accepted Crowthorne's hand in marriage.

He ordered flowers to be procured immediately, and then sat down to compose a brief missive requesting an audience with Marianne. A moment later, he bade one of the footmen to deliver the letter to Grosvenor Square and to await an answer.

Marianne sat at her dressing table, strangely numb. She had risen early when her maid had brought her a message from Lord Crowthorne, reminding her he would be calling on her today, as agreed upon. At the same time, another letter had arrived, and so she stared down at two very different missives, the handwriting of each as different as night and day, yet each bearing the same request—a private audience.

The decision should have been a simple one—deny Jaspar his audience and honor Lord Crowthorne's earlier request. She understood the implications of both missives. There could be no doubt on that score. Jaspar intended to press his suit yet again. As for Lord Crowthorne, there could be no other interpretation for his desire to see her alone than an intention of offering for her.

So she was to choose. Yet she already had chosen, so why was she hesitating? Why was she sitting before her dressing table in her nightclothes, trembling from head to foot? She knew what she wanted. She had always known the proper course for her future, always.

Why, then, did she stare at one missive, then the next, as though there was a decision to be made?

She struggled to breathe and to calm her shaking limbs. She knew why—because Jaspar's kisses tasted of heaven and Lord Crowthorne's seemed so cold and disinterested.

She squeezed her eyes shut. Could anything be more ridiculous than contemplating a refusal of Lord Crowthorne's offer of marriage merely because she had no taste for his kisses? Yet here she sat, trembling and overset.

She rose from the table and began to pace the chamber. She reviewed her tumultuous relationship with Sir Jaspar, from meeting him after so many years at Lady Bramshill's ball in Berkshire to the summer's kiss they had shared by the trout stream to his stormy proposal the day before she left for London to the wicked kisses they had shared after the opera, in Ramsdell's drawing room, at Vauxhall—and, yes, even to the dance they had shared last night.

That was the rub. She should not have danced with Sir Jaspar last night. He had not even kissed her, and she had been filled with the sun, moon, and stars all rolled into one merely by being guided in his arms about a ballroom floor. He had professed his love for her again, and there was something deeply intoxicating about the way he loved her to the point of madness. For a moment, she had almost told him she was in love with him, as well.

She pressed her hands to her cheeks. How had he so beguiled her that she had been ready to confess a love she did not feel? Somehow he had learned to cast spells over innocent maidens and cause them to believe, however momentarily, that they loved him. He must have learned such tricks whilst in India!

She stopped her pacing and drew up short, clapping her hands. That was the explanation she needed to become comfortable again. While Jaspar was in India making his fortune, he had stumbled across some sort of mystical incantation which, with merely a look, would cause the object of his flirtations to tumble wildly in love with him.

She breathed a deep sigh of relief. At last her limbs had stopped trembling. She had resolved everything quite nicely in her mind, and once more she could proceed with her well-calculated plan. She hastily penned two separate letters, sealed them with a dollop of wax and her brass seal, then rang for her maid.

Now, which gown should she wear in order to accept Lord Crowthorne's proposal?

An hour later, Marianne stood before the fireplace in Lord Ramsdell's study, her gaze settled affectionately upon the face of Lord Crowthorne. He was speaking eloquently of his love for her, of his desire that she make him the happiest of men and accept his hand in marriage, of his certain knowledge that one day she would make as fine a countess as his own mother.

She was living a dream. His gloved fingers were warm to her hands, his smile tender, his affection more than obvious in the expression on his face. Surely this was the happiest day of her entire life.

She nodded and smiled in return. "I have no desire greater than to accept your offer of marriage and become your wife, my lord."

He gave her fingers a gentle squeeze. "Ours shall be the marriage which shall set the example for all others to follow."

"I could not agree more." She smiled brightly upon her favored beau.

"May I kiss you now and seal our troth?"

"I confess to no other wish."

How very tidy and polite that he had asked permission to kiss her. Jaspar would not have done so. Jaspar would have . . . No! She had no intention of thinking of *him* just now, the man who used Indian trickery upon the females of his acquaintance.

No, she would think only of Jas—er, Lord Crowthorne and how much she loved him—for she truly did love him—and how much she desired to be a good wife to him.

She leaned into him and he took her firmly by the shoulders and laid a kiss upon her lips.

An eternity passed. Surely an eternity. She could hear herself breathing through her nose. She wished he would stop kissing her or at least attempt to do the job better.

Finally, he released her, then dragged her into his arms to embrace her for a long moment. Tears seeped oddly from her eyes. After another long moment, when fortunately her tears dried up, he begged her to sit with him for a time and drew her toward a chair by the window.

She knew a most ridiculous sensation to ask if she might sit upon his lap, that she might know a little comfort. For some reason she could not comprehend, she felt, given the smallest provocation, she might begin sobbing like a child.

Instead, he led her to a wing chair of plaid burgundy wool and took up a matching chair opposite her. She sat on the edge, like a schoolgirl about to receive a strong dressing down for some misconduct, and folded her hands tightly on her lap. He leaned back into his chair and lounged easily, seeming quite content.

"I hope you feel as I do, that we are fortunate to have all that business behind us."

"Yes, of course." She hiccuped, then covered her mouth with her hands and looked away from him.

Just as a gentleman ought, he overlooked this indiscretion and began another speech. "I vow, the first time I saw you I promised I would one day make you my wife. I recall how quickly you were inundated with hopeful partners at Lady Donnington's ball and how I addressed you so informally. You were right to upbraid me as you did and insist on a proper introduction, but how excited I was just to speak with you. I cannot bring the entire occurrence to mind without remembering the exact tilt of your chin and the elegant sweep of your lashes. You are so beautiful, and I am beyond fortunate you have accepted my hand in marriage. Do you wish me to speak with Lord Ramsdell? I presume the arrangements concerning your dowry should be made with him."

"Yes, that would be the proper avenue to pursue," she responded evenly. Her heart was beating erratically. She felt nervous and uneasy in a way she had never felt before.

He paused for a moment. "You seem a little distressed. Are you well, Marianne? And may I address you by your Christian name?"

"Of course you may. And, yes, I am perfectly well. It is just that I have never been betrothed before."

"Nor I," he responded laughing. "Well, no doubt there will be some awkwardness for a time between us, for we are not well-versed in one another's ways. Is Lord Ramsdell within? Could I apply to him now? I should like it above all things if we were to settle these matters immediately."

Marianne rose to her feet abruptly, grateful for the opportunity to interrupt the disquieting *tête-à-tête*. She rang for the butler and, when he arrived, begged him to send Ramsdell.

A few minutes later, during which time only silence reigned in the small square chamber, Ramsdell appeared. His expression was rather reserved, she thought, and not at all what she had expected from one who must have been aware she was speaking privately with Lord Crowthorne with the intention of hearing his proposals of marriage.

He greeted her softly and met her gaze with a careful, concerned expression. "It is all settled then?" he asked softly.

"Yes," she said, nodding in several short bobs. "I—I daresay you will want to have a discussion with his lordship. I—I shall leave now."

She turned toward her betrothed and bobbed a ridiculous curtsy, then scurried from the chamber. She did not stop in the hallway, but ran upstairs to the first floor and went to her room, where she promptly threw herself onto her bed and gave way to a veritable flood of tears.

This should have been the happiest moment of her life. Instead, all she could think was, *He kisses like a cold fish!* And she sobbed harder.

Eleven

After a few minutes and perhaps a dozen hiccups, Marianne grew more composed. She realized she was merely suffering the attendant shock of having taken so enormous a step without considering how permanent it was. For one thing, Crowthorne would have the mastery of her life, her time, her dowry, even her conduct. The very thought of it, and how she must now be forever asking after his opinions, was nearly more than she could manage with equanimity. She could only wonder how Constance had borne so easily the abrupt change in her life when she had first become engaged to Ramsdell.

She shivered. Whatever had she done? For so many years, her thoughts had been fixed on coming to London, on wearing exquisite gowns and jewelry and having her hair prepared just so, and upon making a brilliant match. She had never given a thought to what would be required of her once she accepted a man's proposals.

Lord Crowthorne was very right. There would be a measure of awkwardness involved during these initial stages of their betrothal, at least for a time. However, his lordship was very kind and patient, and Marianne had every confidence that in time she would rub along tolerably well with him.

After splashing cold water on her face and wiping

the beads away with a soft towel, she finally felt calm enough to begin the process of receiving the household's congratulations on her exceptional match.

She found Annabelle in the hallway, almost at the landing. At the sight of her new friend, charmingly gowned in a soft cream silk dress over which was draped a beautiful silk shawl patterned with roses and an intricate green vine, her heart grew suddenly lighter. Annabelle appeared to such marvelous advantage with her hair swept atop her head and a delicate fringe of curls framing her face. Her cousin was now enjoying every success in London and even had her own small cluster of friends and beaux who immediately sought her out at any function she attended.

Her newfound success was a constant delight to Marianne. Once she had relinquished the notion that Annabelle should form an integral part of her own court, she had swiftly begun to enjoy the pleasures of seeing another person transformed. Nothing would please her more than revealing her most interesting news to her cousin first, for Annabelle had become her confidante and had taken to listening to her every progress with Lord Crowthorne.

Only two nights past, Annabelle had encouraged her in her pursuit of Lord Crowthorne. "If you truly love him," she had said somberly, "then I know you will be very happy, for there is no finer a gentleman in all of England than Lord Edgar."

Marianne had professed her love for Lord Crowthorne and had had the pleasure of Annabelle's sudden embrace, as well as sharing any number of heartfelt tears. How happy Annabelle had been for her, even then. She would surely be ecstatic now that everything was settled.

Marianne called to her just before Annabelle began

her descent down the stairs. "Annabelle, stay a moment. I have something to tell you of great importance."

Annabelle's complexion paled suddenly. "Indeed? Does it involve Lord Crowthorne?" She moved back up the hallway. "Your maid just told me he was in Ramsdell's study even now."

"Yes, it does, very much so. Oh, Annabelle, my every dream has come true. If you must know, I am officially betrothed and will one day become the countess of Bray."

Annabelle weaved strangely on her feet and was only prevented from falling because Marianne hurried to her side and caught her. "Oh, dear! I have given you a shock! Come to my bedchamber, where you might be made more comfortable."

Supporting Annabelle firmly about the waist, she drew her into her room.

"You are to be married," Annabelle murmured, sliding into a chair by the window. She drew in a deep breath and gripped the arms of the chair firmly. "You and Edgar are, indeed, to be married? When?" She shook her head and looked up at Marianne through squinted eyes.

"I do not know," Marianne responded. She could not help but frown, for she could not comprehend why Annabelle was behaving so oddly. "We—we did not discuss the wedding date. Lord Crowthorne was anxious to speak with Ramsdell, to attend to the details of the marriage settlement first. I suppose we will establish a date for the wedding when we have spoken with both our families."

"Yes, of course," Annabelle murmured, her gaze shifting to the carpet below her feet. Marianne watched as Annabelle followed the pretty patterns in the carpet with her eyes. She repeated the pattern several times but remained silent.

"I shall fetch you some tea," Marianne said at last. She rang for the maid and, after placing her request, returned to stand beside Annabelle. "Are you not happy for me? Does your silence mean you do not believe Lord Crowthorne and I to be properly matched? Tell me, Annabelle, for you are frightening me. I have just promised myself to a man who, though I admire excessively, I scarcely know, and I find myself more distressed than I would have believed. You must tell me, do you think I will make him a proper wife?"

At that Annabelle turned to look at Marianne, and finally some of the shock left her face. "Of course you will." She smiled sweetly. "For he would love you, as any man must, who knows your generous spirit, your kind heart, and your clever mind. He will love you, and because you love him you will have a wonderful life together, of that I am certain. If I seem unable for the moment to enter into your joy, you must realize I am suddenly distressed by— by the notion of—of our little family breaking apart."

"Oh, how stupid of me." Marianne dropped to her knees in front of Annabelle and clasped her friend's hands in her own. "I was thinking only of myself and supposing everyone would feel as I do. Yet now that I think on it, I recall quite vividly the day Constance informed me of her intention of marrying Ramsdell, I suffered the very same sort of misery—that the family I knew would no longer exist, particularly since both Augusta and Celeste were to be married, as well. Eventually, however, I came to realize that though my sisters and I would no longer live beneath the same roof, that our lives indeed were changed forever, I would be acquiring in all these marriages brothers where there had been none before. And what is more, both Constance and Augusta are in the family way, so very soon I shall have nephews and nieces, as well.

"You and I must agree to be like sisters to one another from now on, and you must look upon Crowthorne as your brother."

"As my brother." Annabelle's gaze drifted away from Marianne, and tears suddenly filled her eyes and rolled down her cheeks. "As my brother. Of course. I suppose in a way, he always was like a brother to me—nothing more."

Marianne did not know what Annabelle meant, but since it seemed to her her cousin was coming to accept the situation a little more, she did not hesitate to embrace her and gently kiss her cheek.

Annabelle slid a kerchief from the long sleeve of her gown and dabbed at her cheeks. "You are one of the kindest friends I have ever known, and I am beyond happy for you, especially since I know how much you have desired to marry Edgar. Have you told your sister yet?"

"No, but I mean to go to her now."

"Oh, yes," Annabelle said. "And I mean to return to my bedchamber and dry my eyes, for it will not do at all to congratulate Edgar while behaving like a watering pot."

Marianne left Annabelle at her bedchamber door and moved to the opposite side of the town house to her sister's room.

Annabelle sat on the edge of her bed, tears streaming down her cheeks. She opened her reticule and drew from a secret pocket in the lining of the purse a vinaigrette which Lady Bray had given her many years ago.

She had admired the small ceramic box, for on the lid was a miniature of Edgar when he was a lad of seventeen, very nearly the age when she had first met him. Edgar was smiling and appeared very young and not nearly so stuffy as he was now in all his London pomp and propriety.

She had loved him ever since she could remember, but he was lost to her now and her heart was breaking. She did not know how she was to approach him and offer him her congratulations on his forthcoming nuptials.

She had always believed she would one day marry him. Even the gypsies who had once camped near her home had prophesied as much. She had come to London with no other intention than to see Edgar and make him love her, if she could.

There were even moments in the past fortnight when he had seemed much struck by her. Certainly he had complimented her most enthusiastically upon her new coiffure and the fine gowns which Marianne had helped her purchase. He had danced with her on several occasions, had listened to her play the pianoforte at least four separate times, and once when he told her of his desire to become more involved in his father's estate, he had stopped and stared very hard at her.

"What is it?" she had asked after a time.

"I . . . It is nothing. Only . . . Annabelle, I had never thought of you as a beauty, but indeed you are. Your eyes are the color of the sky and your lips have the prettiest shape." He had blinked several times. She had been so caught up in the strong emotions his compliments had swelled within her that she had found nothing to say to him in response.

Indeed, he had seemed to be equally at a loss for words. For the longest moment, he had simply held her gaze, his eyes searching her face, his brow slightly puckered. He had reached for her, too, and his fingers had slid along her arm in a manner that made her tremble even now.

However, the moment had passed abruptly, for Marianne had bounced up to them on the arm of Sir Giles and had playfully demanded that Edgar partner her for the quadrille. Annabelle had been left in a daze that had lasted for hours. Several times that evening, she had found him staring at her, a perplexed expression on his brow. She had not smiled whenever she caught his eye, but willed him to understand that perhaps, were he to truly look at her, truly know her, he might find a woman fully grown whom he could love.

She wiped another tear away from her cheek and slid her finger across the smooth enameled surface of the box.

"Oh, Edgar," she murmured. She gave way to the sobs which had been trapped in her throat ever since Marianne had cried gleefully, *I am officially betrothed and will one day become the countess of Bray!* Falling across the bed, she buried her face in her pillow and determined to spend the rest of the day in her bedchamber professing the headache.

When Marianne entered Constance's bedchamber, she quickly announced her happy news. "He has offered for me, and I have accepted! Do you not think I shall be the happiest of brides?"

Constance cocked her head and after several seconds smiled with obvious pleasure. "It is true, then? But how marvelous. I had supposed you were not inclined to wed him because your sights were set elsewhere, but I am so happy for you. I believe with all my heart your contentment as a bride will be unequaled. To own the truth, now that everything is settled between you and Sir Jaspar, I could never fully comprehend your interest in Lord Crowthorne. He did not seem at all to be the sort of man who could truly know you and appreciate you."

"Sir Jaspar?" Marianne responded, pausing in mid stride. "Why do you suppose I was referring to Sir Jaspar?"

Constance stared at her very hard. In a quiet voice, she said, "Spencer informed me he arrived a quarter-hour past. When you entered just now and spoke of a proposal of marriage, I presumed—that is, are we not speaking of Sir Jaspar?"

"Not by half!" Marianne's spirits drooped once more. "How could you suppose I would ever agree to marry *him?*"

"I am so very sorry, Marianne. Is Lord Crowthorne also below stairs?"

Marianne nodded. So this was her sister's true opinion of Crowthorne's ability to make her happy. She should not be surprised, for to a large degree Constance had championed Sir Jaspar from the first. Why would she not? They had been friends since childhood. Yet she was still stunned.

"I am betrothed to Lord Crowthorne, and I will be very happy with him even if you do not think I shall."

Constance reached out a hand to her, but Marianne's heart felt pinched and sore. She whirled about and quit the bedchamber. She would speak with Constance later and—and force her to see how much she was mistaken. She not only preferred Lord Crowthorne to her father's former stable boy, but theirs would be a marriage far superior to all other marriages. She would somehow make them *all* see this was the proper course for her future.

As for the present, it would seem Jaspar had arrived beforetimes. For the barest moment, she considered sending a message to him to the effect she was feeling ill and would speak with him on the morrow.

A moment's consideration, however, forced her to admit she ought to deliver the unhappy news to her suitor at once. Otherwise he would hear of her betrothal to Crowthorne at some ball or other and that, she felt, would be a less than honorable path.

The butler disclosed that Lord Ramsdell and Lord Crowthorne were still closeted in the study and Sir Jaspar awaited her in the drawing room. She immediately made her way to the latter and saw at once he had brought flowers for her, an enormous bouquet of roses. In his hand was a present wrapped with a violet ribbon.

She grew very conscious, of a sudden recalling that only a sennight past she had kissed him rather wantonly at Vauxhall. Even last night, she had expressed her great delight in dancing with him, so much so that it occurred to her in the most horrifying manner that he undoubtedly expected her to finally agree to marry him.

She stared at him, her hands clasped behind her, her lips compressed.

"Whatever is the matter, Marianne?" he asked, his brow furrowed. He set the gift on a table near the fireplace and advanced toward her. She took a step backward, stumbled unaccountably, and fell. "Oh, dear," she murmured.

She struggled to rise, but her skirts caught on the tips of her pointed slippers, and he extended a hand to her. "Are you all right?" he asked, smiling.

"Yes, of course," she responded weakly, accepting his help and taking his hand. He drew her easily to her feet. When he took yet another step toward her, however, she immediately backed away, then circled to his right, heading quickly toward the windows. "Have you brought more flowers for my cousin?" she asked hurriedly, knowing full well the offering was for her.

"No," he drawled. "These are for you, from my heart, Marianne. Will you not at least look at me?"

She glanced toward him, then quickly averted her

gaze to the square below. "The flowers are quite lovely. I was always fond of yellow roses."

"I brought you a gift as well. May I give it to you?"

"Jaspar, really I do not think—"

"Please, Marianne. It is only a trifle, something I thought might give you a little pleasure."

She did not know what to do. She wanted to blurt out that she was betrothed to Lord Crowthorne, but she could not speak the words. She felt ashamed of her previous conduct and knew in her heart she had behaved badly at Vauxhall, as well as last night while she was waltzing with him.

He brought the gift to her and she took it slowly from his hand. She did not look at him as she pulled the bow apart and unwrapped the small package.

On a small blue velvet pillow sat an elegant brooch in the shape of a butterfly. Its wings were dressed with seed pearls and its body was a thin line of rubies. She felt as though a hand had suddenly taken hold of her heart and squeezed very hard. Something about the butterfly, whose wings were lifted at slight angles, spoke to her soul in a manner she could not explain.

"Oh," she breathed. "I have never seen anything so beautiful. Thank you, Jaspar, ever so much."

She ran the tip of her finger over the jewels and the soft pearls, tracing the shape of the butterfly.

He drew very close to her. "You remind me of a butterfly, so carefree among the world, so beautiful, so delicate."

Finally, she met his gaze and saw in the brown depths of his eyes all the love he possessed for her. She could hardly breathe, so sad did she feel. How was she to tell him she would never belong to him, that she had already given herself to another man?

"Tell me I am not too late," he murmured close to her ear.

She swallowed hard. "Oh, but I fear you are." She stopped breathing.

He did not speak for a long, long moment, and she could not look at him. At last, he said, "You have agreed to marry Lord Crowthorne—even today, this morning?"

She nodded, still fingering the butterfly. Why was no one truly happy for her? Ramsdell had seemed utterly disappointed, Annabelle had shed tears, and Constance had expressed her belief she would never be happy with Crowthorne. Now, here was Jaspar, as silent as a tomb, and she could scarcely bear it.

"I—I have accepted his hand in marriage, but we have not yet set a date. He is even now speaking with Ramsdell."

"He is in this house, at this very moment? My God, why did you not tell me the moment you entered the drawing room?"

"I—I began to see that my behavior toward you has been abominable, that you perhaps were expecting me to give you the answer for which you have been hoping these many months and more because of—of Vauxhall and because of last night. I felt ashamed and distraught. Oh, Jaspar, I am so very sorry, but I cannot accept your lovely gift. Will you ever forgive me?" She extended the blue pillow toward him.

Jaspar took the present back. "I shall leave you," he said. "I wish you every happiness in your forthcoming nuptials. Good-bye."

It was all so abrupt, like a door slamming shut.

Marianne blinked and watched him go. He crossed the room first and left the pillow and the butterfly beside the yellow roses. "I want you to have this," he said. "Consider it a present in honor of your betrothal."

Then he was gone.

* * *

When Jaspar stepped onto the sidewalk, it began to rain. He pressed his hat down hard about his ears and buttoned his greatcoat tightly about his neck. He lived three miles away, but ordered his coach to return to the mews. He intended to walk back to his town house. The postilion merely nodded obediently and set the coach quickly in motion.

Shoving his hands deep into his pockets, he let the rain beat against his chest as he forged his way home against the prevailing wind. The exercise kept him warm even though he wondered whether his heart still beat in his chest, so dead did he feel to all emotion.

She is to be married, and not to me, rang through his head a hundred times.

That evening, Marianne walked beside Annabelle as the residents of Ramsdell's home traversed the short distance to the Earl of Bray's town house two doors down, in order that the two families might celebrate Marianne's betrothal to Lord Crowthorne.

The party was a silent one, and the tension which Marianne had felt all day among Ramsdell, Annabelle, and Constance had not lessened, even a little. She hoped once the countess offered her blessings on the match her sister and brother-in-law might begin to smile in earnest and to realize and appreciate what a triumph the betrothal was.

For herself, she was gradually forgiving everyone for failing to enter into her joy, and trusted that once the betrothal was announced formally and the banns posted a gathering of enthusiastic well-wishers would form about herself and Lord Crowthorne.

Presently, she was grateful to have left Ramsdell's

town house, relieved that Annabelle's headache had finally lessened to the point she could join in the celebration, and happy that now she could concentrate fully on the wondrous miracle of having actually brought Crowthorne up to scratch.

When she entered the countess's drawing room, she was greeted formally and with great respect, if not affection. The earl of Bray, though bowing first to her, offered her a peck on her cheek and welcomed her into his family. "My son has chosen well," he said sedately. "I hope you will be as happy in your marriage as my wife and I have been in ours."

With that, he sought the countess's side, took her hand in his, and brought her fingers to his lips. The exchange between husband and wife brought so much warmth to her heart that she quickly went to them and in a quiet voice said, "I hope I may not disappoint you. I—I love your son very much and intend to make him the best wife possible."

Lord Crowthorne immediately came to her side and lovingly took her elbow. He met her gaze with so much appreciation that all her doubts as to the wisdom of her decision were laid to rest.

From that point on, the evening moved more smoothly and at times even with good humor. The earl of Bray was a warmhearted man in possession of a great number of anecdotes. Throughout the formal removes of a very fine meal, he offered little stories here and there to keep the lively pace of the evening going strong.

He was a tall man with graying hair, startling blue eyes, and a moustache quite at odds with the fashion of the day. Military men were known to wear whiskers, but outside of those who sported of a red uniform, most men were clean shaven. Yet Marianne thought he was particularly handsome. His hair was wavy and his demeanor quite forceful. The more Marianne listened to him and watched him, the more she liked him.

By the end of the evening, he seemed to have formed a particular attachment to her and did not hesitate to tease her a little. "By God, you are the prettiest filly to have graced our halls since I first brought my wife to meet my dear parents."

"You are too kind." She smiled up at him.

"And you have a sweetness about you I find utterly charming. It is no wonder Edgar offered for you so swiftly, for I daresay there must have been a score of young men seeking your attentions."

"Not a score!" She blushed.

Even the countess seemed to have warmed to her. "I have been waiting a very long time to welcome a daughter into my home. I have listened to you speak of your sisters this evening with so much obvious affection that I am persuaded you know what it is to value your familial connections. May I say I could not have chosen better for my son? So long as you love him, truly love him, I am content that you are to be his wife."

For some reason, her words brought tears to Marianne's eyes. "You have made me very happy, my lady," she responded.

Before the party quit the Brays' home, Lord Crowthorne drew Marianne apart. "You conducted yourself beautifully here tonight, Marianne. I must confess I had some concern on that score, given that your spirits are frequently elevated. However, my parents are quite pleased with our decision to marry. Mama has suggested we have the ceremony here, quite privately, with just a few relatives and one or two friends present—in, say, a month's time?"

Marianne blinked several times. The first part of his

speech made perfect sense to her and though she was a trifle put off by his fear she would not know better than to contain her natural liveliness, she was in general pleased. However, the second part of his speech was still sorting itself out in her brain. Had he really told her he wished to be married within a month?

A month!

A month and her fate would be sealed forever. Not that it wasn't sealed already. After all, a betrothal among the *haut ton* was nearly as binding as the marriage ceremony itself. Yet somehow she found it daunting in the extreme that in a month she would be living with the man before her. Lord Crowthorne was little more than a stranger to her.

Because she had for years trained herself to politeness, she said, "A month would be perfection itself."

"Excellent," he responded.

The rest of the evening was quite brief, since Constance was feeling fatigued. Before long, Marianne was walking home with a very quiet Annabelle beside her and her sister and brother-in-law leading the way. Only then did she realize her cousin had uttered scarcely two words through dinner and few more than that the remainder of the evening.

"Are you still suffering from the headache?" Marianne asked softly.

"Only a little," Annabelle responded.

"Tomorrow perhaps you will feel better."

"Perhaps."

Marianne glanced at Ramsdell and Constance, who were still rather somber. *Tomorrow perhaps we all will,* she thought.

Twelve

Once the engagement was announced in the *Morning Post,* the *beau monde* flocked to Lord Ramsdell's home to wish Marianne great happiness in her forthcoming marriage. Though a few young ladies were cool in their attentions to her, she had little doubt that jealousy was at the core of such rudeness. She forgave them all, however, for the simple reason that she had won the prize, and in the winning she had no need to bear ill feelings or grudges toward anyone.

Over the following week, Jaspar continued to visit at the Ramsdells' home, but his entire demeanor toward her had changed. Gone were the passionate glances and the friendly banter which had always characterized her relationship with him. On one occasion, she had tried to reestablish at least some of their former conviviality, but Jaspar merely stared at her, forcing her to become aware of how inappropriate any such intimacy with him would be.

He was right, of course, and she let him drift away from her just as she ought—and, indeed, just as the rest of her hopeful beaux were obliged to do during the first few days of her betrothal. Since Lord Crowthorne during that time was wonderfully attentive, she did not feel overly much the change in her circumstances—at least not until the evening of the Waltham ball.

Crowthorne had been unable to attend the ball, and

she found herself, for the first time since her arrival in London, rather ignored. Even the requests to partner her for the waltz or the quadrille were placed in sedate, reserved manners. Much of the joy of the ball seemed to have evaporated. Worse still was the fact that she remained seated through more than one dance. Imagine, Marianne Pamberley without a partner!

So it was that when Sir Jaspar rescued her, she could not help but thank him. "I was never more relieved about anything in my entire existence," she cried. "Are you aware that of the last five sets I have danced only two? *Two!* Well may you stare. Oh, Jaspar, I feel as though I have crossed into some dark world I do not comprehend."

He nodded. "Now you are betrothed, any number of your beaux must needs pursue other young ladies. I do not mean to give offense, Marianne, but perhaps you should have expected some shift of loyalties once your engagement was announced."

Her lower lip trembled, and though she could see concern in his eyes, he said nothing more, but gently guided her through a quite dull country dance.

Afterward, instead of conversing in his usual warm, hearty manner, he merely introduced her to a friend of Ramsdell's, who politely asked her to go down the next set.

Finally the ball drew to a close, a circumstance which afforded Marianne a great deal more happiness than she would have supposed possible.

On the way home, she expressed some of her distress to Annabelle. "I never expected to be ignored," she said.

Annabelle patted her arm and said, "I daresay you were missing Edgar so very much you could not bear to remain alone for even a few minutes at a time."

Marianne only stared at her, for it was then she realized she had not thought of Lord Crowthorne once all evening.

On the following morning, Marianne decided she must speak with her sister Constance about her growing disquiet concerning her engagement. She found her sister in the drawing room busily arranging an elegant bouquet of daffodils, purple pansies, and feathery ferns. Letting her hand glide along one of the long, elegant fronds, Marianne asked, "When you were first betrothed to Ramsdell, did you suddenly find yourself in a dull state?"

Constance met her gaze with lifted brows. "In a dull state?"

"Yes, you know, with everyone suddenly less interested in you, as though once you had become engaged you were no longer even mildly entertaining when you told your anecdotes."

"I see," Constance murmured. "Well, it is difficult to say, for if you recall, my circumstances were entirely different from yours. For one thing, we were all in the country. For another, Lady Brook had just burned to the ground. I had a great deal to do, and my mind was fully occupied with finding lodgings for everyone, as well as with planning three weddings, including my own." She slid another daffodil into the arrangement.

"I had not thought of that," Marianne mused. "It would be unhelpful, then, to compare my betrothal to yours."

"You seem a trifle overset, my dear. Has Lord Crowthorne behaved properly toward you since the betrothal? Has he been as kind and as attentive as he ought to be?"

"Oh, yes," she returned hastily. "No one could possibly fault his conduct toward me, and his parents have been equally solicitous. Only yesterday, for instance, Lady Bray showed me the pearls which every future countess of Bray has worn on her wedding day since time out of mind. She has been kindness itself and seems to have accepted me as a true daughter. Indeed, I have become quite fond of her." She chewed on her lip and sighed heavily.

"Then what is amiss? I have never before seen so sad a face on any young lady so recently betrothed."

"I do not mean to complain," Marianne said, "but I had supposed a betrothal would be even more amusing than the preceding courtship. I confess, Constance, I believe I am actually bored with the whole of it. Of course, I never expected so many things to change. The worst of it is, I am no longer the object of so much general interest as I was before. Why, even Freddy Shiplake has not asked me to dance once since I accepted Crowthorne's hand in marriage! Are you not shocked?"

"I see what it is," Constance offered. "You were merely missing Lord Crowthorne and his attentions last night. I remember how greatly I longed to be with Ramsdell every moment of every day during our betrothal month. I detested any chore which kept me from his side or prevented me from even thinking about him."

Marianne watched as her sister's color heightened and a secret smile stole over her lips. She frowned, wondering why she did not feel precisely the same way about Lord Crowthorne. If she missed anyone at the moment, it was Sir Jaspar, for no matter what terrible things were occurring in her life, he could always make her laugh and find some new entertainment to lift her spirits, like taking her to Astley's or Bartholomew Fair.

Constance met her gaze. "What were you thinking just now?" she asked.

Marianne shrugged. "I was pondering how differently Sir Jaspar conducts himself with me now I am betrothed. You would think I had contracted the plague, so stiffly does he address me."

"I believe he is attempting to be discreet. I was fully aware of how much he loved you, and undoubtedly still does, and it would no longer do for him to flirt with you now you are to be married. Marianne, you cannot expect your favorites to continue as before. When you spoke of Freddy earlier, I am inclined to believe your betrothal has made him so despondent he cannot be happy in your company."

"I suppose you are right," Marianne said, not in the least comforted by the conversation.

So this was how it was to be—no more flirting or dancing every dance at a ball or depending upon Sir Jaspar to amuse her when she was sad. If this was how the betrothal continued, what would marriage be like?

After shuddering, she was about to quit the drawing room when Constance spoke. "Oh, I nearly forgot. I received a letter from Celeste but an hour ago. She has some very interesting news." She settled another daffodil in the vase, then drew the letter from the pocket of her gown.

Smiling warmly, she handed it to Marianne.

Marianne took the letter, but did not unfold it at once, for she was fully caught by her sister's expression. "Do not tell me!" she cried. "Is she also increasing?"

Constance nodded. "She was hoping we might all be together when she told us, however, sometime last week she realized by the time we all met again, her condition would be so obvious as to make any communication unnecessary. It would seem she could not keep her joy to herself. She and Sir Henry are *aux anges,* as you may well imagine."

Marianne held the letter as though it were a holy document. She touched the vellum with awestruck fingers. "First Augusta, then you, and now Celeste. Is not this the happiest of days?"

"It is indeed," Constance replied, her expression aglow. "And to think only last year none of us were wed. Now by June four of us will have tied the knot, and by Christmas our family will have further increased by three."

"When is Celeste's baby due?"

"October."

"Oh, I cannot credit it's true, yet of course I know it must be! I am so happy for Celeste—for all of you."

"I daresay you will follow suit soon enough."

"I want a dozen children," she announced without preamble.

At that Constance chuckled. "And does Lord Crowthorne hope for the same? If he does, then I know of at least one commonality between the pair of you, and a fine one it would be, indeed!"

Marianne blinked and considered her words. She had never discussed the subject with Lord Crowthorne. Hope suddenly rocketed in her heart. Why, her betrothed might even desire to have a score of children, with her none the wiser. Were he to harbor such a desire, one she shared, there would be at least one reason for them to take greater delight in each other's company.

She thanked Constance for her encouragement and took a moment to read the whole of Celeste's letter, which, besides her announcement and several particulars about Wraythorne, included a recipe for pickled beets which she had tried recently at the vicar's house and had found quite delicious.

"Oh, and Katherine is visiting with them," Marianne said. "I had thought she meant to be in Brighton by now, putting her favorite gelding through his paces."

"I daresay the weather has not permitted, but you are right. I would have supposed she would be at Miss Alistair's home long since. Even though the races will not be held until July, I know Katherine will want her horse to be familiar with the course."

"The Regent will be there by the end of June, and I daresay our sister will find herself surrounded by all manner of genteel and noble persons. I hope she may be invited to the Pavilion, for I have heard tell it is wondrous."

Constance grimaced slightly. "But you know what Katherine is. She has no taste for grand society."

"I suppose you are right. Does Ramsdell's brother mean to attend the races, as well?"

"We have not heard a single word from him since Christmas, and then he was undecided. He thought he might have a chance at winning with a stallion he recently purchased from Ireland, but he seems quite unable to manage pen and ink with which to inform us of his decision. Ramsdell wrote him of our wonderful news, so we are in expectation of hearing from him before too terribly long."

Marianne murmured the appropriate responses. Since she was unacquainted with Captain Evan Ramsdell, she had lost interest in her sister's musings long before she ended her speech.

Once finished, she returned the letter to Constance and went to the library, where she intended to compose a letter of her own.

She desired more than anything to speak with Crowthorne at once in the hope of ascertaining not only if he desired, as she did, to have several children but also to discover any number of other interests they might share. She believed that were she to determine she held even a single pursuit in common with Crowthorne, her heart would finally be at ease.

When Marianne quit the chamber, Constance continued arranging the daffodils and pansies one by one, though with each successive thought about her sister, her movements became slower and slower. She was fully caught up in Marianne's succumbing to a fit of the doldrums within a week of her betrothal to Lord Crowthorne.

She felt a faint ripple of excitement within her as she considered her sister's malaise, for she believed she understood completely why Marianne was despondent when she spoke of her engagement.

Constance did not for one moment believe Marianne was in love with Lord Crowthorne. She had seen no evidence of it. All of Marianne's enthusiasm had been centered upon achieving her brilliant match, which, once accomplished, appeared to pall in the wake of the actual courtship. Marianne, it would seem, had not once contemplated what her life might be past the accepting of her chosen beau's hand in marriage.

This was a delicate time, Constance realized, during which anything might happen, particularly since she had strong reason to believe Crowthorne's affections were engaged elsewhere and had been for years. She wished she had been on more intimate terms with Crowthorne, for then she would have approached him with the notion he was in a fair way to making a grievous mistake in offering for Marianne.

Unfortunately, that path had been closed to her from the start. Whenever she attempted to engage Crowthorne in conversation, he invariably responded in severe monosyllables until she was forced to end

the discourse entirely. She had been struck more than
once with the sensation he did not approve of her in
some manner. She was not even certain he approved
entirely of his chosen wife, for he frequently frowned
at Marianne when she expressed herself in her usual
vibrant manner.

If all she suspected was true, she had but one reasonable recourse. She must speak with Sir Jaspar, and
the sooner the better.

To that purpose, she completed the final arrangement of the daffodils and pansies with greater haste
than artistry and retired to Ramsdell's study.

She quickly penned a note to her good friend and
sent it by way of one of the footmen. She did not know
precisely what she meant to say to him once he arrived
in Grosvenor Square, but she knew a push must be
made to make certain Marianne's marriage never took
place.

Whatever she might think of her sister's interest in
Crowthorne or his reciprocal interest in her, the only
chance she would have to disrupt the relationship was
prior to the speaking of vows. Once the vows were exchanged, heaven and earth could not separate Marianne and Lord Edgar. Only an Act of Parliament could
grant a divorce. In her opinion, that would be more
difficult to achieve than a thunderbolt from Zeus's
right arm.

Marianne twirled her parasol of light blue silk and
glanced nervously at Lord Crowthorne from beneath
the thick dark fringe of her lashes. She sat beside him
in his mother's elegant coachman-driven landau for
the daily procession at Hyde Park. She was always
happy to be noticed and admired and congratulated
on her forthcoming marriage, but since she had a par-

ticular question she wished to put to her betrothed, she hardly noticed those who passed by or who nodded and called out greetings to her.

When she had conceived the notion of applying to him concerning precisely how many children he wished to have, she had felt nothing would be simpler than to engage him in such a conversation. However, each time she brought the question to her lips, her heart quailed.

For the life of her, she could not imagine how she was to ask him. She scarcely knew Lord Crowthorne, and felt it utterly beyond the pale to ask, *And how many children would suit you, my lord?*

She recalled his warning that there would be some awkwardness between them during these early days of their betrothal, but until this moment she had not realized exactly how much.

Finally, she decided to come round to the subject in a circuitous manner. After all, she had many questions she wished to put to him. "Do you enjoy silver loo?" In the past several weeks she had become much addicted to the game.

"Not particularly." He nodded to Lord Donnington, who passed them on a fine bay gelding. "I prefer whist or even hazard."

"Oh," she murmured. He had introduced her to the pleasures of silver loo, and it never occurred to her he had only a moderate interest in the game.

She remembered with much delight all the fun she had with her sisters playing commerce of a snowy winter's evening. "What of commerce? Do you not enjoy the hilarity of that game?"

He laughed outright. "A child's game? I have not played commerce since before I left for Harrow—and that, as you know, was many years ago."

Her spirits felt a trifle ruffled. "I suppose you enjoy cricket, then?" She did not.

"Nothing better than an excellent cricket match."

"Of course," she murmured.

Lady Cowper drove by and nodded in her elegant manner to them both. Marianne felt herself on safe ground now, as she proclaimed, "Is not Lady Cowper one of the finest women of your acquaintance?"

"Yes, indeed, though I have always preferred the Princess Esterhazy. She is much more to my style. Lady Cowper, though well enough in her own way, is far too lively to be my ideal of a lady of quality."

Marianne felt as though he had slapped her cheek by saying so. She stared at him and could not keep from asking, "Then do you find my spirits far from exemplary?"

He smiled at her in an utterly condescending manner. "You will learn in time. Though you are five and twenty, in so many ways you put me in mind of a schoolgirl who has yet to be put through her paces."

"And you mean to put me through my paces?" she asked, bristling. She recalled quite abruptly that Sir Jaspar had said something very similar to her before she departed Lady Brook. She found the whole of it disheartening in the extreme.

"Of course not. I did not mean for you to infer any such thing. You have the heart of an angel, and I am perfectly persuaded that, in time, your spirits will be equally as gentle."

She was somewhat mollified by his response, but something about the general flow of the conversation was not easing her mind the way she had hoped it would. "So tell me, just what is your ideal?"

"I am happy you have asked me, for I believe you will begin to understand a little of what I expect of you as my wife. First, let me say how much I admire you. You have a wonderful ability to make those around you feel comfortable, which in itself is a marvelous gift. However, you might consider practicing the pianoforte a great deal more than you do. I have heard you play and can certainly understand why you do not perform in public. As Lady Crowthorne, and one day the countess of Bray, I will want my wife to be accomplished on the pianoforte."

"Much like Annabelle?" she asked, horrified, for she could not imagine ever excelling as her cousin did.

He chuckled and threw his head back a trifle. "I fear you could never match her skill in that area. Only Miss Caversham approaches her perfection."

Marianne was not precisely offended by these remarks, just a little mystified. She had no musical ability to speak of. "And what if I am never able to perform well for others?"

He slipped his hand over hers. "With a little practice, I am certain you will. One may achieve extraordinary things with a daily, dedicated effort. I have every confidence that with the proper application, you will be everything I could want in a wife."

She thought of the way he kissed and could not help but think, most unkindly, that he should have practiced his kissing a little more.

Though nettled, she pressed on. "And what of my manners? Do you have any suggestions on that score?"

"Why, yes, I do, as it happens. I have considered the subject several times, and I believe you would do well to let Annabelle's example be your guide. She has just the right blend of obsequious conduct and a quiet, reserved recounting of interesting anecdotes which I find to be near perfection in any setting. She never puts herself forward, and one never hears her laughter rising above all others in a drawing room. She waits demurely to be asked to dance, she only engages another person in a conversation when she is first addressed, and her smile is neither too generous nor too timid."

Marianne felt an increasing sense of ill-usage. "Do you often hear my laughter in a drawing room?"

"Yes, quite often. Annabelle asked me only the other day why I was wincing, and I told her because I could hear you even above Sally Jersey—and you know what she is!"

"And, pray tell, what did Annabelle say to that?"

"Only that above all your qualities she admired your *joie de vivre* the most."

"And what did you say?"

"I told her I did not think a peal of laughter a true reflection of one's *joie de vivre.*"

Marianne twirled her parasol rather ferociously. Lady Hurley passed by and offered a curt nod, to which Marianne bowed in response.

"You bow too low," he whispered, once Lady Hurley had gone by.

She jerked her attention to him. "I bow too low?" she demanded hotly. "Crowthorne, how can you say as much?"

"There, there," he murmured soothingly. "Pray do not take a pet merely because I gave you a hint about your conduct. After all, you brought forward this subject, and I have been merely answering your many questions. If you did not wish to hear a truthful answer, then you should not have asked me anything."

"I was not expecting to hear that, for the most part, you despise me."

"What?" he cried. "You have misunderstood me entirely if that is what you believe I said just now. I admire you excessively. If you have a few trifling imperfections which need to be pruned like a fine oak that has outgrown itself, I do not see why I should spare you a little pain. Like the oak, in a year or so you shall send forth just the right branches to balance the entire effect. Your canopy will be a marvel to behold."

Marianne could only stare at him, wondering if he would always be such a bore. "I am not an oak, I am a woman. In future, I pray you will keep your pruning shears in your pocket."

He merely smiled as though he knew she was not in the least serious and responded irritatingly, "Yes, of course, m'dear."

Well, she had attempted to broach the original subject of procreation and had been well bruised for all her effort of being subtle and careful. She might as well discover now just how her betrothed felt about their future offspring, and so she asked bluntly, "How many children do you wish to have?"

He started a trifle before scowling at her. "Do you think this an appropriate time to discuss the matter?" He cast a meaningful eye toward the coachman's back.

"If we can discuss all my faults without blinking, I do not see why we cannot discuss our future children. Do you wish for them at all?"

"Of course I do, though I must say Annabelle would never have dragged such a subject into a conversation anyone might overhear."

At this juncture she not only had little interest in what Annabelle might or might not do, she wanted an answer. "I insist you tell me. To own the truth, all the previous questions I posed were merely leading up to this one. Celeste is increasing—you remember, she is our middle sister—as are Constance and Augusta. I am delirious with joy, and upon learning only this afternoon of Celeste's forthcoming confinement sometime in October, I began to wonder whether or not you took pleasure in children and if you had some preconception about how many of them you might wish for."

His lower jaw was rather stiff, and she admitted he had every cause to be angry. She had pressed him on the subject in a most unladylike manner. However, she was angry, for in all the time she had been flirting prior to their betrothal it had never once occurred to her that he might find her wanting in any particular whatsoever, let alone a host of particulars.

Finally, he said, "I believe two or three would be sufficient to satisfy the entail. Two sons would be best. If you must have a daughter, then one would do perfectly well."

"What if I have three daughters and no sons?"

He turned horrified eyes upon her. "Then, of course, we should attempt to rectify that situation were it to arise. I would trust a son would speedily be born to us."

"And how many children does Annabelle wish for?" she asked, stunned she had dared pose such a question. Yet for all the times he had brought her name forward, she felt in this moment that the question was perfectly reasonable.

"One or two," he responded, without hesitation.

"She has told you as much? When?" she cried, dumbfounded.

"You have to remember Annabelle and I grew up together. I have known her mind these many years and more on any number of subjects."

"I see," she murmured, wondering how it was he actually found Annabelle to be more acceptable in nearly every way than his chosen bride.

She thought about revealing her own desires to have a dozen babes dandling upon her knee, growing into childhood, and becoming wonderful young ladies and strong young gentlemen. However, she decided to wait until he asked her. She cleared her throat several times as the coach left Hyde Park. She fluffed her skirts and twirled her parasol. She waited and waited.

He never asked about anything of interest or concern to her.

Thirteen

Jaspar received Constance's missive at half five and immediately made his way to Ramsdell's town house. He could not imagine what matter of extreme importance Constance must needs discuss with him. He even feared she was unwell in some manner, so much so that he made great haste to respond to her urgent summons. His only reluctance in attending her was in the possibility he might have to speak with Marianne once he crossed the Ramsdells' threshold.

The moment he had learned of Marianne's betrothal, he had vowed to keep his distance and support her forthcoming marriage with honor and dignity. That she seemed very unhappy, especially at the ball last night, tore at his resolution. He had longed to take her in his arms and kiss away the sadness which clung to her so tenaciously.

When she had revealed some of her sentiments to him just before they had danced last night, he had wanted more than anything to slip his arms about her and ease the pain she was obviously experiencing. He did not like to see her sweet innocence or her spirit dimmed by the difficulties of life. One of the things he loved most about her was her childlike way, the simplicity of her feelings and thoughts, the innate goodness even she did not realize she possessed.

Fortunately, when he arrived he learned Marianne

was at Hyde Park at present, so he could relax and listen attentively to Constance's concerns. He was relieved to find Constance in excellent health, but distressed all over again when she began to confirm his own beliefs about Marianne's unhappiness.

"So you are telling me Marianne seems to be in some despair."

"Very much so, though I fear she may never come to understand the source of her sadness."

"You do not believe she loves . . . *him.*"

"I do not." She directed him to a chair near the windows overlooking Grosvenor Square. Once he was seated opposite her, she continued, "Her eyes are so disinterested when she speaks of him. Even though she says she loves him more than life itself, she does not in any manner behave as one who is smitten by Cupid's golden arrow. In truth, if her demeanor were an accurate indication of her circumstances, I would say she feels as though she has been consigned to Hades."

"Strong words!" He chuckled.

"She does not smile," Constance explained. "Scarcely at all anymore. When she is in company with Lord Crowthorne, even though he is quite attentive, she sits beside him like a good little puppy. She is not herself when she is with him."

Sir Jaspar leaned forward. "Do you observe him closely enough to see if he has become unkind to her, perhaps, when they are alone together?"

"There you have my point exactly. They are never alone together. Never. It is as though neither wishes to be exclusively in the other's company. I could understand such conduct if the engagement were an arranged affair, but it is not. Supposedly it is a love match. How, then, can you explain such disinterest?"

"I cannot." Sir Jaspar smiled. "Yet how happy you have made me. I am immensely relieved."

She shook her head and glared at him. "You may only profess the smallest sense of relief when the engagement is broken off," she stated. "Until then, I wish you to know, dear friend, that I fear for my sister's happiness. She can be uncommonly stubborn once she has taken a notion into her head, as well you know. And she has taken the notion into her head that her happiness depends upon wedding Lord Crowthorne. So do not smile at me and tell me you are relieved until she is no longer betrothed to his lordship."

Sir Jaspar met Constance's worried gaze and nodded. "You were very right to give me a dressing down. What would you have me do?"

"I have given this a great deal of thought, and I truly believe you ought to continue with her as you were before, as though you are still courting her. Yes, yes, with perhaps a little discretion to avoid being the object of either the gabblemongers or Lord Crowthorne's notice. Yet to cease your persuasions now would be to end all opportunity for her to see she is indeed in love with you."

Sir Jaspar was stunned and leaned back in his chair. "You believe she loves me?"

"Of course she does, though I can see I have given you a shock. I have no more doubt of her love for you than I do of my own for Ramsdell. She does not know how she glows with life when she is near you, how she radiates such excitement and happiness when even your name is mentioned. Though she complains loudly about what a beast you are and how she has no opinion whatsoever of her father's former stable boy, I have caught her so many times staring at you at a soiree or a ball with such an expression on her face as to make it only the more incredible to me that she does not comprehend her own heart."

"You must be mistaken," he said. "How could she

convince herself she was in love with Lord Crowthorne if even a particle of her heart was given to me or anyone else?"

"You must remember her sad history, which she and I share, and how she came to believe over a period of many years that all would be made right in her existence were she to come to London and make a match like none other before. Well, she has accomplished the deed. If you see any true happiness in her I wish you may tell me, for I have seen none. Never once did she consider what her life would be once she became engaged, and now she is all at sea. Jaspar, I beg you, will you do what you can to alter the course she is on?"

He was silent as he pondered her request. "Constance, you were the one who encouraged me to come to London in the first place, and now you have persuaded me I must act when I feel compelled to let her go. I wish you to know right now that what I intend to do from this day forward, I do because of your persuasions. If all should end well for myself and for Marianne, I will have only you to thank for it. You have been an excellent friend to me."

Constance nodded. "We all need a little encouragement from time to time. I would also suggest—"

Whatever she might have said was disrupted by Ramsdell's sudden appearance in the doorway. "Sir Jaspar! The very fellow I wished to see. I have good news—indeed, excellent news! You've just been voted a member of White's!"

"Is this true?" Constance cried.

"Indeed it is." He crossed the room swiftly and placed a kiss on his wife's cheek. He then turned to Jaspar and added, "Though I daresay your recent knighthood and Prinny's support of you carried the day."

Sir Jaspar rose and took Ramsdell's proferred hand.

"I have you to thank for this. Between you and your wife, I possess no better friends."

"So you've finally come to realize it, eh?" Ramsdell returned jovially.

"No," Sir Jaspar said, "I've known it from the first."

"What is all the celebrating about? I was about to ascend the stairs when I heard all of you speaking so rapidly in the drawing room that I began to believe something of great moment must be occuring."

Sir Jaspar turned to find Marianne standing in the doorway. She was resplendent in a blue pelisse and a matching light blue bonnet covered with white silk flowers. His heart fairly turned over in his chest at the sight of her. She was as beautiful as a fully leafed summer's day.

"Your brother-in-law has made it possible for me to join his club. I am now, apparently, a member of White's fine establishment."

Marianne drew apart the ribbons of her bonnet. "Oh, pooh, what do I care for your club?" she said playfully. "I cannot attend it, can I? Nor can Constance, so how will you bear being away from us? Do you not find the society among just men uncommonly dull? I tell you now I would have no interest in joining a club in which only women were in attendance."

Sir Jaspar regarded the woman he loved and felt his heart soften toward her. He was grateful Constance had spoken with him; otherwise he would not have understood her speech. As it was, he saw the glances she gave him of certain longing and realized she was speaking her heart to him, whether or not she was aware of it.

Constance rose to her feet and turned to her husband. "Ramsdell, a word with you. No, it is nothing terribly serious—only a household matter which needs resolving before six o'clock, and I see by the clock on the mantel that it is nearly half six now. Come along.

You may speak with Sir Jaspar in a few minutes. Mari-anne, will you tend to our guest—perhaps a glass of sherry?"

"Of course," Marianne responded.

Sir Jaspar knew very well there was no matter of ur-gency Ramsdell needed to attend to. He was being given an opportunity to attack Marianne's heart. Once the doors were closed, he followed her to the table near the fireplace, upon which the decanter of sherry sat.

"Do you wish for a little wine?" she asked.

"Yes, if you please."

She settled her bonnet near the decanter and per-formed the office with careful grace, handing him the glass and then filling one for herself.

He leaned very close. "I recall a particular night when you had had too much wine. Do you intend to repeat the evening's indiscretions? I shall oblige you, just as I did that night, if you wish it."

She spilled the sherry and turned to look at him, horrified. "I—I am shocked you would say such a thing to me!" she cried, her cheeks crimson. "You seem to have forgotten I am betrothed." She dabbed at the spilt wine with a kerchief hastily drawn from her reticule.

"In that you are greatly mistaken," he assured her, speaking very close to her ear. "I have thought of noth-ing else since you accepted Crowthorne's hand."

Marianne regarded the stained kerchief for a long, long moment. She thought of her horrid trip to Hyde Park with Lord Crowthorne and how wretchedly her betrothed had laid all her faults before her in relent-less succession. She had pouted all the way home, hop-ing that by doing so he would comprehend how badly he had behaved, but he seemed entirely unperturbed by the beautiful display of her lower lip.

When he handed her down just now, she had smiled sweetly upon him, not wanting him to have even the smallest justification for despising her further, then reminded him he should not be late for dinner. He was dining at the Ramsdells' tonight, a circumstance she wished she could change because of their conversation at the park. For the present, she did not wish to be in Lord Crowthorne's company, at least not until she could make some sense of why he disapproved of her so very much.

When she crossed the threshold into the house, therefore, she had been in the devil's own temper—until she heard Jaspar's voice in the drawing room. How odd that the mere sound of his voice had driven all the anger out of her. She desired only to see him and to hear perhaps one or two compliments from his lips so she might forget the terrible lashing Crowthorne had just delivered to her regarding her manners, her character, and her conduct.

Now, as she turned to look into his warm, dark eyes, her mind replayed his most recent words over and over in her head. *I have thought of nothing else since you accepted Crowthorne's hand.*

Oh, my. She felt overcome with a dozen giddy sensations all at once. Jaspar had been thinking about her. That was more than she would have believed after his recent coldness. Yet why was he suddenly . . . yes, why was he suddenly *flirting* with her again? Oh, she did not give a fig why he was, only that he was! She had missed him dreadfully in the past sennight.

Her heart seemed to melt and all her unhappiness fled like the quick passage of a summer storm. She smiled, dimpling for him, and sipped her sherry. "Then by your speech I can only presume you have not grown indifferent to me?"

"You must know my heart by now. Did you expect me to undergo a sudden shift in my affections for you simply because you agreed to marry another man?"

"N-no, not precisely. I suppose I did not think about it at all. You were so silent I had begun to think we would no longer be able to be friends."

"I shall always be your friend—a true friend, which is why I do not think you should marry Lord Crowthorne."

Her spirits dimmed swiftly. "I knew you would say something I did not wish to hear."

"Then explain to me why, ever since you agreed to marry him, you have lost so much of your verve, your liveliness, even your enthusiasm for a ball."

"You suggest Lord Crowthorne must be at fault, but I will tell you the truth. Everyone sees me so differently now that I am engaged that I have begun to feel I am no longer worthy of all the attention which was used to be showered upon me. Oh, Jaspar, it may be very vain of me, but I do so like to have dozens of people clustered about me, all laughing and funning. I enjoy nothing more than dancing every dance at a ball, and last night I sat out for six sets! *Six sets!* Can you imagine anything more odious?"

He smiled and settled his empty sherry glass near the decanter. "Anything more odious for you?" he asked softly, stroking her cheek with the back of his fingers. "No. You are the sort of woman who loves being at the heart of things. When I saw you that last day in Wraythorne, you had at least a dozen children gathered about you, and I daresay you brought sunshine into each of their lives. They were enjoying your warm presence as much as you were delighting in being in the center of their world."

"Am I merely being vain, though?" she asked earnestly. "Tell me, for if I am, I mean to do better, to not expect to be fawned over at every fete."

"I am not convinced it is all vanity. I believe some people thrive by bringing a number of people together, as you do. No matter where you find yourself, whether at a ball or at the opera or in the front yard of an alehouse, you will always attract a great number of people about you. In return, you will make them feel as though life holds every abundance."

"Jaspar, you are so kind to me!" Tears started to her eyes. "Crowthorne informed me not half an hour past that I had a great many flaws which he believed would be corrected in time if I applied myself to his suggestions and strictures."

When Jaspar remained silent, she thought perhaps he was in agreement with her betrothed. However, a single glance in his direction told her she was much mistaken, for his face had taken on a mulish expression and his jaw was working strongly.

"He cannot have said so," he finally murmured.

She hiccuped. "When we were at the park, I meant to engage him in conversation about those things which he enjoyed and those he did not for the purpose of—well, I suppose my purpose in doing so does not matter. However, the more questions I posed, the more the subject kept coming round to me and all the ways he felt I could be improved. He wants me to practice the pianoforte that I might be able to perform adequately in public—but, Jaspar, I have not the least sense of music. He held Annabelle up as a model for me, not just musically, but in many respects. I—I have a great deal of affection for Annabelle, but I do not wish to be like her."

"He cannot expect you to take on Annabelle's traits," he stated, giving his head a shake. "What you are telling me makes no sense."

"I know," she murmured.

"Indeed, he cannot wish for you to give up everything which brings meaning and joy to your life—your numerous acquaintances, your love of silver loo, your desire to dance every dance at a ball. Surely he wishes you to be happy."

Marianne was silent. "I believe he has a great deal of pride and wishes the next Lady Bray to be as fine a woman as his mother. In that respect, I cannot fault him precisely. Jaspar, I must confess to you how utterly confused I have been since having accepted his hand in marriage. I know he is frequently distasteful of my liveliness, and so I do temper my conduct, yet I begin to think I should not. After all, merely because we are betrothed, I do not expect him to listen more attentively to my opinions than he is wont to do, nor do I make suggestions regarding anything else which characterizes him generally, nor . . . nor do I insist he behave with greater affability toward Constance."

He frowned slightly. "What do you mean, *greater affability toward Constance?*"

Marianne seated herself in her favorite plaid chair, her glass of sherry in hand. She took another sip before answering. "I do not know precisely what has given me this impression, but I have come to believe he does not hold my sister in a great deal of affection, nor does he seem to respect her."

Jaspar appeared stunned as he took up a chair beside her. "What man or woman, once having spent even an hour in Constance's company, would not admire and respect her?"

Marianne smiled, her heart warming to the man before her. "I have thought the very same thing a thousand times. I know of no other lady of the *haut ton* with as much decorum or kindness as my sister. Do you suppose it is because she was so very poor when she wed Ramsdell, or do you think it is perhaps because he has taken a disgust about my father—" She broke off as she realized of a sudden that if Crowthorne did not approve of Constance, then to some degree he did not approve of herself.

Once more, her spirits plummeted and her eyes again filled with tears.

Jaspar rose from his seat and was immediately on his knees beside her. Taking her glass of sherry from her and settling it on a nearby table, he possessed himself of her hands.

"There, there!" he exclaimed. "I refuse to permit you to cry in my presence. You do not know what his true sentiments on the subject might be. You can only conjecture, and that is not wholly fair to Crowthorne."

Marianne swallowed very hard and stared at the man who was wiping tears from her cheeks with his gloved hand and whose face was but a few inches from hers. She did not know what possessed her to do so, but she leaned forward and captured his lips with her own. She kissed him in gratitude for his compassion and gentleness. She kissed him because he had not agreed with her betrothed that she was in need of much improvement. She kissed him for a very long time.

She meant to stop. She meant to let her salute be only an expression of her appreciation, but she found she did not want to stop. She slid her hand about his neck and kept kissing him as though this would be the last time she might ever kiss him—and that was a thought she could hardly bear.

He lifted her to her feet and gathered her up in his arms. She did not struggle in the least, nor did she restrain the wonder which floated up all around her. She loved being held and kissed by Jaspar, and if the thought entered her mind that the kiss was wholly inappropriate, she refused to dwell on it.

Instead, she gave herself to the pleasure of his soft, demanding lips and his tongue which assaulted her so greedily. Her mind drifted about lazily as her hands slid over his arms and down his back. He drew her closer still, and she leaned into him scandalously, delighting in the full length of him. Her heart felt wonderful and full and her exacerbated sensibilities softened to bliss.

Were the sun to pause in place, she could go on kissing Jaspar Vernham forever.

After a time, Jaspar drew back, his expression serious. "This will not do, Marianne," he whispered against her ear, holding her close. "You are betrothed to another."

She almost tried to kiss him again, but then his words sank into her mind like a boulder plunging into a deep pool. She felt sickened both by her conduct and by the truth that not only should she not be kissing Jaspar, she should *never* kiss him again.

"You are right!" She dissolved into tears once more. "Oh, what is the matter with me? Why do I behave so badly whenever you are about?"

She fell into her chair and covered her face with her hands. She wept for several minutes, then began blowing her nose soundly and unhappily into the sherry-stained kerchief.

Jaspar approached her once more. "Do not marry him, my dear. I beg of you. Does not your desire to be in my arms speak of the truth of your heart?"

"B-but I love him," she said haltingly. "However could I have accepted of his offer of marriage did I not?"

"Because for so long you have wished for just this sort of match to right the wrongs of the past. But do you truly love him?"

"Y-yes," she whispered, wondering for the first time whether she really did. She recalled the two times he had kissed her and how those kisses had reminded her of placing her lips against a cold fish—not that she had ever kissed a fish, but she thought the experience would prove quite similar.

She realized with a start she had been avoiding any intimacy with Crowthorne since their betrothal for fear of having to endure his lips upon hers again. Oh, she wished Jaspar had not come here today, for he was confusing her in the worst manner. Perhaps he wished to confuse her to serve his own ambitions of marrying above his station.

She looked up at him and blinked. "Why do you tell me these things? Do you not wish me to be happy, to enjoy becoming Lady Crowthorne? Is it that you are jealous of my success?"

Yes, that was it, she thought, her mind hurrying down this path like a rabbit chased by a fox. Jaspar was merely jealous and had set about confusing her and twisting her thoughts all ajumble in the hope she would jilt Lord Crowthorne.

"I am not jealous of you, Marianne. How can you say such a thing, and why do you look at me in that wild manner?"

She rose abruptly to her feet and swiped at her eyes. "You know I will be happy as Lady Crowthorne, and the very thought of it makes you enraged. Having been a mere stable boy at one time and having risen incredibly to the rank of knight, your ambitions suddenly know no bounds. You wish to marry one of the Pamberley ladies and so fix your place in society as securely as you might. I—I daresay Augusta or Katherine would have served your objectives equally well!"

"You are speaking nonsense! Where do these notions come from? I do not understand in the least."

She whirled on him. "What I do not understand is why you would come here and try to persuade me to jilt my future husband. I am not such a changeable creature as that! I—I love Crowthorne, and I think your words today have been terribly unkind and—and I wish you will go—at once!" She dramatically thrust her arm toward the doorway.

"Is this what you truly believe, Marianne, that I have been pursuing you because I wished to establish a better place for myself in society?"

"Y-yes." She hiccuped anew.

He shook his head, and she could see he was very angry. "Marrying for any reason other than love," he said in a slow, marked manner, "in particular to advance oneself in society, is a notion I find abominable in the extreme."

Marianne was stung, for to all appearances her betrothal to Lord Crowthorne spoke of this very thing. Her pride, however, forced her to lift her chin. "Please leave," she said harshly. Her arm was beginning to ache, for she was still pointing toward the door.

He stared at her for a long moment. "As you wish," he said at last, his every feature solemn and determined. "Before I go, there is one thing I feel you ought to know. I might have served your father as a stable boy for several years, I might have adopted the accents and vernacular of those who spent their lives caring for me while I was a child, but my father was a vicar—albeit an impoverished one—in Yorkshire. When I was orphaned and I came to live at Lady Brook, I brought with me my father's teachings and values. I am very sorry for you if you have judged me unworthy of your hand because of my supposed upbringing.

"However, may I suggest to you that there is something odd in Lord Crowthorne that, although he could have wed the wealthy daughter of a duke, a marquis, or an earl, and although he could have chosen as his future bride a lady who possessed more of the qualities he holds dear, he chose instead an impoverished young lady from Berkshire with meager connections and a dowry provided by the beneficence of Lord Ramsdell. Crowthorne does not strike me as the sort of man who would choose a wife merely because she had a sweet spirit and happened to be very beautiful."

Marianne felt his words to be some of the most hateful he had ever spoken to her. She would not justify even one syllable by responding, but merely averted her gaze and lifted her chin higher still.

A moment later he was gone.

After a few seconds, when she was certain he would not return, she lowered her arm and realized she was trembling all through, from head to foot. She was grateful he had spoken so cruelly to her, for now she need not think of him in kind terms or with even a particle of sadness that once she married Lord Crowthorne she would probably never see him again.

Lord Crowthorne loved her. That was why he had offered for her. She loved him. Besides, as beautiful as she was, she most certainly was worthy of becoming the next Countess Bray.

As beautiful as she was.

When these words finally pierced her mind, she dropped into the plaid chair and let her tears flow freely yet again. What a vain, stupid creature she was. Why had Crowthorne offered for her? Did he love her? She had seen Constance and Ramsdell together, how they were utterly devoted to one another. She had once stumbled upon her sister and Ramsdell locked in a passionate embrace, the air thick with his professions of love for her. She could not imagine ever being locked in an embrace with Lord Crowthorne.

The image came horridly to mind of being held tightly by the flippers of an enormous carp. She shuddered violently at the very thought of it. Her lower lip trembled and more tears marched down her cheeks.

Oh, she did not know what to think. She detested Sir Jaspar. He was cruel and thoughtless and . . . and was so jealous he could only defame her beloved Lord Crowthorne. Yet was it true Sir Jaspar was the son of a vicar in Yorkshire? And orphaned?

She sniffed and wept a little more.

And what was worse, he had turned her into something she detested above all things—a watering pot!

Fourteen

An hour later, Marianne's tears had finally subsided. She reclined in her chair by the fireplace, her knees drawn up beneath her in a completely unladylike fashion. She leaned her head against the wing of the chair and sighed huge sighs, one after another. She had come to no conclusions about anything, except that she was miserable when she should have been happy. She chewed on the corner of a clean kerchief and sighed a little more.

The door opened and Spencer announced Lord Crowthorne. She had forgotten he would be arriving, though she had warned him not to be late for dinner. She wished she had sent him a missive telling him not to come, for she was not in a frame of mind to receive him with any degree of civility, warmth, or affection. However, here he was, his expression concerned as he advanced on her.

She was so exhausted from the encounter with Jaspar that she could not move her legs and only barely lifted her head to look at him. Removing the kerchief from between her teeth, she said, "Oh, hallo, Edgar." She barely realized she had called him by his Christian name for the first time.

"Marianne, whatever is the matter?" he said, moving to stand before her. "Are you ill?" His gaze fell rather scathingly to the sight of her legs squished under her.

She drew them out reluctantly and settled her feet on the floor. "I am perfectly well, merely overset," she responded dully. She wished he would go away. She was in a foul temper and felt she could not endure any more of his reproachful glances, nor did she desire to hear his hints on just how she ought to behave.

"I should leave and return later," he suggested.

So he was able to read her mind. Thank God for that. "Yes, if you please. Perhaps you could call on me tomorrow."

"Of course," he said gently. "Only I do not feel right in leaving you so unhappy. Is there nothing I might do for you before I go?"

She shook her head. "I do not know. You see, when I returned here after having been to Hyde Park with you, I found Ramsdell and—and Sir Jaspar celebrating. It would seem my brother-in-law was able to obtain a membership at White's for Sir Jaspar, and—"

Crowthorne cried out. "What?" He was staring at her as though she had gone mad.

"I—that is, what do you mean, *what?*"

"Marianne, did you not say Ramsdell successfully sponsored a mere stable boy to White's Club and he was accepted?"

"Y-yes, but why are you so angry? You belong to Brook's, do you not, or is it Boodle's? And—and who told you Jaspar had been my father's stable hand?"

"Giles, after your jaunt to Vauxhall. If you will recall, you told Sir Giles yourself."

"I suppose I did," she murmured.

Lord Crowthorne appeared not to have heard her. His face became rather pinched as he shook his head in apparent disbelief at least a dozen times. "Why should that scapegrace be accepted into White's, while I—damme, I thought were I to align myself with someone acceptable to Ramsdell that *I* should be the one he sponsored."

Marianne frowned slightly. "You were expecting Ramsdell to sponsor you into his club?"

"Why should he not? I am wedding his sister-in-law. I should think it would be a mere courtesy."

Marianne, of course, had never understood the notion of men having clubs exclusive to their gender. At the same time, she was bemused by the note of bitterness in her betrothed's voice. She thought it all a storm in a teacup and, with a faint yawn, said, "I do not think Ramsdell admires you very much."

Oh, dear. Had she spoken such a thought aloud? By the look on Crowthorne's face, apparently she had. He appeared as mad as fire.

"I—I mean, I wonder if he does not," she corrected hastily.

"Why do you say as much?" he demanded harshly.

"Merely because he treats you with such formality. Those with whom he is most intimate become like brothers to him—at least, that is my observation."

Lord Crowthorne stared at her for a hard moment, during which time she found her knees were trembling anew. She scooted up in the chair and composed herself a little more. She truly did not understand why he was as overset as he was, all because of White's. Whatever for?

Some of the ire left him suddenly, like a full sail losing wind, and he sank down into the chair next to her. He chuckled and said, "I had thought he would embrace me like a brother once he knew you and I were to be wed. Apparently I was very wrong. Only—I do not understand how he can put Sir Jaspar Vernham forward as he does."

"There is no comprehending his high opinion of Sir Jaspar. I do not understand it in the least. Sir Jaspar is one of the most impertinent gentlemen I have ever known. Were I a man, I think I should call him out. You cannot conceive of how he speaks to me in private. He is a beast. He was here not an hour past, which is why you found me in such an unhappy state. He . . . he said such things to me—you have no idea!"

"You spoke with him privately?" Lord Crowthorne queried.

"Yes, I have on several occasions, for it is the mode in this home to allow him to roam at will like a prowling lion, since he was used to be and still is, of course, a particular friend of my sister's. She was used to correspond with him all during his years in India when he was making his fortune. I despise him." She hiccupped.

"There, there," Crowthorne soothed. "Pray do not distress yourself, my dear. He is gone now. Perhaps you ought to speak with your sister and tell her you think he should be forbidden to come to Grosvenor Square, at least until you and I are wed."

"I should like nothing better," Marianne cried, tears starting to her eyes again. Her betrothed was being so gentle and understanding that she felt she could confide in him a little. She twisted her damp kerchief between her fingers and said, "You can have no notion the things he said to me earlier. He was trying to confuse me, prattling on and on as he was about such dreadful things."

"What was he telling you?" Crowthorne queried softly.

Marianne drew in a deep breath and plunged on. "How he did not believe I truly loved you, nor that you were as devoted to me as you said you were. He felt certain you offered for me for some obscure reason, which of course he could not enumerate on any count! And then he had the audacity to kiss me, although that was before he told me all those terrible things. You *do* love me, though, do you not, Edgar?" She dabbed at her eyes and looked into his face hopefully.

He held her gaze, but did not respond for a very long moment. When he did, he smiled softly and took hold of her hand. "Of course I love you, my precious one. Did he kiss you, indeed?"

"Yes. Was it not abominable of him?"

"Yes, I fear it was."

"You must not pay him the least heed, else he will try to confuse you, as well. The sooner we are wed, the better, I think. Wh-why do you look at me in that manner? Your complexion has grown very pale. Are you feeling ill, Edgar?"

He gave himself a shake and patted her hand. "Not in the least, I assure you. Do try to forget all Sir Jaspar has said to you today. I daresay he is merely jealous that I stole a march on him."

"You must be right, for he has been begging for my hand in marriage since summer last."

"I see. Well, my dear, I shall speak with him just to make certain he no longer annoys you with his useless and quite pointless arguments. You may trust me to deal with him."

"Oh, thank you, Edgar. You are, indeed, the kindest of men." She found in this moment, because of his gentleness, she could forgive him entirely for the horrid criticisms he had dispensed so freely at Hyde Park. When he leaned forward to kiss her, she was so well-disposed toward him that she did not even draw back, not even when his cold lips were pressed to her own.

If the image of being embraced by a carp suddenly rose to mind, she quickly set it aside, even going so far as to kiss him once in return as he drew back from her. Assuring her again that he would make certain Sir

Jaspar did not aggravate her further, he quit Ramsdell's town house.

Marianne was quite pleased with herself as she dressed for Mrs. Warfield's musicale that evening. She felt greatly composed following an afternoon of suffering, since she had renewed within her own heart her love for Lord Crowthorne, as well as her intention of marrying him regardless of the wretched accusations Sir Jaspar had leveled against them both.

She could even laugh about it a little as her maid dressed her hair in a riot of ringlets over the crown of her head. How silly she had been to listen to Sir Jaspar, let alone question her betrothal to Lord Crowthorne. Well, all was settled. Now she could be content again.

She regarded her reflection in the mirror as her maid tucked yet another violet among her curls. Jaspar had been very mean, but her betrothed had been all that was loving, generous, and kind. He had kissed her, as well, and perhaps this last kiss was not nearly so bad as the first two. Perhaps he was improving and, with time, anything might happen.

She frowned, wondering suddenly if she had been wise to reveal to Edgar that Jaspar had kissed her. After a moment's brief cogitation, however, she shrugged. Perhaps the admission of the kiss they had shared was the very reason he had decided to settle the matter for all time with Sir Jaspar, in which case she had done very well to have admitted the truth to him.

How happy she was again, for Lord Crowthorne meant to champion her with Sir Jaspar, and she believed with all her heart she would never again have to speak with that beast of a man—vicar's son or not!— nor would she be tempted to kiss him.

When Angelique pronounced her ready, she studied
her reflection in the looking glass. Her maid was, indeed, a talented abigail. She could not have been better pleased with her appearance had the queen's maid
dressed her.

She wore a gown of lavender patterned silk edged
with delicate Brussels lace. Scattered among her ringlets were small artificial violets. Pearls graced her neck,
and upon her feet were the most delightful slippers of
lavender embroidered with gold thread. Oh, but she
was happy—exceedingly so, for in a scant few weeks
she would be Lady Crowthorne and one day the countess of Bray.

On the way to the musicale, she noted Annabelle
was in fine looks and told her so. "I vow you grow
prettier every day," she said generously.

Annabelle thanked her as she always did, then admitted to some anxiety about performing. "I have not
been practicing as much as I was used to."

Because Marianne was at peace with the world, she
spoke magnanimously. "I am certain you need not be
concerned. Whenever you but touch the ivory keys of
the pianoforte, the music always seems to be yours to
command. I daresay you could not deliver a bad performance if you intended to do so."

Annabelle thanked her profusely for her compliment, and the remainder of the carriage ride was spent
discussing the absolute necessity of paying another visit
to the numerous shops on New Bond Street.

Once within Mrs. Warfield's town house, Marianne
adopted her most gracious manners as she met her
hostess. Mrs. Warfield was a tall woman with a thin
nose and beautiful black hair. Though Marianne had
always thought of her as a gentle, composed lady, tonight she seemed rather nervous.

"Oh . . . oh, M-miss Marianne! How do you do? I

see you are as lovely as ever, as are you, Miss Theale. You will be happy to know Miss Caversham will be performing along with you. I—I am ever so grateful, given the circumstances . . . that is, I have been looking forward to hearing you play again. Will you be performing Beethoven?"

"Yes, if it pleases you." Annabelle bowed slightly.

"It pleases me very much. You may sit toward the front if you like. I believe Miss Caversham has requested you sit beside her. You have certainly won her favor this season. Ah, she is waving to you. No, no, Miss Marianne. I believe you and your sister would be much more comfortable here."

Marianne followed the line of her fan and saw she was pointing toward a rather darkened corner in which Freddy Shiplake was ensconced. She was a little stunned and turned to regard Mrs. Warfield with lifted brows. Mrs. Warfield would not meet her gaze.

There was nothing for it but to go where she was directed. She could not possibly utter a protest. To do so would be tantamount to arguing with her hostess, and that would never do. However, she did not understand why, as Lord Crowthorne's betrothed, she was being treated so shabbily, nor her sister either. She cast an inquiring glance at Constance, who seemed as bemused as she was. In utter bewilderment, she moved toward a pair of chairs cast in severe shadow.

Resigning herself, Marianne smiled faintly upon Mr. Shiplake as she drew near, but received for this effort a horrified, "Good God! Ar-are you to sit here?"

"I beg your pardon?" she asked, utterly mystified.

"That is, f-forgive me, b-but I h-had rather stand over there," he murmured, "by Lady Cowper."

Marianne's mouth fell agape. She could not comprehend Freddy in the least. Why, he was behaving as though to be near her was anathema.

"W-wouldn't want to disturb either of y-you," he explained awkwardly. He bowed stiffly and moved to the opposite side of the chamber. He did not glance in her direction again.

Marianne took up her seat, dumbfounded. Her betrothal had changed many aspects of her social experience, but until now she had not been treated as though she were covered in lice.

"Constance," she whispered behind her fan, "had I known becoming engaged to Edgar would have brought about this manner of isolation, I should never have agreed to marry him. I do not understand what is happening."

"Nor I," Constance murmured. "All of this seems most odd."

"I could not agree more, only—"

Since at that moment two young ladies several rows forward turned around and stared at her for a moment, she fell silent. When the same pair fell to whispering, she was more bemused than ever.

"It is all very strange," Constance said quietly. "When refreshments are served, I shall do what I can to discover if anything is amiss. Do you suppose Mr. Shiplake is feeling piqued?"

"Perhaps, but why does everyone else stare at me so rudely, as well?"

"I do not know."

Fortunately, Miss Caversham approached the pianoforte and all attention was diverted to her. She played her favorite Mozart pieces, then relinquished the instrument to a pair of sisters who performed duets quite brilliantly upon the pianoforte and harp. Afterward, the same harpist played a beautiful solo.

The effect was wholly charming, and Marianne would have enjoyed herself enormously, except that her attention was diverted more than once by other members of the audience turning around to stare at her and engage in more uncivil whispering.

Marianne thought their conduct rude in the extreme, and finally returned glares of her own at the officious gabblemongering which seemed centered upon her. She knew a number of young ladies and even matchmaking mamas were resentful that she had captured a betrothal from Lord Crowthorne, but this behavior, in her opinion, went quite beyond the pale.

After an hour and a half of fine performances, Mrs. Warfield announced a light supper would be served. Marianne was grateful for a chance to seek out some of her acquaintances and to discover, if she could, the content of all the gossip about her. However, when she approached several friends, her acquaintances found every manner of excuse to scurry away. She was left to sit beside her sister and Annabelle—both of whom had grown uncommonly quiet—and partake of the meal in silence.

She was utterly grateful when Lady Cowper approached their small party. She would have launched into a profuse expression of her appreciation, but Lady Cowper merely met her gaze in a direct manner and began a speech of her own.

"I regret to tell you, Miss Marianne, that I will be unable to sponsor you now for vouchers to Almack's. Your conduct, though perhaps overlooked in the country, will not do at all here in London. I trust you will see my actions not so much punitive as instructive. We require a great deal of modesty and propriety among our unmarried young ladies. If we did not, where would we all be?" She bowed formally and moved away.

Marianne wanted to defend herself, but she could not comprehend what horrible thing she had done to offend *everyone*. She glanced at Constance and Annabelle and found neither was able to eat.

"What is it?" she queried. "I do not understand. What is it I am supposed to have done?"

Both ladies shook their heads but said nothing. She would have pressed them, for she rather thought one or the other had chanced upon some information, but at that moment Mrs. Warfield beckoned Annabelle to take her place at the pianoforte.

In solemn procession, Marianne followed Constance to their shadowed seats.

"What have you heard?" she whispered to Constance.

"Nothing to signify," her sister murmured.

"Nothing to signify?" Marianne whispered hoarsely. "Then why have I been rejected for Almack's?"

"I cannot say," Constance replied. "We should discuss the matter at home."

"But, Constance—"

"Not now," she stated firmly.

Annabelle situated herself carefully at the pianoforte, as was her habit, but after playing just a few measures of the sonata, Marianne knew her cousin was decidedly overset. One in every eight notes fell awry. She pressed on, however—a circumstance which would have been admirable, except that her heroism did not in any manner improve her performance. By the end of the first movement, she had missed so many notes as to make the piece barely comprehensible.

Annabelle did not attempt to continue, but rose from her seat and, after dropping a curtsy, begged to be excused, for she was not feeling at all the thing. Mrs. Warfield immediately supported her in her decision and, after expressing her hopes Annabelle would soon recover, brought forward the next young lady.

Marianne became quite angry that whatever gossip was flying around the chamber about her had affected her dear friend so badly. She leaned over to Constance and whispered, "I think we should leave, do you not? Annabelle is in a wretched state, and I am fatigued with being the brunt of so much horrid gossip."

"I think you may be right. Were Ramsdell here, I daresay none of this would have occurred. Ah, here is Annabelle."

Marianne supported her cousin on the right and Constance on the left. Poor Annabelle was trembling from head to foot. Constance immediately told her of the decision to leave, which brought a great sigh of relief from Annabelle.

Once within the carriage, Annabelle cried out, "I am so very sorry, but I could no longer retain my composure, not with so much whispering, besides the horror of having learned—" She broke off and, much to Marianne's shock, dissolved into tears.

She reached for Annabelle's hand. "You must not pay the least heed to the gabblemongers. I never do. When one is as pretty and accomplished as you, of course there will be jealousies—" She broke off as Annabelle met her gaze, her expression utterly shocked.

"Then you do not know?" She shook her head and sobbed. "Constance, did you not tell her?"

Constance shook her head. "No, for I believe Marianne is right. We should ignore the gabblemongers."

"How can you say so?" Annabelle wept uncontrollably. "This is not mere gossip. You know it is not!"

Marianne stared at Annabelle. She had never seen her so completely distressed. "What is it you have heard, Annabelle? I do not understand. Is this not mere jealousy on the part of those who wished Crowthorne to marry elsewhere?"

"Not by half!" she cried. "Do you not understand what you have done?"

"What *I* have done?" Marianne was deeply offended.

"I have done nothing. How could I have, when the gossiping began nearly the moment we entered Mrs. Warfield's drawing room? In what way, from the time we left Grosvenor Square until we arrived in Park Lane, could I have possibly committed so gross an indiscretion as to have set every tongue to wagging? There must be some terrible mistake. And, once we have discovered the error, I mean to call upon Lady Cowper myself in order to rectify the situation." The coach lurched forward slightly and set the ladies bobbing.

Annabelle turned to Constance. "You know the truth, Constance, and you must tell Marianne what is going forward. You must help her see she, and she alone, is to blame."

"You are being unfair," Constance said. "We do not even know if anything we have heard is true."

"It must be true, else Lady Cowper would never have approached Marianne as she did."

Constance hesitated, and an expression of indecision crossed her face.

"Constance, you must tell me!" Fear struck at the pit of Marianne's stomach. "What is going forward? What is this terrible thing Annabelle believes I have done? Why was everyone staring at me so odiously this evening?"

Constance met her gaze. "I wish you to answer a question for me first," she said solemnly.

"Yes, of course, anything, for I know I am innocent. I have done nothing wrong."

"Then tell me, did you kiss Sir Jaspar this afternoon after your excursion to Hyde Park?"

Marianne had forgotten all about the kiss she had placed on Jaspar's lips. "How did anyone come to know of it?" she asked, stunned. "I am completely and utterly mystified."

At these words, Annabelle dropped her hands to her

lap and stared at her. "Then it is true? Y-you *kissed* Sir Jaspar? But you are betrothed to Edgar. How could you have behaved so cruelly to the man you love?"

"It meant nothing," Marianne explained lamely. "It was a ridiculous mistake. Edgar knows as much, and he told me he would speak with Jaspar, or something to that effect, and make certain Sir Jaspar did not importune me again." She felt quite ill suddenly, for she was not telling the truth. She had not even told the truth to Edgar—that she was the one who had kissed Jaspar, not the other way around.

"Then it is all too true!" Annabelle once more dissolved into tears.

Marianne regarded Annabelle and then her sister. "Constance, why has it become public knowledge, this event which occurred between Sir Jaspar and myself and about which only Lord Crowthorne has been informed? I truly do not understand what has happened."

"As to how this kiss has become known to everyone, I cannot say precisely. However, now that you have confessed to the deed, I do feel I should tell you that because of it, Lord Crowthorne felt compelled to call upon Sir Jaspar earlier this evening . . . with seconds."

"With seconds?" She felt strangely numb.

"Yes," Constance responded, nodding once quite firmly. "Do you know what that means?"

Marianne's mouth fell agape as her mind spun around like a whirlpool. "Seconds. You mean, seconds as in a duel?"

"Yes."

"Edgar challenged Sir Jaspar to a duel?"

"So it would seem."

"And he did so because I kissed Sir Jaspar?"

Constance nodded and Annabelle sobbed even more forcefully than before.

"I do not understand. You are saying they are to

cross swords merely because I kissed a man other than my betrothed? But this is absurd! Absurd, I tell you. All was settled earlier when I spoke with Edgar. He . . . he promised me all would be well. He told me he would speak with Sir Jaspar in such a way that Jaspar would never annoy me again . . . oh! He cannot have meant—Constance, does he mean to kill Sir Jaspar?"

"I do not know. Ramsdell should be home by now, and I shall lay the matter before him. He . . . well, when he begged off from this evening's entertainment, I had supposed he meant to go to his club. However, I now believe Sir Jaspar sent for him in order that he might act as one of his seconds."

All the horror of the situation struck Marianne like a storm which had threatened all day, then hit abruptly with a hard blast of wind and rain.

"I am the cause of this," she muttered, "and no one else. What foolishness—all the things I said to Edgar, and he was already so irate that Sir Jaspar had been accepted as a member of White's. Why did I not see what was happening? Why did I think Edgar would be unmoved by—oh, Constance, all the things I told him. I related word for word my conversation with Sir Jaspar because I was piqued. Edgar seemed interested in what I was saying, which usually he is not. What a stupid female I am. What is to be done?"

Annabelle blew her nose. "Nothing," she cried bitterly. "No one is permitted to interfere in a duel. Edgar will probably die, for everyone knows Sir Jaspar is an unequaled shot. His abilities at Manton's are as renowned as Ramsdell's. As for Edgar, he—he can scarcely hold his own on a hunting field."

"How would you know that?" Marianne asked.

"Have you forgotten I have known him all these years? I—I know everything about him—in particular that he may appear to be a rather calm gentleman, but he does have a temper. Oh, Marianne, what wickedness you have done. And the worst of it is the man you love may die tomorrow morning."

The man I love may die? Marianne did not know what that meant.

"Is the duel set for tomorrow, indeed?"

"That was what Miss Caversham told me. J-just before dawn."

"What a kind friend to have told you before you were to perform," Marianne said.

"I cannot account for her cruelty in having done so except her belief I was disinterested, though how she may have thought so I cannot imagine, when I reside beneath the same roof as you."

Marianne had nothing more to say. She was stricken to the very core of her being. Something terrible of her own making, yet not quite of her own comprehension, had rained down on her head. As she watched the foggy shadows of the city pass by, she began to review her previous conversation with Crowthorne. She was appalled now by all she had told him. What husband-to-be, once knowing the content of her discussion with Sir Jaspar, as well as the circumstances of a shared kiss, would have had any other recourse than to call him out?

She shook her head in disbelief at her own stupidity. And the duel was tomorrow, at dawn!

Annabelle continued to weep and shake her head in great despondency. Finally, Constance slipped her arm about Annabelle's shoulder and drew her into a close embrace.

Marianne watched them as one viewing an event inside a dream. Tears streamed like rivers from Annabelle's eyes, never ceasing, and her shoulders shook with uncontrolled sobs. She had never seen Annabelle so upset.

Yet why should Annabelle be upset? She was not risking the loss of her betrothed or of Sir Jaspar. She professed having known Edgar for years and years, but what did that . . .

Marianne averted her gaze and for the first time felt tears of her own bite her eyes. She felt like cursing— indeed, she wished she was a man, that she might let loose with a hundred expletives in order to rid her soul of self-loathing. How could one female be so stupid, so blind on so many counts? She finally saw what Annabelle had been telling her from the first—her cousin was in love with Edgar and had been since she was a child.

Marianne began to weep, as well, but not for the same reason as Annabelle. Instead, she wept because she lacked even the mildest degree of perception. The evening when Annabelle first played the pianoforte, Edgar had insisted on watching Annabelle's performance. She had attended him not because she desired to hear Annabelle but because she wanted to be Lady Crowthorne, and nothing else mattered but achieving that end, not even the fact that Edgar . . . oh, no . . . that Edgar was in love with Annabelle!

Marianne turned from looking out the window and met Constance's gaze. "Do you comprehend the whole of this wretched tangle?" she asked, wiping her cheeks.

Constance nodded somberly.

"Why did you say nothing to me?"

"Would you have believed one word of it?"

Another wave of sickness attacked the pit of her stomach. "No greater fool was ever born than Marianne Pamberley," she muttered.

Fifteen

The forthcoming duel took strong hold of Marianne's mind. She began thinking of nothing else as the coach drew up before the door in Grosvenor Square. Sir Jaspar and Lord Crowthorne—pistols at dawn! The very thought made her shudder.

Constance helped Annabelle down from the coach and supported her into the house. Marianne followed behind slowly, her imagination overtaken with visions of a misty early morning, Jaspar leveling his pistol at Edgar on the count of ten or twenty or however many paces was the chosen distance intended to assuage Edgar's injured pride.

Oh, what a fool she had been! How could she have told Edgar Jaspar had kissed her?

She went to her bedchamber, but did not summon her maid, for she needed to think. She began to undress slowly, removing the violets from her golden ringlets one by one and pulling the pins from her hair. No wonder she had been glared at this evening. By now everyone knew of her terrible conduct, which had resulted in a forbidden duel. For some time, dueling had been outlawed in England. Were the authorities to learn of the duel, both parties could be imprisoned, or, if a death ensued, banished from England.

Worse and worse.

Edgar must have told his seconds of the shared kiss.

Who else could they be but Sir Giles and Mr. Speen? Unfortunately, Henry Speen was a far worse gabblemonger than most of the ladies of the *ton*, and that was saying a great deal.

She paced her bedchamber, her hair dangling about her shoulders, as she considered what she must do to stop the duel. It would be of little use to apply to any of the gentlemen involved. Men could be inordinately stubborn when their pride was involved, and why wouldn't Sir Jaspar and Lord Crowthorne relish the notion of facing one another across a damp field? From the first, their mutual antagonism had been well known to her. That she had been the cause of their dislike of one another centered her thoughts on one objective—how to put a stop to the duel.

By three o'clock that morning, she knew what she must do. She stole upstairs to the servants' quarters and quietly awakened her maid. When she relayed to her the services she would require of one of the footmen, Angelique, though sleepy-eyed, murmured, "We should ask Charlie. He'll know what to do."

"Very well. See to it, then."

An hour later, Marianne was seated in a darkened hackney on the opposite side of the square, with Charlie beside her. At five o'clock, a carriage appeared at the top of the street. At nearly the same moment, Ramsdell emerged from his front door.

"We must leave quickly, the moment the coach turns into the street," she whispered.

"Very good, Miss," Charlie murmured in response. As soon as Sir Jaspar's coach, a rather shabby hired conveyance of some sort, disappeared around the corner, the footman urged the hackney driver to follow it. "And be quick about it, mate. 'Tis urgent. There'll be an extra sovereign in it fer ye."

The hackney driver needed no further encouragement. He set his horses in motion and within a few minutes had Sir Jaspar's coach in sight. Once across Richmond Bridge, the fog grew thick, and it was not long before the driver admitted he had lost the other coach.

Marianne's heart quailed as she tried to decide what to do next.

There were many fields on the outskirts of London where duels could be conducted. Given the direction of Sir Jaspar's coach, she believed him to be heading to Richmond Park. At this hour of the morning, there would be no one about and plenty of shrubbery to conceal the illegal confrontation.

She instructed the driver to take her to the park. They approached two men on horseback coming the opposite direction, and Marianne knew they were curious as to the hackney's presence near Richmond Castle so early in the morning. One of the men bid the driver stop.

"I were ordered to the park," he responded belligerently. "Ask the wench within."

Marianne whispered to Charlie, "You must pretend you are foxed and that I begged you to take me to the park. Call me, er, Molly. There now, lean your head out the window."

Charlie addressed the man who had dismounted. "Wot gives, gov'ner? I be takin' m'missus fer an outing." He hiccupped loudly.

"Charlie, let's be goin'!" Marianne cried in as vulgar a voice as she could summon. "Oy want t'see the flowers at Richmond. It's almost daylight—c'mon, luv!"

"Ye see wot it is," Charlie shouted to the men. "If I don't get Molly there"—he belched for good effect—"she'll be whinin' fer hours."

Marianne could see the face of the man who had

dismounted. Though he seemed suspicious, he finally shrugged and bade them continue.

"Ye've saved m'life!" Charlie cried. "To Richmond, driver, and be quick about it!"

The hackney moved forward. Marianne craned her head to see whether or not the men followed her. When she could no longer see either of the men through the fog, she strained to listen for the sounds of hoofbeats, but heard nothing except the rattle of the traces.

She leaned back in her seat and released a deep breath. "Charlie, I vow you ought to be performing at Drury Lane."

"I'd like that," he returned affably.

The fog suddenly disappeared, as it was wont to do, and a crossroads loomed before them. Charlie begged the driver to stop and descended from the carriage in order to examine the road. He bid the driver take the next right.

In the distance, Marianne could see the shape of two coaches. "It must be Sir Jaspar!" she cried. "Dear God, I hope we are not too late."

When the hackney drew to a stop, she quickly descended. The moment her feet touched the earth, however, two shots were fired in quick succession. She felt as though she had been struck hard by each one, so fearful was she of the outcome of the duel.

She raced in the direction of the sounds, and, passing by an ancient oak tree, found Lord Crowthorne standing very still, his pistol smoking. His face was a mask of white in the growing light of dawn.

"Oh, no!" Sir Jaspar lay in a heap not twenty feet away. Ramsdell was with him, along with—yes, it was Dr. Kent!

Her mind worked like lightning. She raced to Jaspar and saw he was perfectly conscious but was grimacing as Ramsdell unbuttoned his greatcoat and forced the heavy garment back. Blood was seeping into the white of his neckcloth.

She felt ill and swallowed hard to keep from casting up her accounts. She turned away and took several deep breaths, at the same time noting Edgar had followed her.

"What the devil are you doing here, Marianne?" he whispered angrily.

"It does not matter. I am too late." She looked at Crowthorne. Fear etched his eyes and face. She addressed the more urgent matter. "We passed two men on horseback not ten minutes past. Could they be from Bow Street?"

"Probably, but how would they know of the duel?"

Marianne drew him apart, then responded quietly, "Everyone at Mrs. Warfield's musicale, with the exception of myself, knew of your having called Jaspar out. So I put it to you. How could everyone know?"

He appeared very conscious, but clamped his lips shut.

She turned back to Jaspar. "You must leave, at once. There were men about. They stopped Charlie and me, desiring to know where we were going. I am persuaded they were intent on finding you."

Ramsdell looked at her hard. "You must be right. According to my wife, everyone knew of our engagement this morning."

All attention shifted to Henry Speen, whose eyes had grown very wide.

Crowthorne addressed him. "Did you tell the entire *haut ton* what we were about?"

Mr. Speen had the good grace to blush, though he denied having opened his budget—"save to one or two quite reliable friends."

"Your friends," Marianne announced hotly, "made

certain everyone at Mrs. Warfield's musicale knew the duel would take place this morning. Regardless, we must leave. There are runners in the park even as we speak."

Ramsdell hauled Jaspar to his feet. "Come. We'll retire to my house. Crowthorne, you'd best return to yours, along with your friends."

"Will not the runners seek you out?" Marianne addressed the gentlemen in general, but most particularly her betrothed. "Perhaps you should all retire to Lady Bray's, and . . . and, I do not know. Perhaps, engage in the appearance of a card party? I am still in my evening dress and would be happy to help lend the appearance that your mother was hosting her future daughter-in-law."

The gentlemen exchanged glances. Sir Jaspar muttered through clenched teeth, "She's right. If there is even a suspicion of wrongdoing tonight, we'll end up in Newgate Prison."

After this, he fainted, which brought Marianne to a full realization of the horror of the situation. He could die, and the knowledge of his mortality pierced her soul. She did not want Jaspar Vernham to die. He had become quite necessary to her happiness.

"Jaspar," she murmured, touching his face tenderly just before Ramsdell and Sir Giles hauled him to the conveyance.

"Come," Crowthorne said. "We must leave now. You may ride in my coach."

At first, Marianne agreed, for she was overset by thoughts of Jaspar. However, when she was about to mount the steps to his conveyance, another idea struck her as being far more sensible—even necessary, should the runners return.

"I will stay with Charlie for a time. We shall remain here and pretend we are quarreling or some such thing, should the runners stumble upon this road. No, no, we do not have time to argue. You must make this right, Edgar. You should not have shot him. I perceive he deloped?"

Crowthorne nodded. "I was so angry."

"You did very wrong, as did I. Now, please do what is right and make haste to your father's house. He will know what to do, and your mother, as well. I shall be along in fifteen minutes' time."

"Are you certain this is the best course?"

She nodded vigorously. "Very much so. Now off with you. Yes, I know. We have much to discuss, you and I, but not now."

Crowthorne climbed into the coach. A moment later, his well-sprung traveling chariot was bowling down the lane behind Jaspar's hired vehicle.

Charlie waited outside the hackney in preparation for the ruse they had decided upon should the runners come upon them. Marianne ticked off the minutes in her head and when she had reached thirteen, just as she thought, the runners arrived.

Charlie immediately adopted his role and began playing his part to perfection, feigning drunkenness and sickness. He was bent over a ditch, making horrible sounds, when the runners approached him.

"Have you seen anyone about since your arrival? We are in particular searching for two vehicles."

"There were a couple," he said. "Left right smartly not twenty minutes ago, 'eading that way." He threw his arm toward the opposite direction, then leaned over the ditch and pretended to be sick once more.

From the shadows of the coach, Marianne watched as the runners grimaced at the sight. After a moment's discussion, they wheeled their horses about and spurred their mounts in the opposite direction.

Only when they had disappeared into the mounting

fog once more did Marianne breathe a sigh of relief. Charlie hopped in the coach and bid the driver to spring 'em. "To Grosvenor Square!" he cried.

By the time Marianne entered Lady Bray's drawing room, the scene had been set to perfection. Even Lady Bray was present, gowned fashionably as always, though her coiffure was a trifle disordered. Sir Jaspar wore a fresh neckcloth tied at an awkward angle, and his coat was one she recognized as belonging to Crowthorne.

Every detail of an all-night card party was being attended to. Even the cards had been arranged as though they were in the midst of a game of whist. All the gentlemen had exchanged their boots for clean, dry slippers and their damp riding gear for coats and breeches borrowed hastily from both Lord Bray and Lord Crowthorne's wardrobes.

Sir Jaspar sat at the table, white-faced, alternately sipping a glass of brandy and shuffling an extra deck of cards. His eyes were red-rimmed. She thought it ironic that a man who was suffering from a gunshot wound could easily pass for a man in his altitudes.

Lady Bray regarded her carefully and said, "Were you forced to dress your hair yourself?"

Marianne nodded. "I hope it is not too unruly."

"Only a little." She then looked her up and down and gasped faintly. A knock on the door sounded at the same moment that Lady Bray addressed her sudden concerns in a whisper. "My dear—your gown!"

Marianne looked down and saw that the hemline was water-stained and her slippers were muddy. "Oh, no!" she murmured, her heart nearly bolting from her chest.

"Come, sit at the table next to me," she commanded, "and keep your legs well hidden."

Lord Bray left the chamber and each member of the party assumed an assigned role. Lord Crowthorne and Sir Jaspar sat next to one another at the whist table, Sir Giles was busily pouring drinks and placing empty and half-empty glasses about the chamber, and Mr. Speen was reclining in a foxed state on the sofa, his neckcloth askew.

"Edgar," Lord Bray said, returning to the drawing room, "these gentlemen from Bow Street would have a word with you. It would seem they have reason to believe you were at Richmond Park but an hour ago."

"What the deuce?" Lord Crowthorne cried, his speech slurred a trifle as he turned around to glance at the men. "Whatever would I have been doing at Richmond? It is just now light, and the gardens do not open for several hours." He laid down his cards and squinted at the men. "Do I know you?"

"I can't say you do, m'lord."

"What's your business then? I do not understand. And why are you saying I was at Richmond?"

"Rumors, m'lord. A duel between you and Sir Jaspar Vernham."

"What?" Sir Jaspar leaned back and blinked several times. "Did I hear m'name?" He weaved, then hiccuped loudly.

"I knew this was an absurd idea!" Lady Bray suddenly said. "I should never have agreed to play all night. I want my bed." She rose to her feet and pressed her hand against her back. "I am too old for these antics. You young people may be content to greet the dawn with a game of whist, but I shall pay dearly for this indiscretion for days to come. Come, George. I require your support up the stairs. At the same time, we can see these gentlemen out, though I do think you ought to call tomorrow upon the magistrate at

Bow Street and discover why he sent his men to our home so early this morning."

The runners glanced at one another and began to offer hurried apologies. Lady Bray listened with a sense of growing hauteur.

"My son," she stated at last, "would never behave so badly as to engage in an act against the King's Law. Were he to do so, I promise you he would never hear the end of my strictures on the subject. As for you, I would suggest you rely less on rumors and more on observation and the careful discovery of intent before you burst into a private home."

The gentlemen fell into obsequious bows and were soon gone from the house. Lord Bray escorted his wife upstairs, but returned after a few minutes to tend to Sir Jaspar.

"It is only a flesh wound," Jaspar muttered, rising from his chair.

Since he fainted again, Lord Bray cried out, "Take him to the second bedchamber on the left. Dr. Kent is awaiting him."

Marianne accompanied the men to the room and insisted upon making herself of use to Dr. Kent. Because he was well-acquainted with her, he smiled at her over his spectacles and told Lord Bray that he knew the Pamberley sisters to be excellent nurses, one and all, and that the gentlemen would do well to take themselves off. Between Miss Marianne and two of the housemaids, he had all the assistance he required.

Jaspar was unconscious during the entire procedure, during which Dr. Kent removed a pistol ball which had just narrowly escaped piercing the lung near Jaspar's left shoulder. Jaspar had, indeed, lost a great deal of blood and, after being bandaged, was left in Marianne's care.

Dr. Kent took his leave, promising to return that evening to look after his patient. Marianne settled herself very near the bed, gently pressing cool cloths against Jaspar's forehead. She had every certainty he would soon awaken and would be in considerable discomfort. She had been instructed to dose him with a glass of water laced with laudanum. Until he awoke, however, she could only look down at him and wonder how it was she had not understood how very much she loved him, truly loved him.

She recalled the moment when Annabelle had said to her, *The man you love may die.* Only now, as she reviewed her thoughts from that moment through the discovery of the two coaches at Richmond Park and the sound of the two pistol shots until now, did she realize she had never once worried about Crowthorne. Her thoughts, her hopes, her fears had centered solely upon Sir Jaspar, *the man she loved.*

Yes, indeed, there was no greater fool ever born than Marianne Pamberley. She had risen to stir up the coals when her betrothed scratched on the door, then entered quietly.

She turned to him, feeling terribly sad. Directing him to stand behind the screen which had been placed at the foot of the bed, she watched as his eyes filled with sorrow.

"I have made a terrible mull of everything," he stated.

"No more than I," she responded softly. "Tell me this, Edgar, and pray be very honest—did you offer for me in order to ingratiate yourself into Ramsdell's company?"

The look of chagrin which stole over his features would certainly have refuted any protestation he might have offered her. Since none rose to his lips, she nodded and said, "Do you know, it never once occurred to me that your motives in desiring to wed me could have been similar to my own motives in pursuing you."

He seemed rather shocked and she could not help but smile. "We are very much alike after all," she said, "for neither of us could believe that the other was not passionately in love."

Understanding dawned in his eyes and he began to smile. "When you told me he kissed you," he began quietly, "my pride was hurt, abominably so, but nothing more. I fear I was already as mad as fire because Ramsdell had sponsored him successfully at White's. The knowledge he had kissed you merely added to my sense of ill-usage and outrage. I never gave a single thought to you or even to the possibility he might be attempting to steal your heart from me.

"I cared only that he had robbed me of the true prize—you see, from the time I can remember, I have desired to become part of Ramsdell's circle of acquaintance. I desired it more than anything in the world. When you arrived in London, so pretty and so closely connected to Ramsdell, my plan formulated itself almost instantly. I was in need of a wife, and your relationship to Ramsdell could give me what I desired most.

"Was anything more ignoble than this? Not once did I trouble myself over your feelings. My heart, I fear, was entirely untouched. Marianne, I am so very sorry."

"Your heart has been long given elsewhere, has it not?"

He seemed confused and shook his head. "No, of course not. I would never have offered for you or anyone had my heart . . . been engaged . . . elsewhere. Why do you smile in that manner? Oh, the devil take it. I see what you are about. But it is not possible."

"Are you certain? Edgar, I think it is quite possible. Now that I am able to view our betrothal with distance and some perception, I can recall vividly a dozen circumstances in which your attention was wholly captured by Annabelle."

His lips parted as he pondered this possibility. Awareness dawned in his eyes. "I believe you may be right," he murmured, rather astonished. "I have known her forever, and I suppose all these years I have taken her presence in my life completely for granted."

Marianne extended her hand to him, and he held it for a long moment.

"Well, we are a pair, are we not?" she said.

He smiled ruefully. "Yes, we are."

She gave his hand a squeeze. "I must break off our engagement in view of the daunting truth that we do not love one another, but I wish you every happiness, Edgar, indeed, I do. Most sincerely."

"And I, you," he responded softly. "I shall go to Ramsdell tomorrow and explain everything, if that would suit you."

"Very much so." She was surprised he would make such an offer. "I take it very kindly in you, Edgar. I hope I may always count you as one of my friends."

"Yes, of course. I shall depend upon it."

Marianne watched him go and closed the door upon him with a soft snap. Well, her brilliant match had lasted precisely eleven days, which was certainly longer than she deserved.

She could only shake her head at her stupidity and promise herself she would do a great deal better in the future. As she returned to Jaspar's bedside, she again held a cool, damp cloth against his brow, which was growing quite warm.

"Oh, Jaspar," she murmured. "Will you ever forgive me?"

She watched his eyes flutter open for a brief moment

as a faint smile formed on his lips. A moment later, however, the smile disappeared and his eyes closed.

"All I ask," she whispered, "is that you do not leave this earth before I have a chance to properly tell you how much I love you."

Sixteen

A month later, in early June, Marianne found herself in the grove of cherry trees at Lady Brook. She addressed the head gardener. "It is quite early in the season for the blight," she mused, staring up into the trees, "yet I believe all of them will need to be smoked."

Finch nodded in agreement. "I'll see to it right away, Miss Marianne, and may I say how happy I am yer here at Lady Brook once again?"

"Thank you. You are very kind."

"Yer trip to London has been good to ye. Ye seem older somehow, and ye put me wery much in mind of Mrs. Pamberley when she first come to Lady Brook so many years ago."

Marianne wondered in what way she had changed so noticeably that more than one of Constance's retainers had commented on how different she seemed. "I can think of no finer compliment. Did I tell you my mother intends to return for the summer?"

"Aye, at least twice, miss." He smiled broadly and, tipping his hat, headed toward his gardening sheds. She let her gaze follow him. Finch's rolling gait pleased her exceedingly, for it was as familiar to her as the land upon which the new mansion was settled, putting her fully in mind of her history at Lady Brook.

She was so happy to be home. Her London escapade

seemed somehow distant and less worrisome here at Lady Brook, for the rosy brick mansion stood tall and proud against the landscape, fairly daring the winds to blow. Perhaps in time she would be able to forget all that had happened.

Once it became known she had broken off her engagement to Lord Crowthorne, she began declining most of the invitations sent to her. London had lost its savor.

The gossip which the duel had aroused, as well as the broken betrothal, had diminished her delight in the metropolis to the point that unless the event was confined to Ramsdell's immediate circle of acquaintance, she refused to attend. Far too many high sticklers were happy to gloat over her fall from grace.

Following the duel, she had maintained her duties at Jaspar's bedside quite conscientiously. He had succumbed quickly to a terrible fever and delirium, through which she had nursed him steadily, unwilling to leave him even for a moment. She slept in his room, awakened to every tossing and turning, forced bitter draughts down his parched throat, changed his bandages according to Dr. Kent's strict instructions, and whispered her love as well as her remorse to him over and over.

Only when the fever broke and he began a slow recovery did she permit one of the maids to relieve her so she might return to Ramsdell's house to bathe and don a fresh gown.

During her first trip home, she begged to speak privately with Annabelle. When she told her of her decision to break off her engagement to Lord Crowthorne, Annabelle opened her eyes wide, then promptly swooned.

When she awoke, she gave way to a flood of tears.

"You do not love him?" she cried. "But are you certain?"

So many times did she pose the same question that Marianne became convinced Annabelle could not conceive of any lady's failing to love the man she fairly worshiped.

Once Jaspar was recovering safely, he bade her to return to Ramsdell's home. He scarcely met her gaze as he told her he feared for the gossips. She had said she did not give a fig for the gabblemongers, but he had looked at her in a way that brooked no refusal. She could do naught else but agree to leave his bedside.

Before she did, however, she told him she had ended her betrothal to Crowthorne, and in particular, why she had done so.

He had listened to her explanations, but had responded dully, "One should never marry where one's heart is not engaged."

She sat very still, watching him closely. She did not understand in the least why her pronouncement had not had a happy effect upon Sir Jaspar. Somehow she had supposed that once he awoke from his delirium and learned she had broken off her betrothal to Crowthorne, he would naturally extend his heart to her once more. He said nothing, however.

She bid him a very quiet good-bye, wanting more than anything to ask when she would see him again, but he had turned away from her, shifting his head on the pillow so he might look out the window. She left the room, her heart breaking.

Both Constance and Ramsdell were in full support of her decision to take on a quieter existence, especially given the fact that Lord Crowthorne had retired to Hampshire with his parents. Annabelle, now happily but privately betrothed to him, had accompanied them. Marianne had bid the party farewell and, with true tears of regret, had embraced each of them in turn.

"I shall miss your liveliness," Lord Bray had said.

"And I shall miss your warmth and kindness, for you always treated me as a daughter even when you knew your son and I did not suit. And you did know, did you not?"

He nodded in his wise manner. "But these things always have a way of sorting themselves out."

She could not help but agree, though she would have preferred a milder sorting out than one which included a duel with pistols.

She had continued waving farewell until the coach disappeared into the lane at the top of the square. She had lowered her arm, wondering if her situation with Sir Jaspar would sort itself out, particularly since she had not spoken with him since he began his recovery.

As for Edgar, shortly following the duel he had spoken in private with Lord Ramsdell. The interview had the oddest effect, for Ramsdell finally accepted Lord Crowthorne into his circle of intimates.

When Marianne questioned him as to why he had come to embrace Lord Crowthorne, he responded, "For the first time, he did not appear to be a complete bore. He admitted to having entered the betrothal for ignoble reasons, and I came to find I rather liked the man. He was not nearly so stiff-rumped a fellow as I had believed him to be."

He gave the subject a hard turn. "So tell me, Marianne, is everything settled between you and Jaspar?"

Her cheeks had burned painfully. "He will never forgive me," she murmured. "Indeed, why should he?"

Ramsdell chucked her chin. "My dear sister-in-law, you certainly are something of a peahen. Well, well! I will not interfere . . . only, should he come to call, I would not be too hasty in sending him away. In the meantime, I daresay he will not soon forget that you cared for him while he was exceedingly ill." He smiled faintly, then continued. "If I recall correctly, a similar circumstance occurred at Lady Brook. Your sister was quite faithful in tending to my wounds, and I found there was nothing for it—I had to marry her."

Marianne chuckled. "Yes, but you had tumbled violently in love with her."

"So I had," he returned softly, his eyes warm with affection.

A fortnight later, she had returned to Lady Brook with but one letter from Jaspar in hand, a rather indifferent missive which thanked her for her attentions to him while he was ill. He made no mention of wishing to see her again and in no other respect gave even the smallest hint that he still loved her. She could only suppose the events of the past several weeks had turned his heart to stone where she was concerned.

Ah, well, it was her own fault. She had treated him shabbily, had kissed him several times when she should not have, and in the end she had nearly gotten him killed in a duel.

As she took one last look up into the cherry trees, she wondered if all stupid females were destined to live out their years as spinsters. She could only suppose it was true, particularly since she knew full well Jaspar had returned to The Priory a sennight past, but had not come to call nor in any other manner acknowledged her existence. She sighed heavily. She missed him so very much.

Turning toward the house, she was surprised to find Constance walking toward her.

"The blight?" her sister called out.

"Yes, and so early in the season. What brings you to Lady Brook?"

"You know I can never be gone for very long."

Marianne showed her which trees were particularly affected, then joined her on a slow tour about the property. After an hour, they were sitting side by side on the bench by the trout stream.

"Papa was used to love to fish here," Constance said.

"Though I was young, I do recall he did. I also recall this is the place where Jaspar kissed you. I was hiding behind the oak."

Constance smiled. "Speaking of Jaspar, has he called at Lady Brook yet?"

Marianne shook her head. "No, and I do not expect him to."

"And why is that?"

Marianne did not wish to tell her the truth, that the afternoon before the duel she had said horrible things to him. However, she felt her sister ought to know why Sir Jaspar would undoubtedly avoid her society as much as he could.

"That day before the duel, when you and Ramsdell quit the drawing room in order to afford Jaspar and me a few minutes' private speech—well, I am afraid I accused him of wishing to marry me in order to advance himself in society."

Constance drew in a sharp breath, but remained silent. Marianne could feel her sister's disapprobation prickling the air between them.

"You need not tell me what a horrid thing it was to have said. In truth, I was the one who was behaving in that fashion, for I never loved Lord Crowthorne—I was merely anxious to make the most brilliant match of the Season, and so I pursued him relentlessly. I accused Sir Jaspar of the very thing of which I was most guilty and he, though perfectly innocent, took the brunt of my wretched tongue. Did you know his father was a vicar in Yorkshire?"

Constance nodded. "Yes. He wrote of it while in India."

"And you never said anything?"

"It did not matter one whit to me. I have always admired and valued Jaspar. We were fast friends when he resided here."

"You are a much finer person than I am."

"Marianne, have you considered the possibility you did not truly give a fig whether he was a stable boy or not?"

She turned and stared at her sister. "Whatever do you mean? Of course it was important to me—at least, it was before . . . well, before the duel."

"So you say, and yet I have seen none of this attitude in you where anyone else is concerned."

Marianne frowned. "If that is so, then why did I provoke him as I did? I was forever reminding him he had been my father's stable boy."

"I believe it was because you feared loving him."

Marianne blinked and hiccuped. "Oh . . . you must be right, for as I look back on my previous conduct, particularly when he would kiss me and I would feel myself becoming mesmerized by him, only then would I taunt him. I did so quite consistently. I guess I would not allow anyone or anything to deter me from wedding where I wished, and I nearly ruined four lives because of it. Oh, Constance, to think I almost married Lord Crowthorne and—and, if you must know, he kisses like a fish!"

At that, Constance laughed. "Dear Marianne. You always say something that both shocks me yet delights me. Pray, pray never change." She slipped her arm about her sister's shoulders and gave her a warm hug.

"I cannot laugh as you are now, not when I am so very sad. I have come to believe Jaspar will never forgive me. In truth, I would not blame him. I only wish

I could tell him once more how truly sorry I am for everything that happened."

"I know one day you will have that opportunity. You'll see."

Constance then drew a letter from the pocket of her gown. "I have something here which I believe you will find amusing, and, perhaps unfortunately, all too familiar."

"What is it?" she queried, taking the missive.

"A letter from Katherine. She is in Brighton."

Marianne unfolded the single sheet of paper and saw at once that the missive was in Katherine's direct and sensible style.

Dear Constance,

Captain Ramsdell arrived yesterday, which you will be glad to know, since you were inquiring about him in your last letter.

I am not at all pleased with his presence in Brighton. Having understood he would be here, and that he was bringing a horse which I had been longing to see, I was looking forward to meeting him again, for I have not seen him since that wretched day when Lady Brook burned to the ground.

However, the most annoying thing has occurred. Captain Ramsdell has taken a fancy to me.

He seeks out my company at every opportunity, and since your husband is well known to the Regent, we are both invited to the Pavilion quite often. I frequently feel as though I have a dog at my heels and cannot be rid of him.

Dare I tell you he stole up on me one day and kissed me? It was so very wicked, and I struck him with my riding crop. That only made him laugh, whereupon he kissed me again!

I am still stunned by the whole of it. Whatever am I to do? I have told him to leave me in peace, but he seems positively intent upon hugging me whenever he gets the chance.

I wish you will mention the matter to Ramsdell and tell him, on my behalf, that he should instruct his younger brother on how to behave properly.

My horse fares well. I wish the captain were not here.

Yours, etc.,

Katherine

Marianne released a trill of laughter. "She is smitten!"

"Entirely so!" Constance agreed, laughing with her. "Imagine our Katherine consigning the condition of her beloved horse to the mere bottom line of a letter. Yes, she is smitten, indeed!"

"Do you intend to tell Ramsdell?"

"Of course not. He would be sent on a fool's errand were he to respond to her plea, which I doubt he would anyway. No, both Evan and Katherine are fully grown. I shall leave them to resolve their own difficulties, though you might wish to advise her, for you have had a great deal of experience of late which might prove invaluable to her."

Marianne sighed deeply once more. "I know very well my words should fall on deaf ears, just as yours fell on mine. Our sister, if you must know, is more stubborn than even I."

"Indeed, she is. I trust Captain Ramsdell took her measure before he began his flirtations with her. Otherwise, he shall be speedily disappointed."

Marianne met Constance's gaze, and the sisters shared another hearty laugh. Katherine was indeed a most stubborn and willful female.

Constance grew silent, then asked, "Do you mean to visit the Applegate children this afternoon?"

"Yes, of course. I always do on Wednesdays. Do you care to join me?"

"No, I think not," she responded thoughtfully. "I promised Cook I would review the menus with her."

Soon after the ladies returned to the house, Marianne put on her bonnet and pelisse in order to drive the gig to the village.

Constance, however, did not discuss the menus with Cook. That errand would have to be postponed for at least an hour or two.

Instead, she waited until Marianne had left Lady Brook, then went to the stables herself in order to have her curricle made ready for travel.

Perhaps she was going on her own fool's errand, but she felt she must try to bring about Marianne's relationship with Jaspar. Within a handful of minutes, she was tooling down the back lane which led directly to The Priory.

Sir Jaspar sat in his garden in the shade of a large elm, sunshine dappling the ground all about his chair. He felt better every day and was nearly recovered from his wound—at least from the wound in his shoulder.

The wound in his soul was a different matter entirely. His heart, which had been subjected to several weeks of Marianne's indecision and at times contemptuous words, had grown oddly indifferent to her, something he never would have believed possible.

He had been deeply appreciative that she had remained beside his bed during the worst of his illness. However, he had listened to the remarkable news that she had broken off her engagement to Lord Crowthorne with a deadness in his heart that had taken him completely unawares. He should have been overjoyed at her announcement. Instead he felt numb to all sensation where she was concerned. He could be neither happy nor sad.

He had returned to The Priory in order to complete his recovery in the peace and beauty of his home. Several times he had thought about calling upon Marianne merely as a matter of politeness, but found he could not bring himself to the task. For some reason he could not fathom, he did not wish to see her—not now, perhaps not ever.

"And how are you feeling, my dear friend?" a feminine voice called to him from the doorway.

He turned toward the shallow steps of the terrace and smiled broadly as Constance stepped out into the sunshine. "How glorious! I have been wishing for a little company, and now here you are. What brings you to Lady Brook? Are you feeling well yourself?"

"I am in excellent health. And you? I must say, you appear to be completely recovered."

"Nearly so," he responded, rising. "But come, sit with me for a while."

She surprised him with a strong shake of her head. "Another time, perhaps. Today I thought you might accompany me to Wraythorne, for there is something of great importance I wish to show you."

Sir Jaspar recalled vividly the first time she had spoken such words to him. He shook his head. "It is of no use. I do not have the same feelings for her as I did. I fear, however, that in saying so I disappoint you greatly."

Constance nodded. "Marianne is devastated by her conduct and believes you will never forgive her."

"Of course I will forgive her. I have already. How I feel"— here he held a fist to his chest—"has nothing to do with forgiveness. I do not believe I love her anymore. I seem to be dead to all feelings for her, good or ill."

She nodded again. "I understand. Truly, I do. But will you do this for me anyway, if for no other reason than to permit Marianne to tell you herself how badly she feels? She does not expect anything of you, nor do I. However, until she understands you hold no grudge, she will not be at ease. Please come to the village and give her a chance to apologize."

Jaspar looked into her sorrowful, pleading eyes and found he could not refuse her. Besides, he wished to make peace with Marianne, for no doubt very soon he would be meeting her in company. How much better to overcome any awkwardness now, rather than at a soiree or ball.

"I would do anything for you, so of course I shall go. Please be assured, though, that I have nothing left to give her."

"I understand," she said again.

Marianne was holding young Tom in her arms when she saw Sir Jaspar and Constance arrive at the alehouse. The Applegate children were playing a riotous game of tag all about her, and she was keeping the three youngest from getting trampled.

At the sight of Jaspar, however, she bid the children stop, that she might give Tom to Alice. "I shall return in a moment," she said.

As she walked toward Jaspar and saw in his eyes a look of indifference, she suddenly realized all he had endured at her hand during the past year, from the time of his arrival in England until the morning of the duel. He had loved her, and she had treated him brutally, especially by permitting him to kiss her as passionately as he had without ever intending to honor the passion between them.

Now the glove was on the other hand, for now her

heart was full of passion, longing, and hope, while Jaspar remained utterly impassive. His disinterest in her was like fiery coals upon her head. She hurt, terribly so, and with only a forceful effort was she able to keep from yet again becoming a watering pot. At the same time, she could not help but recognize the complete justice of the situation.

"Hello, Sir Jaspar," she said. "Will you have some lemonade or perhaps a tankard of ale with me?"

"Yes, of course," he said. He gave Constance the reins. She, in turn, informed them both that she would be calling upon Mrs. Applegate, since she had brought some honey to give to her. Jaspar joined Marianne on the green before the alehouse, and spying a rose arbor, suggested they walk instead, saying he was not thirsty.

"May the children join us?" she asked.

He seemed surprised. "Yes, if you wish it."

"Indeed, I do. It is a pretty walk, and once we leave the village the path leads in a gentle circuit of Wraythorne. I frequently take the children on a complete tour, especially on a beautiful day like today."

She picked up young Tom and explained the scheme to the children. A quick cheer rent the air, followed by a pounding of feet as some of the older children raced ahead through the arbor and onto the well-used path.

"How are you feeling?" she inquired politely. "The last time I saw you, I fear you were still quite ill. Your complexion I shall never forget, for it was the color of chalk."

"I hoped to thank you in person for your kindness in assisting Dr. Kent. Lady Bray told me you hardly strayed from my bedside."

"I was determined to do nothing less. I felt I owed you that much, at the very least. Jaspar, will you ever forgive me for my wretched indiscretions which led to the duel—first that I kissed you when I should not have, and secondly that I so stupidly told Crowthorne what I had done?"

"I hope you know me well enough to comprehend you need never have posed the question to me. Of course you are forgiven."

Marianne glanced at him. She believed him, yet there was little warmth in his voice. "I knew as much to be true, yet I longed to hear you say so."

Tom wiggled in her arms and demanded to be put down. Young Katie, who was nearly seven and always remained close to Marianne, took up his hand and helped him in his halting steps.

"You are such a good girl, Katie," she said. "And what a fine mother you shall make one day."

"Thankee, miss. Oh! I fear he's wet through. I'd best take him home."

Marianne laughed. "Perhaps you should."

Katie quickly picked up Tom in her arms and, though the toddler squirmed and complained, his older sister soothed him with a song, which soon quieted him. A few minutes more and the pair disappeared toward the alehouse.

"You seem changed," Jaspar said, regarding her closely, a frown between his brows.

"I hope I am," she responded, setting off down the path again. He kept pace with her, the sounds of the children ahead marking the way. "I learned a great deal during my first Season. Edgar once told me I was behaving like a schoolgirl who had not yet been put through her paces. Though at the time I resented his criticism, I have since come to believe he was very right. I thought only of myself from the moment my feet touched the cobbles in Grosvenor Square, never of him or of Annabelle or of you. And you were so right about everything."

He glanced at her, but did not respond.

Her heart sank. She had supposed once he heard her sincerity, he might soften toward her, but it was evident he was unmoved. Ah, well. This was one more lesson, then, that her conduct, just as she had supposed, had completely ruined his love for her.

She turned the subject and asked after The Priory, inquiring earnestly into the many changes he was planning to undertake over the course of the coming year. She spoke of her intentions of acting as Constance's bailiff at Lady Brook and continuing her charitable works in all the surrounding villages.

After a time, the children's voices disappeared entirely, and the path became overshadowed with dense shrubberies and the overhanging branches of ancient elms. She stopped and whirled around.

"I have gone the wrong way!" she cried. "How stupid of me. Back at that enormous anthill, we should have turned to the right. It is pretty here, though, is it not?"

He looked about as well. "I was used to come here when I worked in your father's stables. Beyond is a stream in which I caught the largest fish ever and an occasional eel."

"Show me," she said.

He led her on. They pushed through a rather scraggly thicket of bramble vines and a fine brook appeared in which the quick movements of trout could be seen in the clear water.

"Oh, how lovely! And to think I never knew of this place." She ventured toward a large rock near the grassy edge of the stream and did not hesitate to sit atop it. "Do sit with me for a while," she said. "Look, even the sun is shining."

Jaspar hesitated. He felt certain that with every minute he remained in her company, she would come to believe he had more to offer her than he did. However, she was so changed that he could not help but respond a little to her. The contriteness of her speech and the sincere, womanly expression in her eyes as she looked up at him over her shoulder bade him oblige her.

He sat down on the grass next to her. After gathering up a handful of small stones scattered near the edge of the stream, he began tossing them into the creek.

She did not say anything, but merely sat looking all about her, at the creek, at the tangle of the shrubbery on both sides of the stream, at the blue sky above dotted with puffy white clouds.

"Does your shoulder give you much pain?" she inquired after a time.

"Very little to speak of," he said. "I had a most excellent nurse."

"You had several nurses who doted upon you, including myself. Lord Bray's maidservants were quite enamored of you. More than once when I entered your bedchamber I heard them whispering about how handsome you were and what fine shoulders you possessed."

"What gammon!"

"You doubt me?" She turned an arch look upon him.

He chuckled, but decided not to pursue the subject. "You were very kind to me," he said, directing a rather flat stone in a sharp line against the surface of the stream. It skipped three times. "And I shall not soon forget it."

When she did not respond, he turned to find she had averted her face, but he could see that she was rubbing the back of her gloved hand against her cheeks, each in turn.

"I did not mean to overset you, Marianne."

"It is just that whenever I think back on that time . . .

oh, Jaspar," she said, turning toward him, her expression pinched, "I was never more frightened than when I saw you lying at the base of the oak. I felt certain I would perish were you to . . . well, were you to die. Only then, when I faced the possibility of losing you forever to death, did I come to understand that I loved you. Was there ever a female so stupid? As for caring for you, it was the very least I could do to tend you on your sickbed—the very least, since I was the cause of all the mischief."

"But you were not," he said, "which is something I have been meaning to say to you. I should never have let our *tête-à-tête* linger as it did. When you kissed me, I should have taken my leave. You were betrothed to another man, and I had no right to take advantage of you as I did."

"But I kissed you!" she cried. "It was my fault and my fault alone!"

He rose to his feet, chucking the remainder of the pebbles into the stream all at once. "And if you'll recall, I hauled you to your feet and fairly dragged you into my arms."

"Yes, you did," she breathed.

He saw the longing in her eyes and could see her pulse beating in the well of her throat. He felt very strange suddenly as he looked down at her. Without knowing he had done so, he extended his hand to her. She looked at it and blinked, then slipped her small gloved hand into his.

Lifting her face to him, she queried softly, "Jaspar, do you indeed forgive me? I wish to see in your eyes that I am forgiven, truly."

"You are," he returned sincerely. "Indeed, you are." He stared into her lovely green eyes and felt the change begin deep within his heart, almost as an awakening from a profound sleep. She was different from

the vain young woman who had left Wraythorne two
and a half months ago. She had matured, wonderfully
so. Even her countenance glowed with a womanly presence which had not been there before his duel with
Crowthorne.

His heart began to burn very brightly as he drew
her to her feet. He did not release her hand, but held
it firmly. She met his gaze without the least reticence.
For the first time in his acquaintance with her, he saw
love in her eyes, a pure, fiery love that fanned the
strong burning in his soul.

"Marianne," he murmured softly. The wind caught
at the ribbons of her bonnet, and the pale blue bands
drifted over his chest.

"Yes," she responded, her face merging with the
sun, the sky, and the gurgling of the brook. He felt
oddly at peace as he drew her into his arms, holding
her fast. She slipped an arm about his neck and fin-
gered the curls at the nape of his neck.

"I thought I no longer had any feeling left for you.
I believed somehow that the duel changed everything.
But now, as I see that you have left all your schoolgirl
dreams behind, I find love flooding my heart anew."

He pulled the bow apart and pushed her bonnet off
her head. She smiled as it bounced off her legs and
tumbled onto the grass at her feet. He would have
kissed her, but she spoke first.

"There is something I feel I ought to say to you."

"What is it?" he asked, his voice hoarse with longing
even to his own ears. How very odd!

"I am not a very governable female. I am chastened
at the moment, but if you kiss me now, I promise you
I will not be content and will undoubtedly pester you
the rest of your life to kiss me again and again."

"I love you, Marianne."

"You should not. I am a wretched creature."

He smiled, the whole world suddenly filling with a golden glow. "I will always love you."

"Then you are a greater fool than even I."

She leaned into him, and he found her lips with his own. The kiss which followed caused the burning in his soul to burst into flames. "I love you," he murmured against her lips again and again.

She cooed in response, a wonderful warbling that sounded like the music of the heavens. He entered her mouth and plumbed the soft recesses, which always made him think of her great beauty, the innate sweetness of her spirit, and her *joie de vivre*.

After a time, he drew back slightly. "We have your sister to thank for bringing us together once more."

"She wishes us to marry. She has always believed that I loved you. She was very right."

"Then for her sake," he said with a smile, "I think we should wed. Will you have me now, Marianne?"

"With all my heart," she responded, once again claiming his lips for her own.